DARK QUEEN'S ARMY

THE CHILDREN OF THE GODS BOOK 34

I. T. LUCAS

NOTE FROM THE AUTHOR:
Dark Queen's Army is a work of fiction!
Names, characters, places and incidents are products of the author's imagination or
are used fictitiously and are not to be construed as real. Any similarity to actual
persons, organizations and/or events is purely coincidental.

MEY

*M*ey leaned over the vanity to get closer to the mirror and touched the small pimple that had popped up on her cheek overnight. It had been years since she'd had an outbreak.

Was it because of the stress?

She used to get breakouts during finals in high school, but that had more to do with stress eating than with the stress itself. If finding out that her boyfriend had been cheating on her hadn't ruined her perfect complexion, and neither had her sister's disappearance, stress was not the likely culprit.

It was probably what she'd been eating lately.

Since meeting Yamanu, Mey had been on an emotional rollercoaster. She'd been letting herself indulge in foods she hadn't touched in years and in quantities that were sure to end her modeling career. With the camera adding at least fifteen pounds in addition to what she'd gained already, she would have to go on a severely restrictive diet if she were to model again.

Except, going back to that lifestyle would be difficult. It felt good not to agonize over every bite and to eat until she was sated.

The irony wasn't lost on her.

In the same way that Yamanu couldn't go back to being celibate after taking a break from his vow, she couldn't go back to being hungry after taking a break from her strict diet.

Perhaps she should follow Yamanu's example and abandon modeling like he had abandoned martyrdom.

Both lifestyle changes had an adverse effect on their jobs, but while hers only meant the potential loss of income, Yamanu's meant the loss of his powers and protection for his people.

And stressing about that was probably the reason for the damn pimple.

That and the guilt.

Carrying the burden of responsibility for depriving the clan of their shield was so stressful that it cast a dark cloud over her joy at being with Yamanu.

And then there was the worry of whether or not she was going to transition.

If she wasn't a carrier of the godly genes, then the clan had lost its protector for nothing, and she was going to lose the love of her life. Not only that, if she wasn't a Dormant, neither was Jin, and the clan was not going to help her find her sister.

Despite coveting Jin's spying talent, Kian would not welcome a non-Dormant into the clan.

Not because he was cruel, but because he couldn't.

With a sigh, Mey dabbed a little concealer over the pimple and stepped out of the bathroom.

"How does a Saturday morning stroll through the village sound to you?" Yamanu asked. "We can have breakfast at the café."

"I would love a stroll, but didn't you say that the café was closed on the weekends?" She stepped out of the bathroom and went into the closet.

Leaning against the doorframe, Yamanu crossed his arms over his chest. "Jackson keeps the vending machines stocked. We can have fresh sandwiches, pastries, and even cappuccinos."

"Sounds like a plan." Mey pulled a hoodie off the hanger and shrugged it on. "Aren't you going to put something over that T-shirt?"

As she eyed Yamanu's muscles bulging out of the short sleeves, a tingling warmth started at her belly and traveled south.

Damn, her man was hot. They had made love twice last night and again this morning, but she could easily go for another round. Sex with Yamanu was out of this world, and thanks to the venom, it didn't leave her sore or fatigued either.

Talk about the perks of being with an immortal. At this rate, he was going to turn her into a nymphomaniac.

"I'll be fine. It's not that cold." He took her hand.

As they stepped onto the trail, Mey inhaled deeply. "I love how clean the air here is. I always imagined Los Angeles as a city drenched in smog."

Yamanu wrapped his arm around her waist. "This is Malibu. We are not really in Los Angeles."

Despite it being a beautiful morning, Mey didn't see anyone else taking a walk. Not that it meant that the entire village was still sleeping. The meandering path was surrounded by trees and tall shrubs, so there could have been people strolling the other trails that she couldn't see.

Yamanu, on the other hand, could probably hear their footsteps.

"Are we alone here? Or are there others taking a morning walk?"

"Someone is jogging behind us. I think it's Ella."

That was too specific to deduce from just hearing footsteps.

"Can you sense that it's her?"

He shook his head. "She is still too far away. I can sense that the jogger is a female, though, and Ella is the only one I've seen running this time of day."

A few minutes later, Mey heard the light footsteps getting closer and looked over her shoulder.

"Hi!" Ella waved. "Are you going to the café?" She caught up to them and kept jogging in place.

"Good morning." Mey smiled. "And yes, we are on our way to having a vending machine breakfast."

"Awesome. Julian is there waiting for me. You can join us, and we can have breakfast together."

"We would love to," Mey said.

"I'll see you there." Ella waved again and jogged away.

"She is the one with the missing aunt, right?"

Yamanu nodded. "Personally, I think it's a long shot. Eleanor is Ella's aunt on her father's side, not her mother's, so there is no guarantee that she is a Dormant. In fact, she probably is not, and her being in West Virginia could be purely coincidental." He chuckled. "From a nonbeliever, Kian has gone all the way to the other extreme. He is now seeing patterns where there are most likely none."

Mey's heart sank. Kian was planning to find Jin with Ella's aunt's help. Without Eleanor, they wouldn't know where to start searching. The Quiet Zone and the area around it were sparsely populated, but there were many tiny towns scattered over the plains and mountains of West Virginia. They would need an army of investigators to comb through them.

YAMANU

*M*ey sighed. "I hope Kian's hunch is right. Otherwise, our chances of finding Jin are slim."

"I hope so too."

Yamanu wanted to slap himself. He should not have voiced his thoughts about Eleanor being a long shot and ruined Mey's mood.

Not that her mood had been all that great to start with. She smiled and pretended that everything was fine, but her eyes and her scent told a different story.

Mey was worried, anxious, and not as overjoyed as he was about them finally consummating their bond.

Hopefully, it wasn't about his lovemaking skills.

After six and a half centuries of abstinence, Yamanu was a bit rusty, but he'd still managed to wrest several orgasms out of her each time they'd made love, which had been quite a lot, especially given that it had been only two days.

Mey seemed just as hungry for him as he was for her, eager for every moment of intimacy, touching, caressing, kissing.

He was in heaven.

The only thing that could make his life absolutely perfect was discovering that he hadn't lost his powers. The problem was that testing wasn't simple. First of all, he needed to be around humans.

Secondly, for his test to be conclusive, he needed to shroud a major disturbance that would have otherwise attracted a lot of attention.

Almost every Guardian could shroud to some extent, but to test his blanket shroud, Yamanu needed something big to happen, and he wasn't about to set up explosives in downtown Los Angeles just for an experiment.

But that wasn't the only problem.

The truth was that he was afraid.

As long as he didn't test his abilities, the possibility that he hadn't lost them still existed. But if he tried and failed, then that little bit of hope would be snuffed out.

Mey was going to take it even harder. Besides feeling guilty, she also feared the clan's response once they found out that she was responsible for the loss of his powers.

Not that she was, but that was what she believed.

Yes, he had broken his vow of celibacy for her, but it had been his choice, and he'd gotten approval from the goddess. Hell, Annani had practically commanded him to induce Mey and even provided a valid justification.

If Yamanu angered the Fates by refusing their gift, they might retaliate by taking both his mate and his powers away.

Mey thought that it had been pity talk, but Yamanu knew that Annani had meant every word. Like him, the goddess was a firm believer in the Fates. And just like him, she attributed the good fortune of all the recent truelove pairings to their intervention. After eons without mates, clan members were suddenly finding them one after the other.

Even Kian, the staunchest skeptic, had finally accepted that the Fates had had a hand in arranging the seemingly random discoveries of Dormants.

As they neared the café, the murmur of voices got louder, and after listening to them for a moment, Yamanu could distinguish the speakers.

He pulled Mey closer against his side and whispered in her ear,

"In addition to Ella and Julian, Wonder and Anandur are there, and also Callie and Brundar."

She lifted her eyes to him. "You can sense all of them?"

"I can hear them."

"Will my hearing improve to such an extent after I become immortal? That is if I transition?"

He chuckled. "Are you still doubting that you will?"

Mey nodded.

He leaned and kissed the top of her head. "Don't. Trust the Fates."

She snorted. "Yeah, like you trust them with Ella's aunt?"

For a long moment, Yamanu debated how to answer that. If he told Mey why he felt that Eleanor was a long shot, it would upset her, but he didn't want to lie to her and falsely raise her hopes either.

In the end, he decided that the truth was his best option.

"I talked with Roni and got some more information about Eleanor. Vivian and her family haven't seen the woman in years, and the reason Kian is jumping to conclusions about her is Ella and her brother's extraordinary powers. Their mother is not powerful enough to account for that, so Ella came up with the theory that her father must have been a Dormant as well. Except, I can't see how that could have happened with Dormants being so rare."

"I assume that the father is not around?"

"He died in a helicopter crash while serving in Afghanistan."

Mey sighed. "That's so sad."

"Yes, it is."

Mey shook her head. "What if the Fates brought Ella's parents together? Why is it harder to believe than the other pairings?"

"Because two Dormants are just like any other two humans. So unless we believe that the Fates are involved in every match, not just the clan's, that doesn't make sense."

For several moments, Mey didn't say anything, her strides matching his as they walked along the path. Then she lifted her eyes to his. "Why would the Fates want to help your clan out of all people? I know that you are special, but still. Every person is special in some way."

Yamanu shrugged. "Perhaps we are the key to humanity's continued survival. Or maybe the Fates got involved when they realized that without mates, we were facing extinction. Or perhaps they sought to reward us for all the good we've been doing for humanity. I believe that they have a grand plan and that they choose key players that will help make it happen."

Mey's lips lifted in a knowing smirk. "If we continue along that thread, then the Fates might have had a good reason for bringing these two particular Dormants together. What if Ella and her brother were needed for that grand plan of theirs? Perhaps in order for them to be born with those special powers, the Fates had to pair up their parents first."

His woman was a smart lady. "I can't find fault with your logic."

"I think Kian is right to assume that Eleanor is a Dormant. That, combined with her changing her name and moving to West Virginia, is enough to make her a strong prospect. I wonder what her talent is."

"Ella thinks that she might be a compeller like Parker. She used to work as a pharmaceutical rep, and she must have made a killing. Her bank account, the one in her old name, holds a very impressive amount of money. If she used compulsion on her clients, that would explain her success."

Mey shook her head. "But that's speculation. What if she was just very good at it? Or maybe the money is from her current job? What if she opened a business and is doing very well? It's not that I want to disprove Eleanor having powers. I'm just switching places with you and playing devil's advocate."

"The money is from before she disappeared. According to Roni, it hasn't been touched since then. Still, you might be right, and she's simply an excellent salesperson."

MEY

*A*s Mey and Yamanu entered the café, Callie waved them over. "Come join us."

The group was sitting around two tables pushed together. Other than the six of them, only one other guy was reading a newspaper at a table on the other side of the café.

He reminded Mey of her father.

Every morning, he would read the paper as he drank his coffee, sharing the more interesting tidbits with her mother or whoever else was in the kitchen.

God, she missed her parents. Since Jin had left for her new job, Mey hadn't called them as often as she used to, mainly because she didn't want to worry them. She had no news she could share about her sister, and she hated lying to them. Nevertheless, she should call them tonight.

Anandur got up and added another table to the grouping, while Yamanu grabbed two more chairs.

"Thank you." Mey chose the seat next to Callie, her new BFF. "Having this place to meet up and chat is so cool." She waved a hand around. "This whole village is amazing. Such a wonderful place to live and raise kids in."

Callie nodded. "Yeah. Up until recently, that thought would

have made everyone sad because it was just a dream. But now that Merlin's developed a fertility enhancer, it might be a possible future." She gestured at the playground. "You see that place? That is the saddest spot in the village, but not for long. Syssi and Kian are expecting, and Vivian and Magnus started working on a baby as well."

"What about you?" Mey asked.

"In time. I'm not ready yet. I have all these great plans, and I'm running around like a chicken with no head."

Wonder cast her a guilty smile. "You could have taken more classes if you weren't helping me in the café."

Callie leaned and patted her arm. "I'm doing it for me as much as I'm doing it for you. As Carol has so wisely pointed out, there is a big difference between cooking for fun and cooking in a restaurant kitchen. Working in the café gives me a taste of that."

Brundar shifted closer to his mate. "You need to decide whether you want to be a teacher or a chef."

"Why?" Callie cocked a brow. "I'm an immortal. I can do both and also be a mother, just not all at the same time."

Mey still found it a difficult concept to wrap her head around. Life without time limits required a shift in thinking. Except, she wasn't an immortal yet, so there was no point in getting used to the concept of limitless time.

Yamanu pushed to his feet and put his hand on Mey's shoulder. "What would you like from the vending machines?"

"A cappuccino and a sandwich of your choice, please. I don't care which one."

"Anyone else want coffee or something to eat?" he asked.

"I could use another cup," Ella said.

Julian pushed away from the table. "I'll come with you."

The guy was nearly as handsome as Kian, but he seemed mellow, as a doctor should be, and he lacked the leader's intensity, which made him much more approachable.

"Do you usually run outdoors?" Mey asked Ella to start a

conversation. Perhaps she could later steer it round to the girl's aunt.

"Unless it's too hot or raining, I like running outside. Luckily, so far, it's only happened a few times, and then I used the gym in the underground."

Mey grimaced and patted her stomach. "I should start exercising as well. I need to do something to counteract the amounts of food I've been shoving in my face lately." She cast Callie an accusing glance. "I can't help myself when someone shows up with gallons of ice cream."

Callie puffed out a snort. "It happened once and for a good reason. Desperate times call for desperate measures."

When the guys returned with the coffees, sandwiches, and pastries, Anandur sat down and leaned back in his chair, causing the thing to groan in protest. "Did everyone hear the news about Kalugal?" He crossed his massive arms over his chest.

Ella nodded. "I was in William and Roni's lab when they showed Kian the footage. It was a black and white grainy recording, but the guy looked straight at the surveillance camera, and his face was exactly like the one in the picture the forensic artist drew of him. Well, not exactly, but close enough. I think it's him."

Yamanu shook his head. "This is just another example of the Fates' work. Roni and William were scouring footage from around the country for Kalugal, and then Lokan gets a clue about his brother's whereabouts during a random meeting that had nothing to do with the search."

"I wonder what it means," Ella said. "Do the Fates have a pairing with Kalugal in mind? Or is he needed in the war against the Brotherhood?"

Yamanu put his sandwich down. "From what I've seen so far, probably both. But I don't think the Fates are aiming for war. Maybe Kalugal can replace his father in a bloodless revolution."

Wonder snorted. "Dream on."

Mey was about to support Yamanu's positive outlook when her new phone pinged with an incoming message.

Pulling it out of her hoodie's pocket, she glanced at the screen and gasped. It was a message from Jin.

Sister to sister. What's up with you? I asked for info, something to keep me entertained in this boring place and got nothing. I'm still waiting. Text me.

"Is it from Jin?" Yamanu asked.

Mey nodded.

This was definitely Jin. The sister to sister address was from their childhood when they had fashioned walkie-talkies from empty cans and connected them with wire. Since then, it had become the equivalent of a secret handshake.

Mey typed with shaky fingers. *Sister to sister. I have a new boyfriend, and he is it. What's up with you?*

Holding her breath, she waited for a response.

I'm green with envy. There are a couple of cute guys here, but one is still a kid, and the other one is too old for me. Bummer.

That was Jin. Mey had no doubt.

She typed back. *What's with the communication silence?*

It's like a boot camp. Remember basic training? This is worse as far as rules and chain of command go. Everyone is so severe and strict. But at least we don't have to run around the base with backpacks filled with rocks.

Remembering that part of the training, Mey smiled. *Did you join the army? Is that what your contract is about?*

You know that I can't talk about it. But it's not the military. It's just stupid corporate bonding nonsense. It will be over soon, and then I will have more freedom.

What about the sucky cellular reception?

Still shit. I got the day off, and I'm in a place that has decent reception.

Can you tell me where it is?

Sorry. I can't. Not unless I want to lose my bonus, and you know how important that is for me.

Yeah, the damn bonus was the reason Jin was wherever she was.

Mey typed. *I need to know whether you are okay. This entire thing has gotten me so worried about you.*

Don't worry, I'm fine. I miss you, and I miss my friends, but I'm making new ones. It's a fascinating group of people, very diverse. Things are interesting.

A moment ago, Jin had said that she was bored. Was that a clue?

If you are not happy there, forget about the bonus and come home. I miss you so much.

I can't.

Why not? It's not like we can't live without that money. It will just take a little longer to open our business, or we will need to find a third partner to invest in it.

I can't. I have to stay and do this thing because I'm not a quitter, and I signed a contract. I need to go now. My friends are waiting for me. I love you. I'll text you next week when I have another day off. In the meantime, I want details about that new boyfriend, and by details, I mean everything, including a picture.

Mey teared up and typed back. *I love you too.*

She waited for a long moment in case Jin was going to send another text, but when nothing came, she handed the phone to Yamanu. "What do you think?"

His brows dipping low, he read over the exchange. "I'm trying to read between the lines, but I don't know your sister. You should be able to do it much better. One thing is obvious. Either Jin is curious about me or her bosses are." He handed Mey the phone back.

"I'm sure it was Jin this time, and not someone else using her phone. It sounded like she is there voluntarily, not too excited about it, but not miserable either. Perhaps she doesn't need rescuing after all."

Callie leaned forward. "If Jin knows that her communication with you is monitored, which she probably does, she wouldn't say anything incriminating."

"She could have hinted something. It could have been anything, some anecdote from our childhood that never happened or something like that."

Wonder shook her head. "If I were her, I would have been afraid to do that. What if you responded with 'what are you talking about'?"

That was a valid concern. "What would you have done?" Mey asked.

Wonder shrugged. "Nothing different from what Jin has done. I would have pretended that everything was fine to keep you from worrying about me. I would have tried to find my way out of the predicament on my own. But that's me. I don't know how your sister handles things."

Mey sighed. "Exactly like that. But what if she really wants to stay? I would feel terrible if the clan assembled a team to extract her, and she said, 'thanks but no thanks.'"

Yamanu put his arm around her. "Then we will have to make sure that our offer is so good that she cannot turn it down. I don't think a bonus, no matter how generous, can compete with immortality."

4

YAMANU

*M*ey shook her head. "I can't believe that I'm going to see the goddess."

Standing in front of the long mirror mounted on the back of the closet door, she smoothed her hand over her hip-hugging skirt. "Do you think I'm overdressed? Or maybe underdressed? I don't know what to wear."

"You look great. But perhaps you want to skip the heels. Annani is tiny."

"But her children are all so tall."

Yamanu chuckled. "She must have a thing for tall men."

Mey looked at him over her shoulder. "How does she do it? I mean, you said that she has glowing skin and is so beautiful that it hurts to look at her. Does she just show up at a bar and walk out with a dude?"

He rubbed a hand over his jaw. "She can tamp down the glow. But I have no idea how she picks up guys. And I'm not sure I want to know. It's like thinking about your mother having sex. There is something disturbing about it."

She chuckled. "You said that immortals didn't have the same hang-ups that humans have about sexuality."

"It depends on the context. As long as it doesn't involve my

15

mother or grandmother or the Clan Mother, I can talk about sex with anyone."

She nodded. "It's sad that none of you know your fathers. I bet you would have felt the same about your patriarchs as you do about your matriarchs."

"Maybe. I've never given it much thought. It is what it is."

Mey stepped down from her black high-heeled pumps and put on a pair of flats in the same color. "Is this better?"

"On second thought, you can wear whatever you want. Annani won't mind either way. She will just ask you to sit down."

Mey pulled a black cardigan off the hanger and put it over her blue blouse. "I'm dressed as if I'm going for a job interview, and I feel like it too. I'm so nervous. This invitation was totally unexpected."

It had taken him by surprise as well. Annani usually didn't host dinner parties on Sundays. She had Friday night dinners with her close family and on other days invited clan members for tea, canapés, and a chat.

Yamanu pulled Mey against his chest, careful not to disturb her makeup and hairdo. She'd been fussing over those for the past hour. "The goddess is curious to meet the woman who has captured my heart, and I'm sure Alena had something to do with it as well. She probably told her mother how great you are."

"Do you know who else is going to be there?"

"I don't. When the goddess sends me a text, inviting my lovely lady and me to dinner, I'm not going to text her back and ask who else is going to be there. I can only respond with how honored I am to be invited."

She nodded. "I get it. I just thought that maybe you happened to talk to one of the other guests."

"Sorry, love, I didn't. We should go." He took her hand. "We can be there in less than ten minutes if we walk briskly, but I think that an easy stroll will be good for your nerves."

"I love it here," Mey said as they descended the front steps. "It's a lot like living in a kibbutz, just without the livestock, which is much nicer. I don't like the smell of manure."

"Have you ever lived in one?"

"No, I was a city girl, but I had friends who did and who occasionally invited me to spend the weekend with them."

Yamanu arched a brow. "A boyfriend?"

"Yeah."

He expected her to tell him more, but Mey just kept walking. Maybe it was better this way. The less he knew about her past lovers, the better.

Still, he couldn't help himself. "Did you love him?"

She nodded.

Damn. Weren't women supposed to be talkative? Extracting information from Mey was like extracting venom from fangs.

"Tell me about him."

"Not much to tell. I was eighteen, he was five years older, and I thought he was the coolest guy who ever lived. We had good times together, but when I was discharged, and he stayed on, we had to end it. We stayed friends, though."

Things clicked in Yamanu's head. "He's the one you called about Jin?"

Mey nodded again.

She was keeping things from him, and it rankled. He had told her everything that there was to know about himself and his clan, laying it all out, but she wasn't as forthcoming.

"I sense there is a story there, but that you don't want to talk about it."

She cast him an apologetic glance. "It's not that I don't want to, I can't. It has nothing to do with me personally, but I was sworn to secrecy, and I can't share it with anyone. Not with my parents, not with Jin, and not even with you."

"Did he treat you right? Can you tell me as much?"

"He was awesome. Otherwise, we wouldn't have stayed friends. But although I loved him, it was puppy love. It can't compare to what I feel for you. I wasn't even all that devastated when it ended.

I was sad, but I didn't mourn for long." She sighed. "If I don't transition and have to leave you, that would definitely break me. I was trying to comfort myself, thinking that I wouldn't miss what I couldn't remember, but I didn't really believe it for even a moment. There will be a void in my heart that I won't understand. I will just know that I'm missing a vital part of myself."

A tear slid down her cheek.

Yamanu stooped and hugged her to him. "Don't cry. That is not going to happen, okay?" He hooked a finger under her chin. "I know it deep in my gut."

"Do you want to tell me that you have no doubts?"

"None whatsoever."

Was he exaggerating?

Just a little.

In the back of his mind, a small doubt still managed to hook its ugly claws into his cranium, but Yamanu would be damned if he'd let it poison his happiness with Mey. It was Sunday, for Fates' sakes, and they had been trying to induce her transition only since Friday.

Still, even though none of the other Dormants had transitioned so quickly, he'd hoped that it would happen faster for Mey. It was his damn vanity rearing its head again. Yamanu had thought that he would induce Mey on the first go.

Evidently, the Fates were teaching him another lesson in humility.

Mey smiled. "You're a lousy liar, but I love you anyway." She lifted her face and kissed him, then used her finger to wipe off the red lipstick she'd smeared on his cheek.

5

MEY

*A*s one of the Odus opened the door, light and the sounds of conversation spilled out of the living room.

Mey took a step back, bumping into Yamanu's solid chest. "The soundproofing of these houses is unnerving."

It was about more than just that, but she didn't want to say that the Odu freaked her out or that she was scared of meeting the goddess.

Nevertheless, she needed to remember that normal human expectations were useless in the village, even when it applied to mundane things like hearing things through closed doors and windows.

"Good evening, mistress Mey and master Yamanu." The butler bowed. "Please come in."

Yamanu took her hand, patting the back of it with his other one. "Good evening." He gave a tug.

Taking a deep breath, Mey squared her shoulders, curved her lips into the shape of a smile, walked in, and then froze in place when her eyes landed on the goddess.

Glowing, ethereally beautiful, and with a mass of red hair to rival Rapunzel's, the goddess sat in an armchair surrounded by her children and their mates.

Yamanu put a hand on her back and gave her a small nudge while bowing. "Good evening, Clan Mother. Thank you for inviting us."

Mey followed his example, bowing instead of bending her leg in the tight skirt. "I'm honored by your invitation, Clan Mother."

Rehearsing these words countless times had paid off. Otherwise, Mey doubted anything would have come out of her mouth.

The goddess smiled, revealing a pair of tiny, barely-there fangs. More like pointy canines. "Welcome to the clan, Mey. I am overjoyed for you and Yamanu."

Annani's intentions were good, but Mey hadn't transitioned yet, and it was too early for her words of welcome.

Stifling a grimace, Mey dipped her head. "Thank you."

The goddess rose to her feet and clapped her delicate, glowing hands. "To the table, everyone. You can all exchange greetings over appetizers."

Amanda rolled her eyes but did as her mother commanded, while Syssi gave Mey a small wave and headed to the dining table as well.

Dalhu and Kian nodded their hellos and followed the ladies.

Annani might be diminutive in size, but she filled the house with the power of her presence and her commanding personality.

"Sit right here next to me." The goddess pointed to a chair to her right.

Mey swallowed and glanced at Yamanu for help.

Except, he didn't dare to disobey either. Pulling out the chair for her, he waved his hand. "My lady?"

"Thank you." She smoothed her skirt before sitting down.

This was going to be a long night.

Once the Odus were done pouring drinks for everyone, Kian proposed a toast.

"To Mey and Yamanu."

Everyone clinked glasses.

"I hear that you are a model," Annani said.

Mey nodded.

"My Alena is modeling for the first time in her life, and I wonder what it is like. Do you enjoy your chosen profession?"

As Mey answered to the best of her ability, she tried not to stammer or trip over the words, praying that Annani would be satisfied with that and wouldn't ask about her time in the military.

Lying to the goddess seemed like a very bad idea, but if Annani asked, Mey would have no choice. Or she could just admit that she wasn't allowed to talk about it and hope that Annani would respect that.

"When is Alena coming back?" Amanda diverted the conversation to another topic.

Had she sensed Mey's discomfort and decided to rescue her?

In either case, Mey was grateful that the goddess's focus had shifted away from her.

"Saturday," Kian said. "She is wrapping up her last shoot on Friday."

Annani sighed. "I miss her company." She looked at her children and sighed again. "And I am going to miss all of you once I leave. I wish we were not scattered around the world like we are, but it is necessary for our safety. Everyone living in one location would have made us too easy to destroy."

Mey shivered. She often had the same thought about Israel. On the one hand, it would have been great for all the Jewish people to come back to their homeland. But on the other hand, having everyone in one tiny geographical location would have made it too tempting of a target for the haters and the bigots.

Racism, antisemitism, and all the other isms had never died. In fact, all were on the rise again, proving that humanity hadn't progressed as much as people liked to believe it had. It was still far from enlightened, and the voices of hate were getting not only stronger but also smarter. They were cloaking their bigotry quite ingeniously in excuses that should have been transparent to anyone who cared to dig a little deeper.

Except, it seemed that too many people were happy to jump on the hate wagon, and the 'us versus them' chimp mentality still ruled even those who lacked nothing. The educated, and those thinking of themselves as enlightened.

"When are you leaving?" Kian asked Annani.

"As soon as Alena is ready to go. We have been away from the sanctuary for too long." She looked at Yamanu and then shifted her gaze to Mey. "If you hurry, I can perform a mating ceremony before leaving. I do not know when I will be back again."

Just like Yamanu, it seemed that the goddess was taking Mey's transition for granted.

Yamanu took Mey's hand and squeezed reassuringly. "Thank you for your kind offer, Clan Mother, but Mey needs to find her sister first. She wants Jin and their parents to attend the wedding, and that will take time to arrange."

It was a clever way to avoid mentioning that her transition had to happen before all of that.

"I understand. When you are ready, let me know. I might come back sooner rather than later." She cast a glance at Kian. "But first I need to pay Sari a visit. I do not want her to feel neglected." She smiled at Mey. "Even grown children can feel jealousy when they suspect their mother of favoring some over the others."

Syssi chuckled. "I think mine will suffer from too much of it. I love children, and I'm probably going to be one of those overprotective moms that hover over their kids."

"How many children do you plan on having?" Mey asked.

"As many as the Fates will bless me with."

Kian cleared his throat. "With the help of Merlin's potion, it's not entirely up to the Fates."

"True," Syssi agreed. "I want to have at least three. So, after this precious one is born, I will start on the potion again. After that, I might leave it up to the Fates."

"Smart decision." Annani patted her arm. "Although, in my opinion, the Fates had a hand in this too, guiding Merlin toward discovering the right combination of ingredients to put in it." She waved her hands in a circle. "It is all part of their grand plan."

6

YAMANU

*A*s Syssi and Mey continued their conversation about children, Kian pushed away from the table.

"I'm going outside to smoke. Anyone care to join me?"

Amanda got up. "I'll come with you."

He raised a brow. "You hate the smell."

"I've gotten used to it." She glanced at Dalhu. "Do you want to come?"

Yamanu had a feeling that the conversation was making Amanda uncomfortable.

"Sure. If it's okay with the Clan Mother." Dalhu looked at Annani.

The goddess smiled in approval. "Thank you for asking. I do not mind waiting for coffee and dessert. I am quite full." She put a hand over her middle.

Dalhu dipped his head. "Thank you."

When the three of them stepped out, Syssi leaned toward Mey and whispered, "Amanda doesn't want children."

Annani shook her head. "It is not that she does not want them, she is afraid of having a child and losing it. In her case, it is better to wait for the Fates to decide what is the right time. There is no rush."

"Why is she afraid?" Mey asked.

It was a sad story that Yamanu wasn't in the mood to hear retold.

He dipped his head. "If you'll excuse me, Clan Mother, I would like to join Kian outside and try one of his cigarillos." He glanced at Mey in case she wanted to escape as well.

She smiled. "Enjoy."

Over her initial nervousness, Mey seemed comfortable sitting next to Annani and chatting with her and Syssi.

Outside, Dalhu and Amanda were sitting on the fountain wall and talking in hushed voices, while Kian stood with his back to the house and smoked his cigarillo.

"I wonder how those taste," Yamanu said.

Kian turned around. "I didn't know you smoked."

"I don't. I like a cigar once in a while when it's a special occasion, like a bachelor party. Are those as good as the big ones?"

"Not as good, but good enough." Kian pulled the box out of his pocket and handed it to Yamanu. "What I like about them is that they don't take long to finish. Cigars are too time-consuming."

"That's the whole point." Yamanu pulled one out. "A cigar forces you to chill, and it's twice as good with a glass of quality whiskey." He shielded the flame from Kian's lighter and lit the cigarillo.

"I don't have time to chill." Kian took a puff. "Did you have a chance to test your powers yet?"

Yamanu shook his head.

"You should do it as soon as possible. I need to know whether or not I can count on you for blanket shrouding and thralling."

"I can't do it while I'm inducing Mey. I will probably have to abstain for a couple of days before I attempt a mass shroud or thrall, but I don't want to do so before Mey enters transition. We are in a time crunch, as you know."

Kian took another puff. "Try it without abstaining. I'm curious to see whether it is required at all."

That was actually not a bad idea, and it also removed some of the anxiety he felt about testing his powers. If they didn't work without abstaining, he still had the option to try it again after holding off for a couple of days. And if they worked without that, even better.

"I was trying to come up with a way to conduct a test. Blanket thralling would be easy to stage. I can go to the beach and thrall everyone into building sandcastles. But shrouding is more complicated. I need something major to hide. Any ideas?"

Kian shook his head. "It needs to be something loud or smelly that would normally attract a lot of attention, like a fire or an explosion. But we can't do either without major prep work. We would have to stage a movie set in the middle of a populated area, and that would take time to organize."

"A movie set is a good idea, but you are right about the complexity. It needs to be something simpler to pull off. Maybe I'll just get someone to sing in the middle of the mall with a loud megaphone."

Kian chuckled. "That could work. Or you could have Roni recite his vile slam poetry. That would certainly attract a lot of attention."

"I can work with that." Yamanu tapped on the cigarillo and watched the ash fall and disperse. "I could give Roni a megaphone and put him in front of a college cafeteria during lunchtime."

"I would like to see that." Kian took another puff. "How is the cigarillo?"

"Not bad. Relaxing. And since we don't have to worry about the side effects, it's a good way to wind down."

Kian nodded. "Not knowing whether you still have your powers must be stressful for you."

"It is, but I'm also worried about Mey. I thought she would have entered transition by now."

Kian cast him an incredulous look. "You just started inducing her on Friday. Did you expect it to happen after one time?"

Yamanu shrugged. "I'm an old immortal, and my blood is not as diluted as that of the younger guys."

25

"Brundar is about your age, and Callie didn't transition right away. He also didn't manage to induce Roni. In the end, I had to do it."

"Roni was sick. I don't know what the deal with Callie was, but I'm sure there was something else. Maybe she was ill too."

"As far as I know, she wasn't. In any case, it's too early to worry. I have the purest blood of all the clan males, and Syssi didn't transition right away either."

That was true.

Yamanu let out a breath. "We have only one week left."

"It should suffice. If Mey doesn't enter transition by next Sunday, she most likely isn't a Dormant."

7

KIAN

"Stop beating yourself up." Turner flipped the top of his thermos closed. "What's done is done. You learn from your mistakes and move on."

Kian pushed his hair back. "I wish you'd reconsider my offer and come on board full time. If you do, I will transfer control over all missions to you and dedicate my time to making more money for the clan. That's what I'm best at."

"I'm sorry, Kian, but I can't do that."

"I know that you can't bear the thought of being someone's subordinate, but I promise that you will have complete autonomy. I will defer to you in all things military."

Turner shook his head. "It's not about my need for independence. There is that too, but I might have accepted your offer if this was the only obstacle."

"So what is it? Money? How much are you making in your business, if I may ask? I'm willing to match it and even top it."

"That's very generous of you. But I doubt you can afford me." Turner smiled. "It's not about the money either, although the money is good. It's about helping people who have no one else to turn to. I'm their last resort. Kidnappings for ransom don't make the news unless the family is famous, but a lot of it is going on. I'm usually the only one who can get their loved ones out."

Talk about a checkmate.

But perhaps there was one more move Kian could make before conceding defeat. "Can't you train an assistant? If you have someone capable in your office handling most of the stuff, you can head both the clan's missions and your own."

"Look who's talking." Turner snorted. "I could give you the same advice."

"I tried. I'm either a lousy teacher, or none of those that I hired were up to the task."

"Some things you cannot teach. Did you consider that running the clan's business empire is your special talent?" Turner lifted one blond brow. "You have a natural knack for it, and not all of it is about what you know and how much experience you have. A lot of it has to do with gut feelings and knowing which business is worth investing in and which is not, regardless of how they look on paper."

It hadn't occurred to him before, but Turner might be right about that.

Kian's decisions were seldom based on dry numbers. He often relied on intangible things, like believing a particular technology would succeed while others might fail or seeing the potential for real estate developments where others had seen none.

And the same was true for the improvements and tweaks that he routinely suggested to management whenever he visited a location. He just knew how things should be done. It often baffled him that what was perfectly clear to him was not to others.

No wonder he couldn't teach it to anyone.

"So, you are saying that no one can replace you because rescue missions are your special talent?"

Turner nodded. "I don't know if it's planning missions in general or just rescues, but I have what appears to be a supernatural knack for that. I see all the possibilities for fuckups in my head as if they had already happened and I'm watching a replay."

Taking a deep breath, Kian leaned back in his chair. "I guess we are both stuck then. We need to keep going and do as much as we can because we are irreplaceable."

Turner clasped his thermos in both hands. "I don't know about irreplaceable. I would rather say difficult to replace." He smiled. "I'm trying to keep my vanity in check. Bridget keeps telling me that I appear stuck up to people and that I need to work on my humility. Or at least fake it."

Turner didn't appear stuck up, he actually was, but he had a good reason to feel superior. Nevertheless, it certainly didn't make him likable or approachable. People didn't like know-it-alls any more than they liked martyrs. Yamanu had been smart to keep his sacrifice secret. If he hadn't, he would have been much less popular and well-liked.

"I need to pick your brain in regard to finding Kalugal and Jin."

Turner arched a brow. "I thought you already found the guy."

"I might have found him, but I don't have proof or a way to get it. If the compound is guarded by immortals, we can't get in and check what he is up to. I'm not going to initiate contact until I know who I'm dealing with."

"I like that you are approaching this with caution. You could send people to the area to watch the mansion from afar. When one of his men leaves, they can follow him to wherever he is going and verify whether he is an immortal or not. Proximity should be enough to determine that."

"If one of ours feels one of Kalugal's, the reverse is also true."

"But ours will be there to find that out, while Kalugal's men will not be expecting to encounter other immortals. If our guy gets out fast enough, Kalugal's guy will dismiss the warning prickling."

"Let's say that it works, and we have proof that immortals live in the mansion. What then?"

"Then you will need Jin. Provided her talent works on immortals, that is." Turner shook his head. "It's a creepy one. Someone will have to volunteer for her to test it, and then she will have access to that person forever."

29

Kian chuckled. "For you, it would be the worst nightmare."

"Not the worst, but definitely among the top three."

"What if we can't find Jin, or if her talent doesn't work on immortals? We need plan B."

"Lokan. You will have to send him to talk with his brother and find out what he is up to."

"I don't trust Lokan. Not yet."

"That's why he is plan B and not plan A."

"Anything else?"

Turner shrugged. "You don't want to attack the place. You just want to snoop around. If both plans A and B fail, I'll think of something else."

"Fair enough. Let's get back to plan A then. How do we find Jin?"

"Eleanor is a good start. Before anything more elaborate is planned, I think finding her first and checking what she knows is your best option. You will need a strong thraller, though. The woman has been hiding for a while, and she is probably highly suspicious. Those types are not easy to thrall. Who is your best, Yamanu?"

"Yamanu is good for mass thralls. Arwel is better for individual ones. And if thralling doesn't work, he can employ his empathy. We also have Andrew to tell lies from truths, but I don't like the idea of taking him away from his family."

"Or you can use a truth serum, but then you will need a doctor with you, and they are not as effective as Andrew. On second thought, you don't need to wait for Arwel to come back from New York either. Any Guardian with good thralling skills would do."

"I can send Merlin with the team, but I disagree about the thraller. This is too important for second-tier Guardians to handle, and we only have two head Guardians who are unmated. Onegus and Arwel. The mission is not complicated enough to justify sending Onegus, so it has to be Arwel. Besides, I'm not going to send the team out before Mey transitions, so there is no rush, and Arwel is coming back this Saturday."

Turner chuckled. "At this rate, you will soon run out of bachelor head Guardians. You have to either step up the training and promote some of the others to head positions or start sending your people on missions regardless of their mated status. Those who've been mated for a while can tolerate a short separation."

"Or I can send them along with their mates like I did with Kri and Michael."

"That's also an option. Except, most of the mates are civilians."

8

LOSHAM

"What are you going to tell our leader, sir?" Rami asked.

Losham had been debating that since Shafen had come to him with the disturbing news on Thursday.

His initial investigation had confirmed Shafen's report, but it hadn't proved or disproved the clan's involvement. The official city records contained a report about the raid, claiming a massive drug bust with sixty-seven suspects detained in an undisclosed location.

But that didn't mean a thing.

The clan could have planted that report, either hacking into the system or thralling someone in charge to write it up.

The few neighbors who'd been awake during the raid parroted the same thing. A SWAT team had arrived, stormed the building, and taken everyone residing there into custody.

"I'm going to tell my father the truth, Rami."

His assistant smiled. "And which truth are you going to choose?"

"The real one. I'm going to tell him that I'm not sure what happened and hope for the best. If he is in a good mood, I might still have a job after this conversation. If he is not, we might need to get our things and run."

Rami's smile slid off his face. "I'm with you, sir. Wherever you go, I go."

Losham clapped him on the back. "I know. Your loyalty means a lot to me."

Not that it was all about loyalty for Rami.

Losham suspected that his assistant had feelings for him, but as long as he didn't make a move, which Losham was confident he would never dare, he didn't mind his assistant's harmless infatuation. If Losham swung that way, Rami would have been the perfect companion, but he didn't.

Losham loved women, but unlike other immortals, he didn't need to indulge all that often. He was a cerebral man, not one ruled by his baser needs.

Rami was a great assistant, intelligent, resourceful, and respectful without being sniveling. Losham could count on Rami to tell him the truth even when the man knew that Losham wasn't going to like it.

This was a priceless quality, especially in the Brotherhood, where everyone was terrified of their superiors.

"Could you make the call for me, Rami?"

"Yes, sir."

The calls to his father went through his secretary first, so it wasn't like Navuh was going to be offended by Rami placing the call on behalf of Losham.

"This is Ramael, Commander Losham's assistant."

"Hold the line. I'll check if his lordship will accept the call."

"Thank you."

It was the usual song and dance. Navuh was going to take the call, but he was going to make Losham wait and sweat until he did.

Except, Losham was going to wait with a glass of superb Japanese whiskey in one hand, a Cuban cigar in the other, and he wasn't going to sweat because it was a most pleasant evening in Bel Air.

Rami put the phone on the table. "I'll be in my room if you need me, sir."

Losham nodded.

He hadn't soundproofed the house yet, so Rami was going to be privy to the conversation wherever he went, but Losham didn't mind. Navuh thought himself refined. So even if he was majorly pissed, he wasn't going to shout or call him names.

"Good evening, Losham, or is it morning where you are?"

"It is late morning, my lord. I'm afraid that I have disturbing news. My team was taken out on Wednesday. I held off calling you until I completed my investigation. On the face of things, it appears as if they were arrested in a drug bust, but I suspect the clan's involvement. I think they donned SWAT uniforms to make it look like a police arrest and then planted a fake report in the official database."

While a long moment of silence passed, Losham's forehead beaded with sweat.

"How would they know where to find your men? Did you start abductions in the area, so they got alerted to your presence?"

"No, my lord. The men had just arrived in the building I purchased for them in Koreatown. I chose the location because it is densely populated and relatively inexpensive. I have no idea how the clan could have discovered so soon that we'd arrived in the city.

"Were there drugs on the premises?"

"Naturally. This is part of what we are doing here, my lord."

"Yes, I'm aware of that. But since your men had just arrived, I wondered if there was real justification for the arrest."

"We brought the drugs with us from our previous location."

"I see." There was another long moment of silence. "It might have been the work of a traitor. He could have sold you either to the authorities or to the clan in exchange for money or other compensation."

"I considered that possibility." Losham sighed dramatically. "If the men had been implanted with trackers as I suggested, we might have been able to find them. If the clan has them, the trackers could have led us to them."

"If the clan got them, they killed them and dumped the bodies somewhere in the mountains or deserts. So that would have done us no good. And if the human authorities have them, the men will find a way to get out. In any case, implanting them with trackers would have been a waste of time and resources."

"Yes, my lord."

Bottom line, Navuh was cheap and didn't want to spend the money. Nothing new about that.

"The mistake was letting the men stay away from the island for long periods of time," Navuh continued. "No one should be away for more than a month, and then they should stay on the island for an extended period before being allowed back. I'm going to send you replacements, but you will need to overhaul your entire operation. It is going to be a small group of men this time. Once a warrior escorts an acquisition to the island, he will stay here, and another one will take his place. We are going to establish a rotation."

"Yes, my lord. But that will require training for each new group of men."

More work for Losham.

"Initially, yes. But once you train everyone in the rotation cycle, you are done. It won't require too much effort on your part. I also suggest that you don't house them in the same location again. Rent them apartments in several buildings in different parts of the city, and no more than two warriors in one address. Putting them all together is making them an easy target for the authorities as well as for the clan."

"Yes, my lord. That is an excellent idea." In fact, he should have thought of it himself.

Except, it was easier to keep the men together. Besides, purchasing one old building had saved him a bundle on rent, which he'd pocketed. Now he would have to pay at least double for their accommodations and also rent a warehouse for meetings.

"And, Losham."

"Yes, my lord."

"I expect you to recuperate the monetary loss, so you'd better start thinking creatively."

"Yes, my lord."

The line disconnected without any goodbyes, but that wasn't new either. Navuh rarely bothered with niceties.

Leaning back, Losham puffed on his cigar.

This had gone much better than he'd expected. In fact, Navuh's response worried him. His father was never that mellow or that understanding. Usually, he would express his disappointment and issue a few threats. He must have been in an exceptionally good mood.

Or maybe Navuh appreciated Losham's honesty?

Nevertheless, it was disconcerting because it was out of character. Losham would have to be extra careful and watch his back. If nothing else, his father was going to send an informer with the new group of warriors.

Had there been one among the group that had been taken out? Was that why his father had been so accepting?

That made perfect sense.

If Navuh had an informer among the fallen warriors, then lack of communication from the man had confirmed Losham's report.

9

MEY

"I must be out of my mind." Mey adjusted the silk scarves that were tied to a wide belt slung low on her hips.

She looked sexy, but only when striking a pose, not when attempting to belly dance. The vivid colors went well with her dark hair, and since she didn't really need to wear a bra for lift, only for coverage, the scarf that was tied around her breasts and looped around her neck did the job well enough. Her tummy, although a little rounded after all the big meals she'd been having lately, was still flat enough to put on display.

Besides, the belly dancer in the video was far from slim, and her jiggly belly and wide hips only added to the allure of her dance.

Except, the woman on the screen could move, while Mey's attempts looked like they belonged on one of those animated mannequins that had been popular lately on YouTube.

Feeling silly, she imitated her favorite one, called *Late for a Meeting*, flapping her arms around and bending her body in weird ways.

That was good for a laugh, and for getting her limbs to loosen up, but if she wanted to dance for Yamanu, she needed to practice. Unless she could pull off dance moves that weren't embarrassing, she wasn't going to do it. The idea was to get him excited, not laughing his ass off.

Perhaps she should just do a model walk for him. That would get him all hot and bothered without her having to put much effort into it.

But what was the challenge in that?

Determined to learn, Mey restarted the video and followed the moves as best she could. She practiced until every muscle in her body hurt, and a cramp in her side forced her to stop.

Twenty-five minutes. That was how long she'd lasted this time. What the hell was she going to do with the rest of her day?

Yamanu had to work, so he couldn't stay with her in the house all day, and her new friends were all busy as well. Callie had classes, Wonder worked in the café, and Syssi and Amanda were in the university lab.

Perhaps she could help Wonder out? Without Callie, Wonder had to do everything by herself, making the coffees and cappuccinos and the sandwiches and also serving them.

Now that was an idea.

Instead of sitting at home, being bored and thinking about stressful stuff, she could help a friend and at the same time get to meet new people. The café was the central hub of the village, and according to Wonder and Callie, it was the best place to get to know everyone.

It shouldn't be too hard to learn. Anyone could make coffees and sandwiches, or at least serve them.

Fifteen minutes later, showered and dressed in a pair of jeans and a T-shirt, Mey walked out of the house and closed the door behind her. She didn't have a key, but it seemed like no one in the village bothered to lock their doors, so that wasn't a big deal.

As she strode toward the café, she texted Yamanu to let him know where she was going in case he came looking for her.

Have fun, he texted back. *I'll come to get you when I'm done.*

When she got there, the place didn't look too busy, and Wonder welcomed her with a big smile. "I'm so glad you came. Would you like a cappuccino?"

"Actually, I came to work. With Callie at school, I'm sure you could use a helping hand around here."

Wonder looked uncomfortable. "I need to check with Jackson. I only work here, and I can't pay you."

Mey waved a dismissive hand. "I'm not expecting to get paid for this. The clan is doing so much for me, the least I can do is put in a little work. Besides, I'm bored, and I really suck at belly dancing."

Wonder lifted a brow. "Belly dancing?"

"I'll tell you all about it while you show me how to work the cappuccino machine."

"It's really easy." Wonder pressed a button. "The only part that takes some practice is frothing the milk."

"Can I try?"

"Let me show you how it's done first."

As the machine finished grinding the beans, Wonder filled a metal container with milk and put it under the nozzle. "You need to make sure that it's not too hot and not too cold. You can watch the thermometer. It should be between a hundred and fifty and a hundred and sixty. But soon you'll be able to tell by touch. When the pitcher becomes too hot to hold, you are done"

"Got it."

From the corner of her eye, Mey saw Ella and her mother heading toward the counter.

"It seems like the cappuccinos are not going to be wasted."

"Hi, Mey. When did you start working in the café?" Ella asked.

"Mey is volunteering," Wonder said. "Which is really nice of her but unacceptable." She turned to Mey. "I'm going to call Jackson and ask him to put you on the payroll."

"Don't. I might not be here next Monday."

Vivian frowned. "Why? Where are you going?"

"Probably back to New York."

Vivian's frown deepened. "Are things not working out with Yamanu?"

Mey sighed and leaned against the counter. "Yamanu is amazing, but if I don't transition by Sunday night, I can't stay."

"Said who?" Ella asked.

"Kian. He gave me two weeks. Evidently, erasing memories of a period longer than that can cause brain damage."

Luckily, he hadn't thought to include the week she'd spent with Yamanu and the team before arriving in the village. If he had, she would already be back at her apartment in New York, bemoaning a loss she couldn't remember.

Ella waved a hand. "Don't worry about it. If you don't transition in time, he'll give you an extension. The two weeks is just an arbitrary choice. No one knows for sure how many memories are too many to erase."

Well, that wasn't exactly reassuring. What if she'd already accumulated too many memories and was going to suffer brain damage when Yamanu removed them?

"How long did it take you to transition?" she asked Vivian.

The petite blonde blushed. "From the time we threw the condoms away, it took about ten days."

That was good news. They had started on Friday, and this was only Tuesday.

"Same here," Ella said. "So don't think that my mom took longer because she was older."

Mey let out a breath. "Then I guess I should start worrying only if I don't enter transition by Sunday." She pushed a strand of hair behind her ear. "Perhaps I should ask Kian for an extension. Given your experience, he might consider approving a day or two over the deadline."

10

YAMANU

"No way!" Roni crossed his arms over his chest and leaned into his Batmobile style swivel chair.

"Why not? You did it to aggravate Kian." Yamanu smirked. "As someone who loves getting a rise out of people, you should enjoy this."

"I'm not going to stand in front of a student cafeteria and recite slam poetry. Besides, what's the deal with testing your powers? Did you lose them somewhere?"

Yamanu grimaced. "Love might have weakened them. I have to find out before Kian sends me out on a real mission. He counts on me."

William shook his head. "Why would falling in love make you weak? It's not like you were a grouch before meeting Mey, and your bad temper fueled your abilities. You were always an easy-going fellow."

Damn, it felt bad to lie to his friends, but coming clean and admitting the real deal was not an option. Not only for his sake but for Mey's as well. He didn't want people blaming her for the loss of his protection.

"I can't focus as well as I used to. Meditation always helped, but since Mey entered my life, I have a hard time clearing my mind. I keep thinking about her, seeing her whenever I close my eyes and feeling my heart overflow with love for her. I have to find out whether the lack of focus affects my shrouding and thralling."

Roni smiled, and it was a genuine one, not mocking like usual. "There ain't nothing better than love. Still, you will have to rope someone else into doing this for you. As much as I would like to help, I'm still a wanted man, and I can't risk people pulling their phones out and videotaping my performance. What if it ends up on YouTube?"

"I'll do it," William said. "Just text me the damn thing so I can memorize it."

That was a surprise. William hardly ever left his lab.

"Are you sure?" Yamanu asked. "You don't have a problem with public speaking? Because I might not be able to shroud you."

William shrugged. "I could use some excitement." He chuckled. "Doing something that doesn't involve a computer screen would be great."

He stretched his arms, pushing his big belly out. "Besides, I wouldn't mind mingling with some college hotties. There is nothing sexier than a smart woman."

Roni snorted, his expression reverting to reflect his usual sarcastic attitude. "Being in college doesn't make them smart. I've never gone, and I'm one of the smartest people you will ever meet."

William shook his head. "Your humility is astounding."

"What? It's the truth. Faking humility is the same as lying. I don't feel humble, and therefore I shouldn't act as if I am just so people who are dumber than me won't feel threatened."

William waved a hand. "The problem is that you think everyone is dumber than you, and then you wonder why you don't have friends."

"I have friends." Roni sent William an air kiss. "You are my friend."

Yamanu lifted a hand to stop the bickering. "We are getting sidetracked." He turned to Roni. "Do you still have those poems on your phone?"

"I never deleted them, so they should be there." Roni swiveled his chair around and lifted the device off the table. "Yeah, I've got them. I'm sending them to you, William. Try not to blush when you read it."

A second later, William's phone pinged with an incoming text. As he opened the attachment, his brows dipped low. "Nope, not reading those." He lifted his eyes to Yamanu. "How about I sing opera instead?"

"Can you sing?"

"Not well, but I can sing." He started bellowing a song from *The Phantom of the Opera*.

Yamanu shook his head. "I'm sorry, William, but that will drive people away instead of drawing them closer. To test whether my shrouding still works, I need a crowd to assemble. Otherwise, I wouldn't know whether they dispersed because they could no longer see or hear you or because they didn't want to."

William's face fell. "Fine. I'll search for something cleaner."

"Not too clean or no one will come," Roni said. "Do you think people would watch the news if it was all about nice things happening around the world? People love misery and conflict, as long as they can watch it from the safety of their couches, that is."

Sadly, it was true.

William sighed. "I'll find something to work with that doesn't have the words fuck and bitch in every sentence."

"Good luck with attracting a crowd." Roni turned his chair around to face the screen.

"When do you want to do it?" William asked.

"Now. If you are not too busy."

William gazed up at him with his smart eyes. "You are really worried about your powers, aren't you?"

"Of course. Imagine waking up one day and realizing that you might be losing your knack for technology."

"I would panic." William pushed up from his chair. "Do you have everything ready?"

"I have a crate in my trunk for you to stand on, and I have a megaphone. Do we need anything else?"

"Yeah, I need to memorize some damn poems by the time we get there."

"I don't expect you to do that. You can just read them from your phone."

"That's not going to cut it. If you want a crowd to gather, some showmanship is required. But don't worry, I have an excellent memory. It's enough that I read a thing twice, and I can recite it word for word."

"That's a useful talent."

"For a nerd like me, it certainly is."

11

MEY

"Who is this little cutie?" Mey crouched next to the most adorable little girl.

"I'm Phoenix," the toddler said. "Who are you?"

"I'm Mey. How old are you?"

The girl lifted two fingers. "I'm two."

The mother smiled. "Almost. She is going to be two in two months but hearing her talk, you'd think she is twelve. I'm Nathalie." She offered Mey her hand.

"I know. I met your mother in New York." Mey shook her head. "I flipped when Yamanu told me that she was a grandmother. But even more impressive than that were her makeup skills. The way she transformed Alena's face to make her look like Areana was awe-inspiring."

Nathalie snorted. "That's just one of her many talents. My mother used to be a DEA agent, and after taking a long break to raise me, she opened her own detective agency. Now she's taken another break to be with Ethan."

Mey couldn't help the grin spreading over her face. "He is such a sweet baby. He let me hold him and kiss him, and he didn't make a fuss about it. Usually, babies don't like being passed around."

"He's used to that." Nathalie sat down and lifted her daughter into her lap. "And so is Phoenix, but lately, she's become more selective about who she allows to kiss her." She planted a kiss on top of the child's head. "But I'm the mommy, so I get dibs."

"What's dibs?" Phoenix asked.

"It means that I am first in line for your kisses."

"Nah-ah, that's Daddy."

Nathalie rolled her eyes. "Girls and their daddies. It's not fair."

"Why?" Phoenix asked.

Nathalie ruffled her daughter's dark hair. "Because I'm the one answering your *why* questions all day long, so I deserve kisses first."

The child scrunched her nose. "You get my kisses all day long, Mommy. But when Daddy comes home, it's his turn."

Mey laughed. Phoenix was just precious. "What can I get you, ladies?"

"Did they put you to work already?" Nathalie lifted a brow. "You just got here."

"It's boring to sit around the house and wait for Yamanu to come back. I volunteered."

"I want ice cream," the girl said.

Nathalie hugged her closer. "They don't have ice cream in the café, sweetie." When Phoenix's face fell, she added. "We can get some at the supermarket later."

The smile was back, accompanied by a happy clap. "Oh, goodie."

As mother and daughter discussed flavors, Mey wondered whether the child was an immortal already. Yamanu had said that girls turned at a much younger age than the boys and that it was enough for them to be around the goddess to do so.

No venom required.

"I guess you don't worry about her getting stomach aches or things like that."

"No, I still worry," Nathalie said. "But I believe in moderation. Even if Phoenix weren't so special, I would have allowed her ice cream and sweets. Just not too much or too often."

It made sense not to mention the word immortal in front of the girl. She was too young to understand the need for secrecy, and if Nathalie was taking her on supermarket excursions outside the village, she might say something incriminating.

"I wish I could go with you. I need groceries, but I can't leave the village."

"Why?" Phoenix asked.

Mey smiled. "I don't have time to go." She waved at the direction of the café's serve-out counter. "I have work to do."

"Oh. Mommy can get you gwoseris. Do you want ice cream?"

"That's a great idea," Nathalie said. "Make a list of what you need, and I'll get it for you."

"You're shopping with a toddler. That's hard enough without schlepping things for me as well."

Nathalie waved dismissively. "Don't be silly. Phoenix loves shopping, so that's not a problem, and I give the boy who bags my groceries a couple of bucks to load everything into my car. When I get back to the village, there is never a shortage of helping hands to carry everything home."

Mey still felt uncomfortable about Nathalie doing this for her, but if she wanted to make a nice dinner for Yamanu, it was her only option.

"I'll take you up on your offer." She pulled out her wallet and handed Nathalie a hundred-dollar bill. "But I owe you. Once Eva comes back, I'm inviting all of you to dinner."

"That would be lovely." Nathalie pushed the bill back at Mey. "I didn't get you a welcoming present, so let me cover the groceries."

"No way. If you don't take the money, I'm not going to give you the list." Mey pushed it back and crossed her arms over her chest.

Phoenix burrowed into her mother's chest. "Why are you and Mey fighting, Mommy?"

"We're not fighting, sweetie. We are having a discussion."

"It sounds like a fight, and Mey made an angry face."

Damn. Apparently, she still had a lot to learn about raising kids.

Were girls particularly sensitive? Or were all young children so easily upset?

"I'm sorry, Phoenix. I'm not angry, I was just pretending so your mommy will take my money."

"Why?"

Mey stifled a groan. "Never mind. I was just being silly. Everything is okay."

The girl smiled. "I like you. I want you and Mommy to be friends."

"Me too, sweetheart." She lifted her gaze to Nathalie. "The village and the people living in it are all incredible. Everyone is so nice and eager to help. I really want to become part of this community."

Nathalie reached for her hand and gave it a gentle squeeze. "You already are."

12

YAMANU

*A*s Yamanu placed the crate on the lawn in front of the cafeteria, a few people cast him and William curious glances before entering the building.

"Are you ready?"

William nodded. "I found some good ones. But without practice, my delivery is not going to be spectacular."

"It doesn't need to be. All you need is to grab people's attention for several minutes and then step down. A moment later, you are going to step up again, but I'm going to shroud you so it will look like you are still sitting on the lawn and resting. If they leave, we will know that the shroud worked. If they stay, it didn't."

William tugged on the bottom of his Hawaiian shirt. "They might leave because they are bored, or because they don't want to look at a fat guy reciting poetry."

William was nowhere near as heavy as he used to be, but he was still heavyset. Nevertheless, he was an immortal, with an immortal's perfect skin and handsome face. Yamanu had caught several young ladies casting him covert glances.

He clapped the guy on the back. "You are much better-looking than you give yourself credit for. I've seen the glances you've gotten from girls."

William snorted. "They were looking at you. No one noticed that I was even there."

"Not true. I saw where their eyes went, and they were looking at you."

With a shrug, William took the megaphone out of the duffle bag and stepped onto the crate. "Let me know when you want me to stop."

"Go for it." Yamanu gave him the thumbs up.

As William started reciting, Yamanu's eyes widened in surprise. Not only had he memorized everything during the one-hour drive, but his delivery was also superb.

Soon, a small crowd was gathered around the crate, and people were smiling, nodding, and praising the performance.

When the crowd grew substantially, Yamanu decided to start with a thrall, planting in their heads that it was about to rain and making them see dark, heavy clouds heading in their direction.

Several people lifted their eyes to the sky, shook their heads, and stayed. Others did the same and then hurried away.

It seemed like his thrall had worked on some but not all, meaning that he could still blanket thrall, but he wasn't as powerful as he used to be.

It wasn't bad news. As long as he could still affect many people at once, he could work on adding juice to his thralling by abstaining for a couple of days, or meditating, or both.

He waited until William was done reciting his first poem before motioning for him to step down.

"How did it go?"

Yamanu tilted his head toward the depleted crowd. "You've seen it. My thrall worked on some but not others. It didn't have enough power, but I can still do it."

"I don't know why you were worried that you couldn't in the first place. What's next?"

"Let's wait until most of them start walking away, and then you go back up. If they return or even look over their shoulders, it means that my shroud failed. If they keep walking, it means that it worked."

When people got tired of waiting and started leaving, Yamanu motioned for William to get up on his improvised podium. "Use the megaphone." He handed it to him. "But wait for my signal. Don't start until I activate the shroud."

William nodded.

There weren't many people left on the lawn, but the cafeteria doors were kept busy, with students going in and others leaving. If the shroud didn't work, a new crowd would assemble in minutes.

Yamanu closed his eyes and concentrated on the familiar feeling of spreading his awareness like a cloud to blanket the area. Usually, it exploded out of him like a thunderstorm, but this time it felt more like a gentle breeze.

He nodded, motioning for William to begin.

Long moments passed before he dared to open his eyes and look around.

Only a small group remained on the lawn, but they weren't paying attention to William. People exiting the cafeteria kept on going without sparing him a glance.

William stopped his recitation and stepped off the crate. "It worked."

Yamanu let out a relieved breath. "It would seem so. But shrouding one person is easy. I need something bigger."

"How about fireworks?" William suggested. "They make a lot of noise and cover a large area in the sky. Would that work?"

That was a great idea.

"Those would be perfect. Lots of noise and a light show in the sky would be a bitch to shroud. The question is how to do it safely. I don't want to cause an accidental fire."

William put the megaphone back inside the duffle bag. "We can do it from the mall's parking lot. The one they use for Fourth of July celebrations."

"Can you help me set it up?"

William's eyes shone with boyish excitement. "It would be my pleasure."

"Have you ever done that before?"

"No, but it shouldn't be complicated if kids do it." He rubbed a hand over his jaw. "I can really go wild with this. I just hope your shroud works. Otherwise, we will be running from the police."

"Let's hope that it does." Yamanu looked around the lawn. "It seems that I've still got it. I just need to work on producing more juice to feed it."

MEY

*M*ey took a step back and looked at the table she'd set up. It was nothing fancy, just a roast chicken with potatoes and a salad, but that was all she'd had time for.

Nathalie had dropped the groceries off hours ago, leaving them on her doorstep, but Mey had worked in the café until it closed, and that didn't leave her enough time to prepare anything elaborate.

Not that she knew how to make any fancy dishes. Her mom cooked simply, and that was what Mey and Jin had learned to do while helping her in the kitchen.

If she'd had time, though, she could've searched for recipes on the internet.

Look at me. So domestic. She smiled.

Preparing dinner for the man she loved felt good, and if there were a couple of children running around, it would have been even better. It was certainly a change of pace from her hectic modeling life. She and her roommates hadn't cooked, mostly eating out and occasionally ordering takeout.

Mey didn't miss any of it. It hadn't been real.

This was.

Phoenix was so adorable, but her never-ending *why* questions could try the patience of a saint. It hadn't seemed to bother Nathalie, though. On the contrary, she had seemed proud that her child was so incredibly advanced at such a young age and had answered each question lovingly.

Mey wondered what kind of mother she was going to be.

Would she be as tolerant as Nathalie?

She certainly hoped so. Her own parents had provided a great example. Mey and Jin hadn't gone through the rebellious phase that many teenagers tormented their parents with. It was probably because of the easy-going atmosphere at home, and the trust and respect with which they had been treated. There had been rules, but not too strict, and the consequences of breaking them had usually been long talks about what had prompted the undesirable behavior.

Like her mother's gentle reproach for the scarcity of phone calls when Mey had talked to her last night. She'd claimed to be very busy with work and social obligations, which hadn't been a straight out lie. Her mother had accepted it, telling her not to work too hard.

As the front door opened, Mey turned around and looked at Yamanu's handsome face. He was smiling, which meant either that he had good news or that he was happy to see her. Or maybe both.

"How was your day?" Mey asked as she walked up to him and wrapped her arms around his neck.

He put his hands on her hips and pulled her close against his body. "It was good, but coming home to you is the best part." He bent and took her lips in a hungry kiss.

When his big hands cupped her bottom and squeezed, the heat from his kiss intensified, but she wanted to feed her man first and make love to him second.

Pushing on his chest, she leaned back. "The chicken is getting cold."

"I don't care." He pulled her to him again.

"But I do. Let's eat first. I want to hear all about your day."

Reluctantly, he let go of her. "Bossy lady."

She slapped his arm playfully. "Don't complain. I know that you love it."

A sly smile lifted one corner of his lips. "I do. You are so sexy when you get stubborn. But that only makes me want to throw you over my shoulder and carry you to bed."

"Hold that thought for after dinner." She took his hand and led him to the table. "Would you like a beer with your meal?"

"You are spoiling me."

"It's my pleasure." And it was.

Mey remembered her father waiting for her mother with dinner on the table when she'd come back from her shift at the hospital. He didn't know how to cook and usually just reheated what she'd made the day before, but it was the gesture that mattered.

It showed that he cared.

Mey pulled out a beer for Yamanu and a can of Diet Coke for herself.

"How was working at the café?" Yamanu asked when she returned.

"It was fun. I got to meet so many people, but the highlight was Nathalie and Phoenix. That girl is so adorable. And Nathalie is so nice. She bought groceries for us."

He looked at the chicken. "I wondered where you'd gotten that from, but I assumed that Callie brought it."

"Na-ah. This is my cooking." She cut the chicken in half, put one half on his plate, and added a mountain of roast potatoes. "Do you want some salad?"

"Sure." He lifted the bowl and scooped a small portion onto his plate. "I have to say that I'm impressed. And thank you. I haven't been pampered like this since I left my mother's home." He chuckled. "Not that there was dinner on the table every night. She worked as a midwife, delivering babies in the nearby villages."

"What does she do now?"

"The same. But now she works in a hospital, and she's gotten a degree in nursing."

"That's awesome. My mother is a pediatric nurse."

Yamanu grinned. "They will have something to talk about when they meet at our wedding."

To hide the sudden flare of anxiety that had gripped her, Mey cut a piece of chicken and put it in her mouth.

Yamanu was such an optimist, taking for granted that everything was going to turn out okay. She wished she could be like him.

"I tested my powers today," he said.

Mey's stomach flipped and then sank low. She hadn't known he'd been planning to do that.

"How did it go?" She croaked and reached for her drink to wet her throat.

"Not too bad. I managed to blanket thrall and shroud, but it lacked power. I think I can fix that with short abstinence. A day or two should do that." He smiled and reached for her hand. "With you around, my sexual energy recharges at lightning speed."

Mey felt light-headed with relief. "You have no idea how happy this makes me. I think that I worried about this more than I worried about my transition. I love it here, and I love the people. I couldn't stand the thought of being shunned because everyone hated me for destroying their protector. Not to mention the guilt I felt for being your kryptonite."

"You're not my kryptonite. You are my superconductor. And once your transition starts, I'm going to test my powers again and prove it. But until then, we need to focus all of our energy on activating your dormant genes."

KIAN

*A*s Kian entered the war room, several of the Guardians raised their brows in surprise, while excitement registered on the faces of others.

The day-to-day rescue operations and security detail for the village as well as the old keep were handled by Onegus. Kian's presence meant something new was brewing, and it seemed that the rumor about Kalugal's suspected whereabouts had not spread yet.

He waited for Onegus to be done before stepping in front of the assembled Guardians.

"For those of you who haven't heard yet, we have new information about Kalugal. Lokan discovered it during a business meeting with a guy who heads one of the top cybersecurity firms in the country. He told him about an installation he'd done for a reclusive billionaire, who had a large underground compound built on the grounds of his mansion. Lokan thought it was worth investigating, and I agreed. I had William and Roni divert their resources from the country-wide screening of airport security feeds to those from bars, cafés, and restaurants in the vicinity of said mansion. They found a match."

Excited murmurs started, and a couple of Guardians raised their hands to ask questions.

"Yes, Reibert."

"Do we know if he has his men with him?"

"For the sake of brevity, it would be best that I continue to tell you what we know at this stage. Kalugal's picture that was captured on the security camera was grainy, but the computer gave it a high probability of being a match with Tim's sketch. I still have my doubts, though. We don't have an actual photograph of the guy, and as good as Tim is, he is not a camera."

Kian waited for the snickers and comments about Tim's talent to die down before continuing. "I want to send a team to the Bay Area to investigate and bring back proof that this is indeed Kalugal. If it is him, he probably has his men with him, and that was why he built the extensive underground compound. If we can follow anyone leaving that place and verify that he is an immortal, we will have our confirmation."

"What if those are Doomers?" Duncan asked.

"According to Lokan, all the Doomers from the Bay Area moved down here, including his brother Losham, who is the head of their operations in California. We took out the rank and file, so the only ones left at the moment are Losham, his assistant, and maybe several of his bodyguards. Lokan doesn't have details on that."

He scanned the faces of his men, stopping when he reached Magnus. Of all the second-tier Guardians, he was best suited for the mission. The way he dressed and carried himself would fit in well with the population of the affluent city the mansion was in. The question was whether he would be willing to leave his wife behind. Especially since they were working on a baby.

"Magnus, are you up for a low-key out-of-town mission?"

The Guardian nodded, but given his expression, he wasn't overly excited about the prospect. "If we get confirmation that immortals live on the premises, do you intend to engage?"

Kian shook his head. "Not until I find out what Kalugal is up to, and in any case, I don't plan an assault against him. At this time, I just want to find out if he is indeed the guy who owns that mansion."

"A recon mission," Magnus clarified.

"Yes. It's crucial to keep the investigation discreet. I don't want to alert him to the fact that we know where he is. That's why I think you are a good choice for it. You can pretend to be a rich guy looking to buy a home in the area. This will give you an excuse to drive around. One of the other Guardians can pretend to be a real estate agent. Another two can be municipal workers tending to the electrical wires or whatever else you can come up with. You are in charge. Assemble your team and let Shai know how many, so he can arrange accommodations."

Magnus scratched his beard. "My cover will seem more believable if Vivian is with me. A husband and wife looking to buy a house is more common than a guy doing it alone. And since this is only a recon mission, she will be in no danger."

Kian nodded. "I like it. Tell Shai to put you up in a luxury hotel. The rest of your men should lodge somewhere else."

There were a few murmurs of protest and comments about unfairness, but they were intended as jabs at Magnus and not actual criticism. The Guardians were all well aware of the financial strain the rescue operations were putting on the clan, and the most significant component in that expenditure was their salaries.

"When do you want us to head out?" Magnus asked.

"Whenever you are ready."

"I can leave tomorrow."

"Don't you need to check with Vivian first?"

"I will, but I'm sure she will jump at the opportunity to get out of here. As lovely as the village is, it's like living on a freaking island, and that includes island fever."

Kian didn't like the comparison. Anything that alluded to similarities between the clan and the Brotherhood, even superficial ones, aggravated him.

"That's on you, Magnus. You could have taken your wife on vacation anytime you wanted."

"He prefers to do it on your dime," Reibert groused.

"It's not his dime, it's ours," someone else commented.

Kian lifted a hand to stop the ribbing. Guardians were like boys. What started as a joke, could quickly escalate into fistfights.

"Anyone have more questions before we adjourn?"

"I do," Anandur said. "What if Kalugal turns out to be a decent fellow who detests his father and everything he stands for? Are we going to invite him and his men to join our ranks?"

The room fell silent as everyone waited to hear Kian's response.

"No."

"Why not? We could use reinforcements. The enemy of my enemy is my friend, true?"

"I'm not in a rush to welcome a bunch of ex-Doomers into our clan. First, we need to find out what they are up to, and then each man will get evaluated separately and over a long period of time. Besides, perhaps Kalugal enjoys his autonomy. He might prefer to stay neutral and as far away as he can from the conflict. The fact that he doesn't see eye to eye with his father doesn't mean that he wants to fight him."

Or take over the island, as Lokan hoped to do with his brother's help.

If Kalugal hadn't made a move yet, he was probably not planning on making one.

YAMANU

As the men started to disperse, Yamanu followed Kian outside. "I feel bad for not going out on rescue missions, but I'm thankful to you for relieving me from duty. Not going out at nights allows me more time with Mey."

Kian clapped him on the back. "Right now, your number one priority is to induce your lady's transition."

"I know. But still. Without Arwel and me, the guys have to manage the rescues, and they also need to reassure the girls after getting them out. Sometimes that's the hardest part. They are so frightened."

Kian nodded. "We also don't have Kri and her calming influence. But the men manage. Vanessa gave them a crash course while you were in New York."

Yamanu chuckled. "I heard about it. Donell says it helps him with picking girls up in bars."

Kian's lips lifted in a ghost of a smile. "That guy needs all the help he can get. I don't know how he manages to seduce anyone with his lame one-liners."

"Pity?"

Kian shrugged. "He is good-looking enough. I hear that nowadays ladies take the initiative, so he can get away with saying nothing."

"I wouldn't know."

Kian cast him a sidelong glance. "Don't tell me that you've never had women hit on you because I won't believe that."

"I might be a handsome bastard, but I'm too tall, and my eyes are too pale. Humans are wary of me."

For several long minutes, neither of them spoke as they exited the pavilion and headed toward the office building.

"We've rescued several boys recently," Kian said. "It's no longer just girls. Vanessa organized another shelter for them."

Yamanu shook his head. "This is so fucking sad. I don't care how much this effort drains our resources. I'm glad we are doing this."

"Me too. But instead of feeling good about it, I feel even worse knowing that we can't get everyone out, and that whatever we do, it's not enough. I hoped that we could at least clean up this city, but it's hopeless. We eradicate one hellhole and another one springs up in its place. There is just too much money to be made in this business to deter the scum that deals in it."

Yamanu often felt the same, but unlike Kian, he was a glass-half-full kind of guy. Rescuing some was better than rescuing none.

"I wish we had legions of people," Kian said. "But I know that Kalugal and his men will never join our ranks in this. Even Lokan, who is as enlightened as a Doomer can be and strives to change the way the island gets its sex providers, is not all that concerned about the trade. They have little regard for humans."

"Can you blame them? Why should they care when humans do not?"

Kian raked his fingers through his hair. "I know. And it frustrates the hell out of me. It always has."

Yamanu wondered what had prompted Kian to share his thoughts with him. They had never been close. Cordial was the best way to describe their relationship. Even Anandur and Brundar, who had been Kian's bodyguards for centuries, weren't all that close to him.

Perhaps Yamanu's confession about his abstinence had changed the dynamics between them?

They both kept people at arm's length, but for different reasons. Kian's position as a leader created a natural barrier between him and his subjects, and Yamanu's secrets created a barrier between him and even his closest friends.

Was that going to change now that it was no longer an issue?

Except, it still was. He hadn't told anyone he didn't have to about his sacrifice, and if he could help it, he never would.

Kian cast him a sidelong glance. "You didn't tell me about the results of your experiment yet."

"Right, I was about to. Roni refused to help, claiming that he needs to remain incognito. William volunteered to go in his place and did a damn good job."

"That's not what I was asking about."

Impatient man.

"I was getting there. It was better than I expected but not as good as I hoped. I can still do blanket thralls and shrouds, but they don't last as long, and they don't affect as many people. I need more power behind them."

Kian let out a breath. "That's better news than I had hoped for. At least you can still do that."

"I think I can get to nearly full power if I abstain for a couple of days. But as you've said, inducing Mey is my number one priority right now, and we don't have much time left. You gave us until Monday."

Actually, it was until Sunday, but Yamanu hoped that Kian wasn't going to be strict about his deadline.

"I'll give you an extension. The two-week timeframe is arbitrary, and its purpose is mainly to protect Mey in case she doesn't transition. None of us want to risk her suffering brain damage from erasing too many memories. But if she is willing to take the risk, I'm willing to give you another week."

That was a huge relief, but not without reservations. What Kian had said was true. "Is this your way of telling me to test my theory sooner?"

Kian nodded. "I have to know if I can still count on you to shield operations. I don't like hanging in limbo. It's either a yes or a no. If it's a no, I'll start working on a substitute, but I don't want to waste time and effort on this if it's not necessary."

"Perfectly understandable. I'll talk to Mey and see what she thinks. It would have to be her decision."

"Absolutely. I wouldn't have it any other way."

16

MEY

*M*ey took her apron off and balled it up. She hadn't brought a purse, so there was nowhere she could put it. "This thing needs washing. I'm taking it home to put in the laundry."

"I can do that," Wonder offered. "I'm washing mine and Callie's anyway. You have better things to do than that." She waggled her brows and then blushed.

Mey pretended not to get her meaning. "I still have to make dinner, but it will have to be something quick. Yamanu texted me that he is heading home in a few minutes. It might have to be a pizza night."

"I wasn't talking about that." Wonder swiveled her hips, performing a damn good belly dance move. Much better than Mey had managed so far. "Are you going to show him what you've learned?"

"Maybe." Mey handed her the apron.

She'd practiced, and her movements were more fluid today than they were yesterday, but she still wasn't good enough.

"I need more practice."

Wonder waved a hand. "Don't be a perfectionist. He's going to love it no matter how well you do."

65

"If I were a perfectionist, I would have given up after the first ten minutes. I'm a realist."

"Well, good luck. I'll see you tomorrow." Wonder pulled her into a quick hug.

Working in the café had been a brilliant idea. Wonder, Callie, and Mey were becoming best friends, and the stories Wonder had been telling her about the young Annani were pure gold.

The goddess had been quite a character, and according to Wonder, she was only a little less wild and impulsive now than she had been as a girl. It was so sad that Annani had lost the love of her life, though, and that she had never allowed herself to love again.

A goddess.

Mey shook her head. She'd met a real goddess.

Life was indeed stranger than fiction.

On the way home, she passed several people and was delighted that she could address each one by name because she'd met them either at the café or at her welcoming party. Only a week and a half had passed since she'd arrived in the village, and it already felt more like home than any other place she'd ever lived in before.

Damn, it was already Wednesday, and she had only until Sunday night to start transitioning.

No pressure.

Hopefully, the belly dancing was going to make Yamanu super randy, and he would bite her every time he climaxed. As she'd discovered, he didn't require recuperating time to have sex again, but he needed it to produce more venom.

When she got home, Yamanu wasn't there yet, but he was due back at any moment.

Mey threw a pizza in the oven, cut a few vegetables for a quick salad, and then hit the shower. Today's dinner was going to be a simple affair eaten at the kitchen counter, but the seduction later on was going to be spectacular.

Hopefully, she wasn't going to trip over her own feet.

When she got out of the bathroom, she found Yamanu sitting at the counter and sipping on a bottle of Snake Venom.

"Is everything okay?" she asked as she leaned to kiss his lips.

He put his hands on her waist and pulled her to sit on top of his thighs.

"That depends. Kian gave us a one-week extension."

Mey felt like the rock that had been sitting in her belly had shattered into dust and evaporated. "That's great news. I was so stressed that it's already Wednesday and nothing's happened. Now we have more time."

"We do, but as you know, the two-week time limit wasn't about Kian being unreasonable. It was meant to protect you. More memories mean a greater chance of brain damage if, Fates forbid, I have to erase them."

She smiled. "What happened to your optimism? I thought you were certain I was going to transition. No memory erasing is going to be needed."

He grimaced. "There is a reason Kian volunteered the extra week. He wants me to abstain so I can test my powers again. He wants to know if I can still shroud and thrall as well as I did before."

"Are you upset about it?"

"Yeah, I am. I don't want to abstain. Not now, anyway. I was planning to test my powers while you were transitioning, when we couldn't do anything anyway. It seems like such a waste to sacrifice even one day of lovemaking for that, let alone two. But if I wait only one day and then the test results are so-so, Kian will want me to do it again."

Smiling, she cupped his cheek. "I know how to shrink the suffering to one day only, but it's going to be excruciating."

He cocked a brow. "What do you suggest? Keeping me on the brink?"

"You guessed it. I'm going to tempt you like you've never been tempted before, but no touching will be allowed."

"You'll have to chain me."

She laughed. "No, I won't. Your mighty beast is a tame pussycat. He just wants to be loved."

"Ouch." Yamanu pretended offense. "That's not a good way to tempt me. My ego just suffered a terrible blow. I'm not even sure I can rise to the occasion."

"We will see about that. But first, we will have dinner, and you are going to tell me about your day, and then I'm going to tell you about mine."

His grin was radiant. "Other than lovemaking, this has become my favorite time of the day. Coming home to you, talking with you, sharing our lives with each other, I've never imagined this part of being a couple would be so satisfying."

Mey sighed. "You didn't have the benefit of growing up in a home with a father and mother who loved and cherished each other. I had an excellent example of how a couple should be together."

"I need to meet your parents and thank them for raising you so well."

"Same here. Your mother did an amazing job with you. You are more than I could have ever hoped for."

YAMANU

*M*ey dimmed the lights in the living room and put on music. "Don't peek," she warned before ducking into the bedroom.

What was she up to?

Just thinking about the torturous seduction Mey had promised made Yamanu hard as a rock, and that was without knowing what she was planning.

Could it be a striptease?

Whatever it was must have required a lot of preparation because she'd been gone for way too long. Or perhaps time just moved slower for him while waiting for his lady's return.

When she finally reappeared, Yamanu sucked in a breath.

"Dear Fates." He rubbed his hand over his jaw to stop from gaping. "Have mercy."

Mey was dressed in scarves. Or rather undressed. She was holding one between her outstretched arms; another was looped around her neck, crisscrossing over her perky breasts and tied in the back. The rest were tied to a belt slung low on her hips.

Swaying while snaking her arms, she shimmied her shoulders and twirled around on bare feet. All Yamanu wanted to do was get up and start removing those scarves one by one with his teeth.

Was that what she'd planned?

He started to push up when she twirled up to him and pushed him back down. "Don't move."

"Those scarves are just begging for me to pull them off."

Mey laughed. "If you manage to catch one while your butt is still on the couch, you're allowed. But if you lift off even an inch, it stays."

Damn, this was even sexier.

Yamanu loved a challenge.

Teasingly, Mey alternated between undulating her torso and shaking her bottom, but after a few minutes of that, she switched to freeform dancing, which seemed less fatiguing to her.

As she twirled toward him, Mey lifted her foot, and the scarves parted, exposing her leg all the way up to her skimpy panties. She was almost within reach, but as he lunged forward and tried to grasp a scarf, she danced away.

"Butt on the couch, Yamanu. Even if you get it off, you will have to give it back."

With a groan, he sat back down. "Can we talk about the rules?"

She laughed and twirled, spreading the scarf she was holding in her hands like a sail. "That's the only rule. You are not allowed to get up."

"I'll make you a deal. Every scarf you remove, you can tie me with."

"No deal."

She kept dancing, going faster and faster, her dark hair whipping around and her scarves lifting from the centrifugal force of her twirls.

Lost in the music and in her wild moves, Mey wasn't as careful and got close enough for him to grab a scarf and pull it off without lifting off the couch.

"Aha! I scored one!" He wrapped it around his head like a turban, inhaling the scent she'd left on the fabric.

Mey laughed. "My own gorgeous sultan." She got close again and bent to plant a kiss on his lips.

Yamanu caught her, lifted her up, and plopped her onto his lap. "I've got you. You are not going anywhere." He cupped the back of her head, holding her in place as he kissed her.

When he let go so she could suck in a breath, Mey pouted. "You were not supposed to touch."

"Game change. I get to touch, but you don't."

He pulled out another scarf, clasped her wrists, and tied it around them. "You are my captive."

The scent of her arousal flared. "I can play this game. The question is, can you?"

He knew what she meant by that. "I've done it before."

"You were celibate back then, and you were drinking your potion. You might not be able to hold off now."

"Do you question my willpower?" He pushed off the couch with her in his arms.

"I guess I shouldn't." She snuggled against his chest. "You are a rock."

He chuckled. "Now, you are just buttering me up."

"Is it working?"

"Of course. I'm a vain man."

"You have every right to be."

Sitting on the bed with Mey in his arms, Yamanu untied the scarf crisscrossing her breasts, pulled it off her, and bent his head to take one puckered nipple between his lips.

Mey let out a soft moan and arched her back, pushing more of it into his mouth.

Chuckling around her nipple, he cupped her center. "This is mine," he murmured and then flicked his tongue over the small turgid peak.

She pulled her hands out of the loose binding he'd fashioned and put one on the back of his head. "Don't stop."

He did, but only to switch to the other side.

18

MEY

*M*ey had been worried about Yamanu's ability to hold back, but she hadn't thought it would be difficult for her as well. Dancing for him had made her feel sexy, and the rampant desire in his gaze only fueled the embers of her need.

Agreeing to him pleasuring her was selfish and weak, but she just couldn't bring herself to refuse.

Besides, this had given him pleasure before.

It was going to be so much harder this time, though. Then again, charging up his sexual energy without giving it an outlet was the entire point of what they were doing.

He was going to suffer no matter what.

"Kiss me," she whispered.

His mouth left her nipple with a wet pop. "I thought that I was doing just that."

Sweet Yamanu. Always ready with a smile and a joke.

"Kiss my lips."

He pretended to bend down to her throbbing core, but then lifted up and claimed her mouth. His tongue warm and commanding, he somehow managed not to nick her with his protruding fangs.

It still amazed her how good of a kisser he was, navigating without letting those sharp points detract from the experience.

She melted against him, surrendering to the sweet invasion and curling her tongue around his.

His hand was still cupping her center, which by now felt molten, and as he deepened the kiss, he pushed his fingers under the gusset of her panties and stroked her swollen folds.

Her hips moved like they had a mind of their own, undulating in response to his gentle touch and begging for more.

He hugged her closer to him and slid one finger inside her wet sheath.

The groan that escaped her lips was a plea for more.

"What do you need, my lady Mey?" He murmured at her lips. "Tell me what to do. Another finger? My mouth? My tongue? Everything is yours to command."

Mey didn't want to command, she wanted to surrender. "More fingers," she whispered.

He retracted his digit and came back with two, eliciting a throaty moan.

"Like that?"

"Yes. Keep going."

He added a third finger, stretching her, and then curled them inside her, lightly rubbing that sensitive spot that no other man before him had discovered inside her.

The orgasm that exploded out of her took Mey by surprise. He hadn't even touched her clit.

Yamanu kept pumping his fingers in and out of her, prolonging her pleasure, until she collapsed against him, boneless.

Wrapping his arms around her, he kissed her closed eyelids. "I love you so much that it hurts."

A soft chuckle escaped her throat. "Right now, I believe it." She lifted her hand to his cheek. "My poor baby. How are you going to survive until tomorrow?"

"The same way I survived for the past six centuries. But if you think that we're done, you are mistaken." He lifted her off his lap and laid her out on the bed. "You're still wearing too many scarves, and they are just begging to be removed."

Ducking between her legs, he closed his fangs around one scarf and tugged, then shook his head like a beast to get rid of it.

Mey laughed. "If you make holes in them, you'll have to buy Callie new ones."

He paused, letting the next one fall out of his mouth. "These are Callie's?"

She waved a hand. "Forget I said anything. I'll get her new ones. Keep going, tiger."

His fanged grin let her know that he liked her calling him that, and when he attacked the delicate silk fabric with renewed vigor, Mey had no doubt he was going to tear apart at least some of them.

When all the scarves were gone, he slid her panties down, and all that remained on her body was the belt.

He left it where it was and crouched between her spread thighs. "Now, that's a sight to behold." He licked his lips.

Her core fluttered in response, her desire roaring into life as if she hadn't been wholly sated mere moments ago.

Evidently, Yamanu was supercharging her sex drive as much as she was supercharging his. As her mother used to say, with the meal came the appetite.

Well, Mey's appetite had never been more ferocious.

Sliding his big hands under her bottom, Yamanu lifted her to his lips and planted a soft kiss on her plump lips. "So silky," he murmured, and then treated her to a long lick. "And so tasty."

Unhurriedly, he explored every crease and crevice, every fold, dipping shallowly into her sheath and then retreating and going back to his explorations.

How could he be so patient when he was no doubt hurting?

"You are incredible," she whispered. "I don't know how you do it."

He lifted his head and smiled. "With love."

For long moments, his tongue teased and probed, his lips

rubbed and kissed, and his hands kneaded her buttocks. He avoided her clit, though, letting her simmer but not ignite.

"Yamanu," she whispered. "Please."

He planted another soft kiss on her petals, and then flicked just the tip of his tongue over that most sensitive spot at the apex of her slit.

Mey jerked up, the gentle touch feeling like a bolt of lightning.

He slid two fingers inside her and at the same time sucked that sensitive little nub into his mouth.

As Mey's core convulsed, his hands tightened on her bottom, holding her up as she shuddered and shook, releasing noises she'd never heard herself making before.

When the tremors subsided, he treated her to another soft kiss. "My sweet lady Mey."

"Yamanu," she breathed.

Sliding up her body, he took her mouth in a soft kiss. "I love you." He braced on his forearms and gazed at her lovingly. "You are always beautiful, but you are absolutely extraordinary with this blissed-out expression on your face."

"I love you." She wrapped her arms around his neck. "More than I thought was possible."

19

MAGNUS

"*I* could get used to this." Vivian adjusted her sunglasses. "Riding in a Porsche, wearing designer clothes, I feel like a celebrity."

Magnus smiled and took her hand. "Do you want to drive?"

"Oh, no. I would be terrified of damaging it."

"It's a rental, and we paid for full insurance. You can have fun with it."

She shook her head. "Being driven around is more fun."

"So, I guess you don't want me to buy you one."

She chuckled. "And what would I do with it? Does the clan have an auto shop that retrofits vehicles to comply with the village's rules?"

"I'm sure something could be arranged."

"Look." Vivian pointed. "The gate is opening."

It was their third pass by the mansion, but this time they got lucky. A gardener's truck was leaving.

Magnus slowed down, letting it pull out into the road in front of him. "I'm going to follow them to their next stop."

Vivian pursed her lips. "You should ask them for a business card and let them remember that you are a future homeowner in the neighborhood. If we were caught on camera while passing by, the gardeners would confirm our story."

"I don't think anyone is going to ask them anything, but I can do that."

The truck stopped several houses down the street, and Magnus had to hurry before it disappeared behind another gate.

He stopped behind the truck and waved his arms. "Can I bother you for a moment?" He stepped out of the car.

Vivian followed, trotting behind him on her high-heeled shoes.

The driver of the truck jumped down. "How can I help you?"

"I just want your business card. My wife and I are looking for a house in the neighborhood, and we will need a gardener. I saw your truck and figured I might as well start collecting phone numbers."

Vivian took her sunglasses off and smiled. "We noticed that you had the latest and best tools for gardening work." She put her hand on his truck. "My father used to say that the mark of a professional is the kind of tools he has. He was a carpenter before he retired." She offered him her hand. "I'm Viv."

"John." He shook her hand.

Good move. Letting the guy know that she hadn't been raised rich made him more comfortable with her and his mind easier to access.

While Vivian distracted John, Magnus reached into his mind and went for a tour.

Nothing out of the ordinary had happened on the mansion's grounds today. In fact, John thought that it was odd for a place this big to be so devoid of life. The only person he ever met while working there was the security guard. It wasn't the same one every time. He knew at least four, all decent fellows who treated him well. Not like some of those affluent homeowners, who didn't even notice that he was there, let alone acknowledge his presence with a hello.

In those homes, John told his helper to use the leaf blower for the entire time. This was his small revenge for being treated like the dirt he worked with.

Magnus liked the guy, and he felt bad for probing deeper and checking if any of John's memories were erased, but there were no suspicious gaps in the last month or so, and Magnus didn't want to go further back than that.

His only interactions had been with the guards, and other than them, John hadn't met any of the mansion's inhabitants.

He knew about the underground bunker but thought that it was a bomb shelter and had no idea how big it was.

Magnus put his hand on Vivian's shoulder. "We should get going."

Vivian smiled at the gardener. "It was nice talking to you, John. We will give you a call once we close on a house."

"Good luck." He got back in his truck and drove through the opened gate.

"Anything?" Vivian asked when they were seated in the Porsche.

"He sees only a security guard each time he comes to work on the grounds. So far, he's met four different ones, and he didn't notice anything peculiar about them. They were friendly."

"Do you think Kalugal and his men are hiding when John and his crew work on their yard?"

"First of all, we are not sure it's Kalugal. And secondly, they might all be working in the underground while John is there."

"Let's go back and buzz the intercom. We can say that we are looking at properties in the area and that we want to check out their front and back yards for landscaping ideas."

"I can't do that. If the guard is an immortal, he would know right away that I'm an immortal as well."

"Then I'll go by myself. You can stay in the car, pretending to be on a business call."

"What are you hoping to achieve?"

She shrugged. "If the guard is indeed an immortal, I can probably sense him. But he can't sense me because I'm a female, and we don't have any tells other than arousal, which is not going to happen because I'm mated to you."

"He might smell me on you."

Vivian reached into her purse, pulled out a container of perfume, and sprayed herself liberally with it. "Now, he can't."

Magnus waved a hand in front of his face to disperse the smell. "It's dangerous."

"No, it's not. He will probably not even open the gate, but it's worth a try. Let's go." She crossed her arms over her chest and jutted her chin out.

When Vivian got that stubborn expression, it was futile to argue with her.

With a sigh, Magnus put the car in reverse and executed a K-turn. "He is not going to let you in."

She shrugged. "He might. Perhaps he will want to check me out and come to take a closer look. That's all I really need. I don't have to get inside."

As Magnus parked near the gate, Vivian stepped out of the car and walked over to the intercom.

"How can I help you?" a male voice answered.

"Hi, my name is Viv Dubronski. My husband and I are looking for a property to buy in the area, and we were wondering if you could kindly let us take a look at your landscaping. We are looking for ideas."

"I'm sorry, Mrs. Dubronski, but the owner is not here, and I can't allow anyone on the property without his permission."

"Can you perhaps call him and ask? We don't mind coming back later if he insists on being here while we take a look at the grounds. We could schedule an appointment."

"Again, my apologies, but the owner is out of the country, and I don't know when he is coming back."

It sounded like a lie even through the intercom.

"That's a shame." Vivian affected a disappointed tone. "I really wanted to see the grounds. From the street, they look so well maintained. Can I leave you my business card? If by any chance you talk to the owner, and he agrees, could you give me a call?"

It was a smart move. If the guard came out to take the card, it would suffice.

"Of course. You can drop it in the mailbox."

"Thank you."

Vivian reached into her purse and pulled out one of the fake cards they'd had printed for this purpose. After dropping it in the mailbox, she opened the door and got back in the car.

"I told you so," Magnus said once he pulled out into the street.

"Go slow," Vivian said. "I have a feeling someone is going to follow us."

Her intuition was spot on.

There weren't many cars on the road, so it was easy to spot their tail. The guy wasn't even trying to be overly discreet.

"How did you know?"

"Women's intuition. The longer I talked to the security guard, the more stressed he sounded. I figured he would send someone to check us out."

"I'm going to find a restaurant, we are going to order, and then I'm going to sneak out and corner the guy. I bet that he will be sitting in his car outside and waiting for us to leave so he can follow us home."

"That's not a good idea. What if the tail is an immortal too? I should be the one to check him out."

"Not going to happen."

"Why? I think I handled the security guard pretty well."

"You did. But this is different. What possible excuse can you give for approaching him?"

"I'll think of something."

Stubborn woman.

"Let's go into the restaurant first and see what he does. He might just drive away. If he doesn't, I'll call Kian for instructions."

Kian was most likely going to tell them not to engage. But since the order would come from the boss, Vivian couldn't get mad at Magnus for not allowing her to check out the guy trailing them.

20

KIAN

"*D*on't engage him," Kian said once Magnus was done telling him about the tail he and Vivian had picked up. "When Kri comes back from New York this Saturday, I'll send her over with a couple of guardians."

"I can do it," he heard Vivian in the background. "He is right here, parked in front of the restaurant. I'll walk over, knock on his window, and ask him for directions to somewhere. If he is what we think he is, I can probably sense it, and we will have our answer right away. Why wait?"

"It's too dangerous. This is not a job for an untrained civilian," Kian told Magnus.

Before, when he had dangled her and Ella as bait for Lokan, he'd had no other choice. Lokan had thought to set a trap for Ella, and Kian had used that to trap him instead. He hadn't liked having to resort to putting civilians at risk, and Lokan had nearly succeeded in abducting both mother and daughter.

Once was enough. Kian was not going to risk either of the women again.

"That's what I'm trying to tell her, but she won't listen to me."

"How can it be dangerous?" Vivian asked. "We are in the middle of a busy street. What is he going to do, kill me for asking him a question? Drag me into his car and drive away? You guys are being ridiculous. After what Ella and I did in Washington, this is really nothing."

Kian didn't like that Magnus and Vivian were discussing this in a restaurant where they could be overheard. Magnus knew to be careful, but Vivian might blurt something about immortals.

As it was, they were probably attracting attention they shouldn't.

"The difference is that back then we didn't have a choice, and it was the only way to get Lokan. This time we have other options. Besides, this is not an argument we should be having while you are in a restaurant. People can overhear you."

Thankfully, Vivian had listened this time and kept quiet, but Kian could only imagine the daggers she was shooting from her eyes at Magnus.

Perhaps it would be better if he talked to her directly.

He didn't know her well, and whether she was the impetuous type or not. She might decide to approach the guy despite his instructions.

It wasn't like Vivian feared retribution for disobeying his command.

First of all, she wasn't a Guardian and had no obligation to obey. Secondly, she knew he would never retaliate after what she and her daughter had done for the clan. It had been courageous of them both to offer themselves as bait to capture Lokan, and it had nearly ended in a disaster. He owed them, the clan owed them, and Vivian knew that.

"Give the phone to Vivian. I want to explain it to her directly."

Magnus released a relieved breath. "Thank you. Here she is."

"I got it the first time." Vivian sounded miffed. "I'll keep quiet."

"I want to explain, so you don't think I'm being unreasonable. When you buzzed that intercom, your face was caught on camera, so they know what you look like. Right now, they are just being cautious, and they sent someone to follow you around to check who you are and what you are up to. As long as you keep behaving according to your cover story, they will let it go. But if you approach the man tailing you, you will confirm their suspicions that you are not who you claim to be and that you are investigating them. It's crucial that they remain unaware of that. Kalugal might take his men and run, and we will lose the only thread we have."

Hopefully, that was enough to deter any ideas she might have had for playing detective.

"I understand. So, what are we supposed to do?"

"Keep acting like a rich couple on vacation, looking to buy a property in the area. You've done enough snooping around the mansion for today. Later on, you can go to a bar or a nightclub in the area and snoop there. Keep doing the same tomorrow and the day after. If our guy has about a hundred men with him, your chances of bumping into one of them are good. It's a small town."

"Got it. Do you need to talk to Magnus again?"

"He heard me. Just stay alert. As soon as either of you senses an immortal, Magnus needs to get away fast."

"I understand. So basically, we are staying until Kri comes to replace us?"

"You can come home anytime you want. But for now, I need Magnus in charge of the operation."

"I will probably have to head back Sunday. Parker is staying with Ella, but without me there to supervise him, I'm sure he is not spending enough time studying."

That reminded Kian that Vivian was with Magnus not only because she wanted to be with her mate, but because she was doing them a favor, and he needed to thank her for it.

"It's up to you, Vivian. And thank you for helping. Without you, Magnus's cover story wouldn't have been as good."

"I'm always glad to help out in any way I can. The clan has done a lot for my family and me."

Ending the call, Kian was proud of himself. He'd been patient, he'd explained, and he'd even remembered to thank Vivian.

Syssi would be happy with his progress.

21

YAMANU

*Y*amanu glanced at his watch. It was seven in the evening, and so far, he had been abstaining for thirty-six hours. It should have been easy, what was a day and a half compared to six and a half centuries?

And yet, it was the hardest stretch he'd ever experienced. Even the first week of his banishment to the uninhabited island hadn't been that bad, and at the time, he had thought that it was the worst part of his punishment.

He'd soon realized that loneliness was much harder to endure than the lack of sex, but it had taken him a couple of weeks on that godforsaken place to reach that conclusion.

The difference was, of course, Mey.

Previously, he had stayed away from temptation, and it hadn't been too difficult to do with the potion's numbing effect. But now temptation was right there with him. Not only was he hungry for Mey twenty-four-seven, but he also had to suffer through her merciless taunting that was meant to recharge his batteries.

Was it enough, though?

It felt like it was. He was practically buzzing with it, not to mention that walking was uncomfortable with a third wooden leg stuck in his pants.

Mey was in for one hell of a workout when he returned home from his experiment tonight. This time, he was sure that his energy stores were so full that they could power a mass shroud with enough left over to give his mate the ride of her life.

With a smirk, he pulled into a parking spot next to William's van, got out, and opened the sliding passenger door. "Are we ready to roll?"

William lifted his head to the sky. "It's not dark enough yet. Let's wait for another half an hour."

Anandur waved his hand. "Hop in. We can all wait together."

As soon as the guy had heard about the fireworks, he'd volunteered to help. The problem was that Anandur hadn't bought the same explanation as readily as William had. Anandur had been suspicious of Yamanu's sexual inactivity for a long time, and the guy wasn't stupid despite trying hard to convince everyone that he was.

The need to test his ability right after Mey had entered his life would clue Anandur in. Except, the guy was a mensch, as Eva liked to say, and he hadn't said a thing.

So far.

"Where am I supposed to sit?" Yamanu asked as he eyed the cluttered interior.

The back of the van was full of equipment, and the floor space in between was taken by the boxes of fireworks. William had gone overboard with that. The amount he had in there was enough to replicate the Fourth of July celebrations.

"There is a rolling stool under the desk." William pointed.

"We should park the van in the back of the mall," Anandur said. "If the shroud fails, someone is going to call the police, and we will need to be close to our escape car."

Yamanu chuckled. "This van can barely move. We will have to thrall the police."

"I can do one, maybe two." Anandur scratched his head. "How about you, William? Are you any good at thralling?"

"I haven't thralled anyone in a while. So I might be out of practice."

"That's a problem. If our boy expends all of his energy on the shroud, he will have nothing left to thrall the policemen with."

Yamanu stifled a groan. It seemed that he had been right about Anandur figuring out his secret.

"The shroud is going to work. I feel supercharged."

Anandur eyed him from under his bushy red brows. "What did you do to recharge, have a huge fight with Mey?"

The explanation he'd given William and Anandur was that his love for Mey affected his ability, so Anandur's question was in line with that. Perhaps the guy actually believed it.

"Something like that. But just in case I'm wrong and my shroud falters, let's drive to the other side.

They parked next to the loading dock of a large supermarket that had moved to another location and now stood empty.

As William and Anandur unloaded the boxes of fireworks, Yamanu started shrouding them right away. It would do them no good to get caught before they had a chance to set them alight.

Not many cars were parked in the back, and so far, no one had stopped to ask what they were doing, so the shroud was working.

Once everything was set up, Anandur clapped William on the back. "I'm going to the front parking lot to watch people's reactions. Give me five minutes to get in position."

Nodding, Yamanu closed his eyes and concentrated.

It was vital that he didn't cover the entire shopping center, just the sky above it, and not all sounds, but only the loud ones from the rockets as they shot to the sky and then exploded.

"Five minutes are up," William said. "Anandur should be in position."

Yamanu nodded.

Focusing his power into a tight spot inside his belly, he spread his arms and let it explode out of him.

This was the signal William had been waiting for.

As the rockets started shooting up one after the other, their explosions were so loud they were deafening. With his eyes closed, Yamanu couldn't see the display, but by the happy sounds that William was making it was a sight to behold.

Yamanu had no concept of time while he was focusing on shrouding, but so far, he hadn't felt like he was about to run out of juice. The power just kept pouring out of him in waves.

Except, it might have been all in his mind.

The way it worked, he had to imagine it happening and keep it up until he either ran out of energy or someone told him that it was okay to stop.

A hand landed on his shoulder, and he heard Anandur tell him it was over, but it took him several long moments to suck back the waves of energy emanating from him and open his eyes.

"Did it work?" he asked.

"Beautifully. No one even lifted their heads to the sky. It was like nothing at all was happening."

The relief was so profound that Yamanu's knees buckled, and he had to sit down on one of the boxes. Or maybe it was the exhaustion.

Anandur crouched in front of him. "Are you okay, buddy? Do you need anything to drink? Orange juice, beer, water?"

"I'm fine. I just need a moment."

"Take as long as you need. Shrouding a massive event like this must have completely drained you. I'll get you some orange juice."

"Thanks."

He should be drained, but he wasn't. The current was no longer sizzling manically inside him. Instead, it was buzzing pleasantly, reminding him that his work for the day wasn't done. The most fun part was still ahead of him.

Mey deserved a big-time reward.

Sending him out of the house with a raging hard-on hadn't been pleasant, but it had been effective.

He should thank the Fates for letting him keep both his powers and Mey. It was more than he had ever expected.

Thank you. He lifted his face to the sky. *I'm forever in your debt. Whatever you require of me, I will do and not question why.*

"Here you go." Anandur handed him the orange juice.

"Where is William?"

"Inside the van, organizing the space. We will give you a ride back to your car."

"Thanks."

Anandur scratched his head. "Maybe it's a good idea to stop by the supermarket and buy your lady flowers and chocolates. If you had a fight before leaving the house, you shouldn't go back without ammunition."

"That's a great suggestion. Let's do that."

Not because he had to placate Mey, but because today's successful test results called for a celebration. A bottle or two of champagne were in order, the best chocolates he could find, and a flower bouquet that was tall enough to reach the ceiling.

22

KIAN

"So here is what I've found out about Aunt Eleanor." Turner pulled a yellow pad out of his briefcase.

Kian put down the two beers he'd taken out of the fridge on the conference table and sat down. "I'm listening."

"The name on her driver's license is Marisol Ortega, but she might be using another alias because there was very little under that name. She doesn't have a physical address, only a PO box in a shared office space in Harrisonburg, Virginia, not West Virginia."

"Is that significant?" Kian asked.

"Possibly. On the face of things, it looks like she is getting her mail in one place and lives in another. Her driver's license is from West Virginia, and our hackers didn't find another match with her face, so this is the one she is using for driving. Except, she doesn't have a car registered in her name either. I assume that she lives in a government facility and uses a government vehicle to get around. She doesn't have a credit card or a bank account in that name either. Roni checked."

"Why rent a box in another state, though? Do you think she is running from someone?"

"She might be, but then her fake identity should be enough to protect her. I guess that she has a reason to be in Harrisonburg often enough to justify it. It's the closest urban center to the Quiet Zone. All the rest are little towns where everyone knows everyone."

"If the facility is somewhere in the Quiet Zone, then the Harrisonburg mailbox makes sense. Although I'm sure that she can get mail where she lives too. They must have a delivery system."

"She might wish to keep her private correspondence at least semi-private. If she rented the box using the alias they gave her, it's not exactly a secret."

Kian wrapped his hand around the cold beer bottle. "Is that standard? I mean the no address, no car, no bank account, no credit cards? She is basically a ghost?'

"It's not uncommon for undercover agents, but it's a lot of security for someone who is not involved in that kind of work."

"Perhaps she is? After all, Jin's talent makes her a perfect spy. The proximity of the Echelon system implies that whatever Eleanor is into has to do with a spy organization rather than with paranormals."

"It's probably a combination of both. What other use could the government have for paranormal talent?"

"Finding hidden deposits of oil?"

Turner chuckled. "Can any of us do that? Because that could be really helpful for refilling the clan's coffers."

"I wish. How far is Harrisonburg from the center of the Quiet Zone?"

"About an hour by car."

"And you say that there are dozens of small towns scattered around the area?"

Turner nodded. "We can either post guardians to watch that mailbox twenty-four-seven and hope that she shows up or find out more information to narrow the search."

"Let me check with Vivian what she knows about her sister-in-law. She and Magnus are in the Bay Area, sniffing around the mansion, but at this time, they might be back at the hotel already."

"How is that going?"

Kian leaned his elbows on the table. "They picked up a tail. Vivian walked up to the gate and buzzed the security guard, asking to see the grounds. She and Magnus are pretending to be looking at properties in the neighborhood, and she said that she wanted to get ideas for her future garden. Naturally, she wasn't allowed in. But when they drove off, someone started following them. I told them not to engage and pretend like they are exactly who they claim to be, go to cafés and bars, and have a good time."

"Smart move. Are they still being followed?"

"Let me check." Kian typed a quick text to Magnus. *Where are you now?*

A moment later, his phone chimed. "We are back at the hotel, getting ready for a night on the town."

"Are you still being followed?"

"He followed us back to the hotel and then drove off. You were right about that."

"Good. Can I talk with Vivian? I need to ask her about her sister-in-law."

"Sure. Here she is."

"Hi, Kian," Vivian said. "What would you like to know about Eleanor?"

"Anything you can think of. What did she enjoy doing, hobbies, interests, the kind of men she dated. Basically, anything that might help us find her."

Vivian sighed. "I never got to know her well. She was the older sister, and she wasn't friendly. Not to me and not to her brother. She and Josh didn't get along. What I know is from bits and pieces of stories I've heard over the years. Eleanor was into sports and very competitive, but she didn't excel in any of them. She settled on skiing, which she was very good at, but not good enough to participate in any competitions. I think she chose to work as a pharmaceutical rep because of the flexible schedule, and the travel involved allowed her to take frequent ski vacations in different parts of the country. If there is a good ski resort in the area, with slopes for advanced skiers, there is a good chance you'll find her there."

"Bingo." Across the table, Turner was grinning like he had won the lottery.

"Anything else you can think of?"

"Not at the moment, but if I remember something, I'll give you a call or text you."

"Thanks, Vivian. You were very helpful."

"Any time."

"There is a ski resort in the area," Turner said. "One of the best in the country, and snow season has just started. I suggest that you send several Guardians on a ski vacation. In fact, I would have loved to join them, but unfortunately, I have a couple of rescue missions to plan for private clients."

"Do you know the name of the place?'

"It's easy to remember. Snowshoe."

"Have you ever been there?"

Turner shook his head. "I like to ski, but I don't have time for ski trips. The local slopes are good enough for me when I have some free time." He sighed. "Which I haven't had in a long while."

Kian raked his fingers through his hair. "I haven't skied in many years. I was damn good at it."

It was one of the numerous things that he had sacrificed for his all-consuming work of heading the clan's business empire and being regent of the clan's American branch.

"Then perhaps you should join your men and have some fun. Take Syssi with you."

"I don't think she should ski in her condition."

Turner waved a dismissive hand. "Pregnancy is not a handicap, and Syssi is still in the first trimester, so her center of balance hasn't shifted yet. Besides, your wife is not a daredevil. She is a careful woman, so it's not like she is about to go wild on the slopes."

"Syssi used to ski with her family."

"There you go. So, she's not a beginner. Take your wife on vacation, Kian. She'll enjoy it, and you will not feel overly guilty about missing work because technically, you'll be on a mission."

23

MEY

*M*ey's poor nails were a mess, but she didn't care. Waiting for Yamanu to return from his test was nerve-wracking in the extreme, and she'd been biting them and chewing at the skin around them like there was no tomorrow.

Maybe there wasn't.

If the test had succeeded, Yamanu would have called her to let her know. The fact that it was after eight and he hadn't called told her all she didn't want to know.

Everyone was going to hate her once they discovered that Yamanu's powers were gone. What if she transitioned and they voted her out of the village?

It could happen. Being immortal didn't guarantee acceptance. Well, it did except for the clan's enemies who obviously weren't welcome, but things might change.

The clan had just not encountered a problem like her before. An undesirable Dormant or immortal was a concept they didn't understand yet.

But they would.

Crap, what was she going to do?

Take a deep breath and get a grip.

She was panicking instead of thinking and planning. Besides, the experiment might have been partially successful, like the one Yamanu had done before, and that would be better than total failure.

They would hate her a little less if Yamanu could still function on some level.

When the door opened, Yamanu strode in with an enormous bouquet of flowers clutched to his chest and a shopping bag from Godiva hanging on his arm, which meant that he had good news.

Unless he'd gotten her flowers and chocolates as a consolation prize.

"It worked," he said.

Those were the best two words she'd ever heard. Squealing with happiness, Mey ran up to Yamanu, but the flowers were in the way of her jumping on him.

He dropped them unceremoniously on the floor and opened his arms. "Go ahead, jump."

She did, wrapping her arms around his neck and her legs around his waist. "It worked." She peppered his cheeks with kisses. "You were able to shroud the fireworks."

"I did and then some." He carried her to the couch and sat down with her in his arms. "Anandur said that no one even lifted their eyes to the sky. It was like it never happened."

"You have no idea what a relief this is for me. I was contemplating a future as a lone immortal living among humans because I was certain the clan would vote to get rid of me once they discovered what I had cost them."

"Silly girl." He tweaked her nose. "You would have never been a lone immortal because I would have gone with you. Where you go, I go. We are a team. Inseparable, invincible, undefeated."

Mey smiled. "I love you too."

"I know."

"Did William and Anandur believe your story about love making you weak?"

"I embellished a little. I told them that I was too happy and in love to concentrate. Then Anandur asked what I'd done to make the results of today different from before. He thought that you had picked a fight with me to get me annoyed and not as stupidly happy."

That was such a flimsy explanation that Mey doubted an intelligent guy like William and a perceptive one like Anandur had bought it.

They'd been humoring Yamanu.

"They probably suspected something, at least Anandur did, but he is a good friend, and he didn't prod." Yamanu glanced in the direction of the discarded flowers and shopping bag. "Then again, he suggested that I buy flowers and chocolates, saying that coming home after a fight required the right ammunition. So maybe he believed me."

"I'd better put those flowers in water." Mey pushed out of Yamanu's arms. "And I don't mind celebrating with some chocolates."

"I brought champagne as well." He waggled his brows. "Let's take that and the box to the bedroom. I came up with a few interesting ideas on my way home."

Mey's core tingled with excitement. "Aren't you spent after such a massive shroud?"

"The way you charged me up, I have energy to spare. I told you, together we are invincible. You are the charge, and I am the cannon, together we are undefeated."

"I like it." She cast him a bright smile over the bouquet. It was such a nice thing to say, making it sound like they were a team and that his powers were somehow dependent on her participation. But it wasn't true. All she had done was torment him.

"I see that you don't believe me."

"You are very sweet. But all I did was make you suffer. For a good cause, but still. My part was marginal."

He shook his head. "I disagree. My hunger for you is so much more powerful than just a basic need for sex. No one else could have charged me up like you did. It's a pretty simple equation. My sexual energy fuels my thralls and shrouds, and you fuel my sexual energy, which means that you are directly responsible for their potency. And let me tell you, I've never felt more potent than tonight."

24

YAMANU

*A*s Yamanu watched Mey put the flowers in a big cooking pot that she'd filled with water, he realized how neglectful he had been. His and Arwel's place was the typical bachelor pad, and it lacked the niceties women appreciated.

Like a proper vase.

And that was probably just one item in a long list of things that Mey would have liked but hadn't asked for. His mind had been so preoccupied with her transition and his faltering powers that he had barely functioned at his job, let alone thought of necessities like filling the house with groceries and making sure that Mey had all she needed.

Right now, though, all he wanted to do was get her in bed as fast as possible. Hopefully, she wasn't going to insist that they eat dinner first. The only thing he wanted to eat tonight was her, and all he wanted to feed her were champagne and chocolates.

With a smirk, Yamanu got behind Mey and wrapped his arms around her. "I want to take you to bed." He nuzzled her ear.

She shivered. "What about dinner?"

"We will have champagne and chocolates instead." He nibbled on her earlobe.

"I can live with that."

That was all the consent he needed. Swinging her into his arms, he carried her into the bedroom and deposited her on the bed. "Don't move. I'm going to get the shopping bag."

"Okay." Smiling, she lifted on her forearms. "Don't forget the wine glasses."

"I won't."

When he returned fifteen seconds later, he found Mey nude, with just one silk scarf draped over her glorious body.

"Dear Fates, you are magnificent." And fast.

Yamanu put the wine glasses on the nightstand and then uncorked the champagne. As the bubbly geysered up, some of it spilled on Mey, wetting the silk and making it transparent.

Yamanu swallowed.

Talk about sexy.

And then she went ahead and smeared the champagne, spreading it over her throat, her chest, and her belly.

He groaned. "I'm going to lick it all off you."

Dipping his head, he lapped up the small puddle that had accumulated in the hollow of her throat and kissed her, letting her taste the champagne on his tongue.

"Hmm." She licked her lips. "I want more."

He poured the champagne into the flutes and handed her one. "To us."

"To us." Mey emptied it down her throat and gave him the glass to refill. "I love it."

Glad that he'd splurged on the best bottle of champagne in the liquor store, he refilled her flute.

"Only the best for my lady."

Which reminded him that he still hadn't opened the box of chocolates, which he'd handpicked piece by piece.

Tearing through the wrapping, Yamanu opened the box and pulled one out. "Open wide." He popped it into her mouth. When she was done chewing, he kissed her, tasting the sweetness of the chocolate and the tanginess of the liqueur inside of it. "Tasty."

She reached for the box and pulled a piece out. "You can have one for yourself."

He shook his head. "It's much tastier combined with your sweetness." He kissed her once more.

Two more chocolates. That was all he was going to feed Mey before feeding off her.

He popped another one into her mouth and took a sip of champagne before kissing her again. The tastes mingled.

"Last one." He offered her a heart-shaped white chocolate filled with caramel. "For now."

Taking another long sip from the champagne, Yamanu pulled the silk scarf down Mey's body and bent his head to take a nipple into his mouth.

"It tingles," she shivered. "Your mouth is cold."

It was going to get hot soon, but he was about to chill it down with more champagne and switch his attentions to her other breast.

Yamanu had no idea where the patience to play was coming from. On the way home, he'd planned to take just long enough to tease Mey, but he was enjoying this too much to stop.

Even the pulsing heat in his straining shaft couldn't force him to rush.

She threaded her fingers into his hair, fanning it out over her body. "This is better than the scarf. I love your hair."

He lifted his head and smiled. "And I love everything about you."

"Take your clothes off." Mey gazed at him with hooded eyes. "You have no more reason to keep your pants on."

He smirked. "Admit that you want to see me in all my naked magnificence."

"Dressed or not, you are always glorious. But, yes. I want to gaze upon your magnificent body and touch it all over." Her eyes drifted down to the bulge in his pants. "Someone is eager to say hello." She licked her lips.

Fates, he almost erupted as he imagined them wrapped around his shaft.

Yamanu had let Mey pleasure him this way before, but only a few teasing licks because they were on a mission to induce her transition, and that wasn't going to happen with oral sex.

But now that they had gotten an extension from Kian, the pressure was off, and he could indulge.

Taking his clothes off with immortal speed, he climbed on the bed and lay next to Mey. "Come, give me a kiss." He patted his chest.

She turned on her side and leaned over him.

"Not like that." He reached for her waist and lifted her on top of him, her long, lithe body a perfect fit for his. "Now, kiss me."

Mey's lush lips curved in a smile as she dipped her head and carefully pressed them to his.

He'd forgotten about the damn fangs.

It took practice to navigate around them, and Mey was still learning. He, on the other hand, was an expert despite his prolonged abstinence. It was one of those things that once learned was never forgotten.

Taking over the kiss, Yamanu flicked his tongue over Mey's lips, and when she parted for him, he lazily pushed into her mouth.

For long moments, he teased her back and bottom with soft caresses, reveling in the sweet pain of delayed gratification.

Except, Mey wasn't as patient as he.

Lifting her head, she looked at him and smiled. "You are an excellent example of a man being of two minds. The one on top wants to take it slow and tease me to death, but the one below is strongly disagreeing."

He laughed, hugging her close but careful not to squeeze too hard. "I think it's time to let the one below take over."

25

MEY

*Y*amanu's strong hands lifted Mey up and flipped her around as if she weighed nothing, and suddenly she found herself facing his impressive shaft.

He pulled on her hips, lifting her up, so her core was right where he wanted it.

Sliding his hands up the back of her thighs, he reached her bottom, squeezed it tight, and parted her lower lips with his thumbs.

Lost in the sensation, Mey gazed at the hard length bobbing in front of her eyes but didn't reach for it. It was impossible to think while he teased her flesh like that.

"Take me into your mouth," Yamanu commanded, breaking her daze. "But don't let me climax."

Yeah, she was well aware of how important it was that every drop of semen ended up in her womb. Still, Kian had given them another week, so maybe this time she could go for it and have Yamanu finish in her mouth?

It was tempting, but he'd told her not to.

Wrapping her hand around his shaft, she licked the tip. There was no way she could take the entire length of him, but she was going to do her best.

His hands tightened on her bottom, urging her to keep going.

As she sucked the tip in, he groaned, the breath leaving his mouth tickling her heated flesh.

She tightened her hold and added a second hand before sucking a little bit more and then pulling back to circle his shaft with her tongue.

He arched up, signaling what he wanted her to do, but this time it was Mey's turn to torture him sweetly by going slow.

"Patience, my love," she murmured against his velvety skin.

Dragging her tongue slowly up the hard column, she took him in her mouth again. His powerful thighs tightened under her.

As she took him deeper yet, his tongue parted her folds and licked into her sheath.

Mey wanted him inside her so badly, but this was fun too. She liked having complete control over Yamanu's pleasure. It gave her a heady sense of power.

Finding her rhythm, she sucked and rubbed in tandem, synchronizing her up and down movements with what he was doing to her on the other end.

Their bodies moved in perfect harmony, her bottom gyrating in sync with his hips, and her groans and moans echoing his. They were both climbing toward the inevitable climax. Except, Yamanu's iron will and determination meant that he wasn't going to allow it to happen.

"No more." He stopped and gently kissed her swollen lower lips.

When he lifted her and turned her around, Mey was disappointed but not surprised.

"After your transition," he said before taking her mouth.

As his tongue breached her lips, she tasted herself on it, her essence mingled with his, sweet and tangy at the same time. Could he taste himself on her? Did he like it?

Still kissing her, Yamanu rolled her beneath him and settled between her spread thighs. As the tip of his shaft probed her entrance, her hunger spiked, and she arched up, wedging the head inside her.

As Yamanu pushed the rest of the way, they both groaned in unison.

"I love you," she whispered. Wrapping her arms around his broad back, she held him to her tightly.

He retreated and surged in again. "I love you too." Another rest and another surge.

Tightening her fingers on his shoulder blades, she lifted her legs and locked her ankles in the small of his back.

At first, Yamanu set a slow and steady rhythm, but his iron willpower could stand only so much. Soon he drew his hips back and began to thrust faster and harder.

She tried to keep up, but he was too strong, too fast for her, and in the end, she let go, giving herself up to him.

Surprising her once more, Yamanu rolled them over, so she was on top. "Ride me," he commanded.

She did, pushing herself up and slamming back down with strength and ferocity she didn't know she had in her.

He reached between their bodies and pressed his finger to her clitoris. "Come for me, my lady," he ordered.

She shook her head. "Not yet."

With a wicked, fanged smile, he closed his hand on her hip and rubbed his finger over the center of her pleasure. "Now."

As he thrust up, Mey was powerless against the climax that sprang free and rippled through her. The keening moan that accompanied it was a sound she'd never heard herself make before.

Boneless, she collapsed over his chest.

He kissed and caressed her gently, then rolled them again, so he was on top.

"Yamanu," she breathed.

"I've got you."

Gripping both her hips, Yamanu let loose, pounding into her with the force of a battering ram. As Mey climaxed again, so did he, and knowing what was coming, she turned her head and elongated her neck.

The pain was sharp, but she no longer feared it. Between one sucked-in breath and the next, the pain was gone, and another orgasm ripped through her, then another, and another.

When she could take no more, euphoria swept away the intense arousal, calming her and lifting her up on a cloud of bliss.

26

MEY

*M*ey woke up feeling sore, which was odd. Usually, the venom took care of all the little aches and pains that vigorous lovemaking could leave in its wake.

Except, she wasn't sore in that way. Her muscles hurt as if she'd exercised for too long and hadn't adequately stretched after. But other than bed sports, she hadn't done anything strenuous in weeks, and she hadn't felt like that the other times.

Was she coming down with something?

Yamanu had told her that the start of her transition would trigger flu-like symptoms. Could it be that it had started?

Hope fluttered in her chest, but Mey was afraid to let it fly. It was probably nothing. She'd been working long days in the café and then not sleeping much at night. No wonder her body was starting to protest the strain she was putting on it.

Yamanu's side of the bed was cold, which meant that he'd woken up long ago and had gone to the gym. She smiled, and her eyes went to the nightstand, where he always left a love note for her before leaving.

Waking up in Yamanu's arms was the best, but getting a love note every morning was nice too.

She lifted it up and unfolded it, smiling at the lopsided heart he always drew at the bottom. Usually, the note said that he was in the gym and was going to bring breakfast on his way back, and this time it was no different.

Mey brought it to her lips, kissed it, and then put it inside the nightstand's drawer. Once she transitioned and was allowed out of the village, she was going to buy a nice box to store them in. She'd looked online but hadn't found anything that was pretty enough as a keepsake and could also preserve her notes.

The question was where to find the kind that they used in museums to preserve old scripts. If she and Yamanu were going to live practically forever, the notes would have to survive a very long time.

Paper didn't last long at all. Luckily for history, old texts were written on clay, which lasted much longer. If not for that, people would have assumed that the ancients hadn't had writing at all. She wondered how many more civilizations had writing, but nothing of it survived.

With a groan, Mey turned on her side and closed her eyes. Maybe she should just go back to sleep. Could it be that Yamanu's venom hadn't worked well last night because of the massive shroud he had performed?

They had made love only once, which was atypical for them, but that was because of her. She'd floated away on a cloud of bliss and hadn't come back until morning. Yamanu could have probably gone for another round or two.

Another possibility occurred to her. What if she was getting accustomed to the venom, and it was losing its effect on her? She should have asked Callie and Wonder about it. Or maybe just Callie. Wonder had been an immortal already when she and Anandur became a couple. Callie started her relationship with Brundar as a human, and she had experienced his venom bite as one. Had it lost its effect on her as well?

That would be a shame.

Mey loved waking up invigorated rather than exhausted, feeling great rather than achy. She'd even entertained a few naughty thoughts about visiting Brundar's club, not only to observe but possibly to make use of one of the private rooms. Knowing that nothing was going to hurt once playtime was over made it much less scary to try.

Yamanu might not be on board for that, though. He was a gentle soul and not into kinky games.

She would have to suggest it in a roundabout way, so he wouldn't feel pressured into it. Her man loved to please her, and he would do his damnedest to fulfill her every fantasy, even if it meant going to a club that he would have never set foot in otherwise.

Besides, it wasn't on the top of her list of things to try. She hadn't had fantasies about bondage and wasn't into pain. But she was curious and liked to try new things. Otherwise, how would she discover her passions?

There were many things on her list. Like visiting places that she hadn't visited yet, learning to surf, on water and on snow. Learning how to belly dance for real, sky diving, and swimming with sharks. None of it was crucial to the enjoyment of life, but Mey liked collecting moments, experiences. And overcoming her fears felt good. She was terrified of jumping out of a plane, but she wanted to try it anyway. And the same was true for swimming with sharks.

If she transitioned, she would have infinite time to collect as many experiences as her imagination could come up with.

7

YAMANU

hen Yamanu entered the house, he expected to find Mey in the kitchen, sipping on her coffee as she had done every morning since she'd started working in the café.

As he usually did after the gym, Yamanu had stopped at the vending machines and gotten pastries for them to share with a cup of coffee before both of them headed out.

Today, though, no smell of coffee had greeted him, and the coffeemaker sat silent and empty on the counter.

Was she still in the bathroom?

He glanced at his watch, making sure that he hadn't miscalculated the time. Just as he'd thought, it was seven-thirty.

Perhaps she was getting dressed.

Worried, he hurried to the bedroom and found her sleeping. The note he'd left on the nightstand wasn't there, though, so she must have woken up and put it in the drawer with the others he'd written for her.

It was such a sentimental thing to do, and he loved her for it. Mey cherished those notes as if they were precious gifts.

"Wake up, my sleeping beauty." He put down the bag of pastries on the nightstand and sat next to Mey on the bed. "You are going to be late."

She groaned and turned on her side, pulling the blanket over her head.

He tugged on it. "It's seven-thirty. You should be on your way by now."

She turned around to face him and opened her eyes. "I'm not feeling well. I think I caught the flu." She started to lift her arm and then let it plop back down. "Everything aches."

Hope surged in his chest. Could it be the start of her transition?

"I'm calling Bridget." As much as he liked Julian and Merlin, he didn't want their hands on his woman.

It was a stupid sentiment, and if Bridget wasn't available, he would have called either of them without hesitation. But as long as he had a female alternative, he was going to use it first.

"Don't call the doctor," Mey said. "It's probably nothing."

"Let her decide that."

"Fine. I'm too weak to argue." Mey turned on her side and tucked her hands under the pillow.

Pulling out his phone, he selected Bridget's number.

She answered right away. "Is Mey transitioning?"

"That's why I'm calling you. She's not feeling well."

"Does she have a fever?"

"Let me check." He put his hand on Mey's forehead. "I don't think so."

"Did you just use your hand? Never mind. I need to stop by the clinic to get my things, and then I'll come over."

"Thank you. I know you are not working in the clinic anymore, but since you have the most experience with transitioning Dormants, I feel better knowing that you are taking care of Mey."

"That's why I'm still on call for when a Dormant transitions. Besides, I love it. It's like delivering new babies, just fully grown. I'll be there shortly." She disconnected.

Yamanu chuckled. "Bridget is on her way."

"What's funny?" Mey asked.

"She said that helping Dormants transition feels to her like delivering fully grown babies."

Mey turned on her back and put her arms over the blanket. "I get it. She's delivering new members to the clan."

"True. Can I get you something? Would you like me to make coffee? I brought pastries from the vending machine."

Mey grimaced. "I don't want anything to eat and thinking of coffee makes me nauseous. Tea would be nice, though. But before that, can you text Wonder and let her know that I'm not coming in?"

"Sure."

He pulled out his phone again and fired a quick text.

Wonder's response came a few seconds later. *I'm keeping my mental fingers crossed.*

He texted back. *Thank you. A prayer to the Fates would be greatly appreciated as well.*

Naturally. Kiss Mey for me and tell her that I will pray for her to transition smoothly.

"Wonder sends you kisses and says that she is going to pray for you."

A tear slid down Mey's cheek. "That's so sweet of her. Everyone is so nice to me here."

Yamanu frowned. Perhaps his hand wasn't good at detecting fever because Mey was not the overly emotional type, and he'd heard that a fever sometimes had this effect on humans.

"I'm going to make tea."

"Thank you."

When he was done, a knock on the door announced the doctor's arrival.

He opened the door for her.

"Hello, Yamanu. I assume Mey is in bed?"

"Yes. Please, follow me."

Two things occurred to him as he led Bridget to the bedroom. One was that the place still smelled from last night's lovemaking, and the second was that he should have offered the doctor tea as well.

There was nothing he could do about the scent, but he could make another cup of tea.

"Hi, Bridget," Mey said. "Thanks for coming to see me, but I'm sure it's regular flu and not the transition."

Yamanu put the teacup on the nightstand. "Can I make one for you as well, doctor?"

Bridget arched a brow. "Since when am I Doctor to you? You always call me Bridget."

He shrugged. "Seemed appropriate for the occasion. What about tea? Do you want some?"

"Maybe later. Right now, I want to see what's going on with Mey."

She opened her bag and pulled out a thermometer. "Can you move your hair so I can put it in your ear?"

Mey lifted a shaky hand and did as the doctor asked.

Bridget waited until the device beeped. "A hundred and one," she read the display.

Yamanu smiled sheepishly. "It seems that my hand is not good at measuring fever."

"No, it isn't." Bridget turned to Mey. "Tell me what hurts."

"Mainly my muscles. They feel like I've overexerted myself exercising. But now my throat hurts too." She cast a glance at the teacup. "Maybe I'm just thirsty." She reached for it.

"Hold on," Bridget said. "Let me take a look first."

"It's not inflamed," she said after shining a small flashlight into Mey's throat. "You can drink your tea."

Mey took a sip and sighed. "That's much better." She lifted her eyes to Bridget. "Maybe it is just regular flu or cold?"

Bridget shook her head. "The incubation period for the flu is two to four days. You've been in the village for much longer than that, and you couldn't have caught anything from us. We don't transmit human diseases. But let me do a thorough check-up first."

"What about the sore throat, though? Yamanu told me that the symptoms are usually fever and muscle aches."

"Well, that's the odd thing out. Guys get sore throats because

113

they start growing venom glands. They also get gum pain because they are growing fangs. Transitioning is harder for men, but then they don't have to give birth, so I think we are even." She winked. "Although giving birth is not a big deal for an immortal female."

Mey perked up. "It doesn't hurt?"

"Oh, it hurts, alright. But we heal much faster."

Mey sighed wistfully. "Yamanu and I want a lot of children."

Bridget cast her a stern look. "I recommend waiting at least six months after the transition. But some people are in a hurry and don't listen. Vivian and Magnus are taking Merlin's potion even though I advised against it."

Mey grimaced. "I hate potions."

Standing behind Bridget, Yamanu shook his head, reminding Mey not to talk about the potion he had been taking to help with his abstinence.

As understanding dawned, Mey's eyes widened for a moment. "I heard that it tastes awful."

Bridget smiled. "It does. Turner and I are taking it too. Now, sit up so I can listen to your lungs."

When the doctor was done, she put her things back into her black bag. "I think you are transitioning, Mey." She turned to Yamanu. "I need Mey moved to the clinic. Do you want to carry her, or should I send over a gurney?"

He frowned. "Do you expect complications?"

"I've learned that you never know with Dormants. Just to be safe, I'd like to hook Mey up to the monitoring equipment."

MEY

"I don't know what's more embarrassing," Mey said as Yamanu picked her up. "You carrying me in your arms to the clinic or wheeling me in a wheelchair."

"Neither. You are not the first Dormant to arrive like that to the clinic. Magnus ran all the way with Vivian in his arms because she passed out and he panicked." Yamanu adjusted the strap of her duffel bag, so it swung behind him. "Think of it as tradition. It's like a bride crossing the threshold of her new home for the first time in her husband's arms."

She snuggled against him. "I would have preferred to walk into the clinic, but I'm too weak."

"And deprive me of the pleasure of delivering you there in my arms?" Yamanu pulled the door closed behind him and descended the steps from the front porch to the pathway.

"Can you stop by the café? I want to tell the good news to Wonder in person."

"A moment ago, you were embarrassed to be seen being carried by me."

She lifted up and kissed the underside of his jaw. "That was before you gave it such a nice spin. I like the analogy of a bride crossing the threshold into a new beginning."

He bent his head and kissed her forehead. "We still have one champagne bottle left unopened. I need to ask Bridget if it's okay for you to consume alcohol during your transition. If she approves, I'll bring it to the clinic to celebrate."

"I'd like that."

As they reached the café, it didn't take long for people to realize what was going on. In moments, everyone got to their feet, clapping and cheering.

Wonder ran up to Yamanu and Mey and wrapped her arms around both of them. "I'm so happy."

Mey laughed. "I didn't transition yet."

"You will. This is how it starts for everyone, and since you are young and healthy, you will have no problem transitioning. You didn't even pass out."

Mey lifted a brow. "Was I supposed to?"

"I don't know how it was for everyone who's gone through it, but most of those whose stories I heard had passed out."

That was encouraging. Mey felt weak, feverish, and achy, but it wasn't too bad.

Several people came over to say good luck, and then Yamanu was walking again.

In the clinic, Bridget showed them into a patient room full of monitoring equipment.

"I'll leave you two alone to get settled." She pointed at the hospital johnny neatly folded on the bed. "Put it on and call me when you are ready."

"Do I have to? I have my comfy home clothes on."

"I need to attach wires to you, and if you pass out, I need to put a catheter and an IV in. Unfortunately, it's not going to work with your comfy clothes." She smirked. "Besides, it's an opportunity to moon Yamanu."

"Well, if you put it that way."

With a wink, Bridget stepped out of the room and closed the door.

"Do you need help undressing?" Yamanu asked.

She'd been so weak that he'd had to get into the shower with her, wash her, towel dry her, and then put clothes on her. Things hadn't changed much since then. After all the well-wishing, Mey felt more upbeat and hopeful, but her limbs still refused to cooperate.

"Yeah, I do."

He helped her out of her clothes, including her underwear, and put the hospital gown on without taking the opportunity to cop a feel.

Mey didn't know whether she should appreciate that he hadn't touched her or feel offended by it. Her guy was a gentleman, and that was nice, but she wanted him to desire her no matter what state she was in.

Was it insecurity?

Perhaps.

Yamanu helped her lie down and covered her with the blanket. "Comfortable?"

"Can you raise the back of the bed a little?"

"Sure." He pressed the lever until she told him to stop. "I'll let Bridget know that you are ready."

"Okay."

While the doctor attached the wires and checked the equipment, Yamanu leaned against the wall and pulled out his phone. "I'm going to text Kian and tell him the good news."

"Isn't it a bit too early?" Mey asked. "What time does he usually start his day?"

"He's in the office already."

Mey wondered if the boss would come to visit her.

"Kian says congratulations," Yamanu said. "And he wants to see me once you are settled in."

Mey didn't want to be left alone in the patient room, not yet, but on the other hand, she didn't want to appear clingy and interfere with Yamanu's work.

Except, she didn't have to say anything. Yamanu read her like an open book.

"I'll stay a little longer." He pulled out a chair and brought it closer to the bed.

"All done," Bridget said. "Here is the remote for the bed." She handed Mey the device. "And here is the remote for the TV." She gave her another one. "It gets boring to just wait. So, you might as well entertain yourself. We have internal streaming with all the latest movies."

When the doctor left, Yamanu reached for Mey's hand. "Are you okay?"

"Yeah, I just don't want to be alone. But you can't keep Kian waiting."

"He said to come when you are all settled. You are not settled yet."

Someone must have knocked on the door because Yamanu got up to open it. Mey didn't hear the knock, but that wasn't unusual. The soundproofing they used in the village was the best there was.

"We heard the good news. Can we come in?"

Mey recognized Ella's voice. "Yes, please come in."

As Yamanu opened the door all the way, Ella and Callie rushed to her side.

"I'm so happy, I could cry." Callie bent down and kissed Mey's cheek. "Finally. We were starting to worry."

Mey chuckled. "And yet you tried to convince me that there was nothing to worry about."

Callie shrugged and hopped up on the bed. "There was no reason to stress you even more."

"I wasn't worried." Ella got up on the other side of the bed. "I knew you were going to transition."

"Alena and her team are coming back on Saturday," Callie said. "Which is perfect because you are going to transition by then and we can have a party to celebrate."

"Awesome. I can't wait to hold Ethan in my arms. He is such an adorable little boy." She smiled. "Besides, there is an old wives' tale that if you want to have a boy, you should hold one as much as you can." She glanced at Yamanu and smiled. "I want a boy who looks just like his daddy."

YAMANU

*Y*amanu's heart swelled with love and gratitude. There was no better expression of Mey's love than her wanting a boy who looked just like him.

He pushed away from the wall and walked up to her.

As Callie moved aside, making room for him next to Mey, he bent and planted a soft kiss on her forehead. "And I want a bunch of girls who look just like their mother."

Mey smiled. "Let's have five of each. How about that?"

"It's a deal." He looked up at Ella, who was wiping a tear from the corner of her eye. "Are you going to stay here for a little while longer? Kian asked me to come up to his office, and I don't want to leave Mey alone."

Ella sniffled. "We will stay until you come back. Take as long as you need."

He looked down at Mey. "Are you going to be okay with Callie and Ella?"

"Yes."

He kissed her again. "I'll be back as soon as I can."

She nodded.

It was a beautiful day outside, and as he walked over to the office building, Yamanu thought that it was a good omen for Mey's transition to start on such a cloudless day.

It was a silly superstition, which he would have never voiced in front of his fellow Guardians, but he believed in it, and it helped ease his anxiety. Several of the transitioning Dormants had had a rough time, some slipping into a coma that had lasted days, and in Turner's case, weeks. They had almost lost the guy, but he was a stubborn sucker and had somehow pulled through.

Mey was young and healthy, and she hadn't even passed out, so chances were that her transition would go smoothly, but it wasn't a sure thing. She could still slip into a coma.

Yamanu found Kian's office door partially open, but he knocked anyway.

"Come in," Kian said. "We have a lot to celebrate today." He pulled a big cigar out of his desk drawer and offered it to Yamanu. "Congratulations on the outcome of your experiment and on Mey entering transition."

"Thank you." Yamanu looked at the fat Cuban, not sure what to do with it.

Next, Kian pulled out a bottle of whiskey and two glasses. "We can't smoke in here, but we can on the roof." He put the glasses in his pockets and motioned for Yamanu to follow. "I usually don't invite people up there, but I'm making an exception for you."

"I'm honored." Yamanu dipped his head.

Kian chuckled. "It's a one-time invitation."

Yamanu followed Kian out of the office. "Still, I feel special for being invited even once to your sanctuary."

At the top of the stairs, Kian opened the door and stepped out onto the rooftop terrace.

"Nice setup you've got here." The boss had two wooden rocking chairs, and a side table brought up to the roof. There was even an outdoor umbrella to provide shade.

"I still don't know who arranged that for me. The chairs and table came first, and then a couple of weeks later, the umbrella. No one is taking credit for it. I thought it was Amanda, but she swore it hadn't been her." Kian put the whiskey bottle on the side table and pulled the glasses out of his pockets.

"What about Syssi?" Yamanu asked as he sat down.

"It wasn't her, either."

"Perhaps Shai?"

Kian's assistant was a quiet guy who didn't like to attract much attention to himself, but he cared about his boss. Before Syssi had entered Kian's life, Shai had been the one who'd ensured that Kian had new clothes custom-made and delivered for him, that he hadn't forgotten to eat, and that he hadn't fallen asleep at his desk from exhaustion.

Kian sat down on the other rocker and pulled a box of cigarillos and a lighter from his pockets. "I suspect that you are right. It's down to Shai or Bridget."

It was sad that Kian didn't have close buddies who he could have suspected of doing a nice thing for him. But maybe he was wrong.

"It could have been Anandur and Brundar."

"Nah." Kian lit his cigarillo. "They are not that thoughtful."

"I'll try to find out who did it."

"Thanks. I need to know who I owe a favor."

As Yamanu unwrapped the cigar, Kian poured whiskey into the glasses.

He handed one to Yamanu. "I heard that you successfully shrouded a massive fireworks display. How did you pull it off?"

"With Mey's help. When I told her that you'd given us an extension, she insisted on me testing my powers right away." Yamanu chuckled. "I wanted to wait until she entered her transition, but she refused to wait. I can't say that her antics to make me randy weren't fun to watch, but it was damn difficult not to do anything about it. I thought that I was a pro at self-denial, but those were the most torturous thirty-six hours I've spent in a long while."

Kian dragged a hand through his hair. "I can imagine. The pull of a fated mate is stronger than any other. I applaud you for holding back. I'm not sure I could've done it when Syssi and I were just getting to know each other. I craved her nonstop. I still do, but now it's more manageable."

Yamanu wondered how long it had taken for the insatiable craving to subside, and whether it had anything to do with the addiction. "Did it become more manageable after the addiction set in?"

Kian rubbed a hand over his jaw. "I don't remember when it happened precisely, but I think it was unrelated to the addiction. It took much longer than that." He smiled sheepishly. "Get ready for a wild year."

Yamanu had thought in terms of a month, like a honeymoon. But hey, it was all good.

"A year, you say?"

Nodding, Kian lifted his glass. "Let's make a toast. To Mey for saving the day."

Yamanu clinked his with Kian's. "To Mey's smooth and uneventful transition."

"Indeed. To Mey's transition." As Kian sipped the whiskey, his expression showed his pleasure.

Yamanu took small sips as well, savoring the exquisite taste. The whiskey was one of the best he had ever had. "What brand is it? It's excellent."

"It's Japanese. As with most things, they take the best of what the Western world produces and make it better."

"I need to get myself a bottle."

"I'll get you one. I didn't get you a housewarming present yet."

Yamanu cocked a brow. "I didn't move."

"You didn't, but you changed housing arrangements. Did you talk with Arwel about his accommodations when he comes back?"

It hadn't occurred to Yamanu that Arwel might not be comfortable cohabiting with him and Mey. With the excellent soundproofing, privacy was not an issue.

Except, Arwel's empathy might make things difficult for him. Nevertheless, Yamanu wasn't going to tell Arwel that he had to move out. It would be his decision whether he wanted to stay or not.

"As far as Mey and I are concerned, Arwel doesn't need to move. This is his house as much as it is mine and now also Mey's."

Kian laughed. "You are still thinking like a bachelor. A mated couple need their privacy, and with Arwel's special gift, it would be like having a third partner who is privy to everything the two of you experience. You should call him and make the proper arrangements."

Yamanu shook his head. "I can't. When Arwel comes back, he will decide what he wants to do. He is my friend, and I'm not going to kick him out."

"I understand." Kian leaned sideways and refilled their glasses. "Now that Mey is transitioning, we can go search for Jin."

Yamanu took the glass and cradled it in his hands. "Do you have a plan?"

"I do. Once Mey is back on her feet, what do you think about taking her on a ski vacation?"

That was an odd change of subject. "I don't know if she can ski."

"But you are a good skier."

"Where are you going with this? What does skiing have to do with finding Jin?"

30

KIAN

*K*ian took a long puff from his cigarillo. "Vivian gave us more information about her sister-in-law. Turns out that Eleanor is an avid skier. Vivian says that she chose to work as a pharmaceutical rep because the flexible schedule and travel involved allowed her to visit all the best ski resorts in the country. One of those resorts is smack in the middle of the Quiet Zone." He took another puff. "Well, not exactly in the middle, that would be the observatory and the naval base, but close."

Yamanu, who had been holding the cigar more than smoking it, tapped on it to release the ash. "Isn't it a long shot to hope we will find her there? It's not like we can spend the entire snow season waiting for Ella's aunt to show up."

"No, we can't, and that's not what we are going to do. The idea is to show her picture to people working in the resort and find out if they have seen her around. If they recognize her, it will give us confirmation that she is in the area. Also, there might be someone who befriended her and who knows where she lives or maybe heard her mention how long it takes her to get to the resort, so we can narrow the search to the corresponding area. I think it's a good start."

Leaning back, Yamanu took a shallow puff of his cigar. "Sounds like a plan. I hope Mey knows how to ski." He grinned. "I'm not cheap, but I like the idea of a honeymoon paid for by someone else." Then his expression turned somber. "On the other hand, perhaps I should pay for Mey's and my stay. After all, the clan is doing this for us."

Kian shook his head. "We are doing it for the clan. Even if Jin didn't have a talent that I can make use of, she is a Dormant who could be someone's mate. That's crucial to the clan's survival, and therefore is number one on the list of priorities."

"I'm glad you see it this way, but I still feel like I should pay for what I can."

Stubborn, prideful man.

"Forget it. I'm thinking of coming as well and bringing Syssi with me. We haven't been on vacation in a while, and my wife could use one."

"What does it have to do with my sharing in the costs?"

"Think of it as a corporate retreat, which is what we are going to pretend it is. I'm going to find a large cabin to rent, so we are all going to stay in one place, and we are going to keep a low profile."

That seemed to finally mollify Yamanu. "Who is going? I mean besides Mey and me and you and Syssi?"

"I don't know yet, and I haven't asked Syssi if she wants to go either. Turner and I haven't finalized the plan yet."

Lifting his half-smoked cigar, Yamanu grimaced. "This thing will take another hour to smoke, and Mey is waiting for me."

"Don't worry about it." Kian waved a hand in dismissal. "Just put it in the ashtray, and it will die out. Go to your lady."

"Thank you." Yamanu finished what was left in his glass and rose to his feet. "For everything."

"You are welcome. I'm relieved that you can still summon your powers when needed."

"Yeah, me too. Mey is relieved as well. She feared that the clan would hate her once people realized why I didn't have my powers anymore."

"Hate is a strong word, but there might have been some resentment. People are people, and they are mostly selfish."

Yamanu nodded.

Once the Guardian had left, Kian pulled out another cigarillo, leaned back in the rocking chair, and debated who he wanted to take with him.

If he and Syssi were going, Anandur and Brundar were going as well, and if they were going, they would naturally want to bring their mates.

He smiled.

Organizing a retreat for the Guardians and their new mates hadn't occurred to him before, but it was an excellent idea. They were more than a bunch of people working together, they were a family, and sometimes he forgot that.

They would also need Arwel and his empathic skills, but that wasn't a problem since the New York team was coming back on Saturday. Mey wouldn't be ready for travel before that anyway, and he'd promised her that she could join the search.

Mey had made a good point about Jin not willing to go with them otherwise. Having Mey with them would save them a lot of explanations for which there wouldn't be time.

They could thrall Jin, but that was morally iffy. If the girl didn't want to leave, they were not going to force her.

Pulling out his phone, he called Anandur. "Can you and Brundar come up to the roof?"

"Sure, boss."

When Kian didn't have meetings outside the village, his bodyguards were helping retrain the new Guardians. Most of the fellows had left the force when swords had been the weapons of choice. A lot had changed in the world since then, not only in weaponry but also in fighting techniques. They had a century or two of catching up to do, and it was almost like starting from scratch.

Still, it was much easier to do than training newbies. These men had fought before and had honed the hard attitude and quick responses warriors required.

As the rooftop door opened, Kian turned to look at the brothers. "I hope I didn't pull you out in the middle of a training session."

"No worries, boss," Anandur said. "We sat them down to do homework."

Kian lifted a brow. "I didn't know the Guardians had home assignments."

"They are watching a video on how to disarm explosives," Brundar said. "What did you want to see us about?"

Kian smiled. "A ski vacation."

After he was done explaining, Anandur shook his head. "If it was on the weekend, Wonder could come. During the week she has to work in the café. There is no one to take over for her, which sucks."

Kian tapped his cigarillo. "The village can survive a few days without the café."

"Are you kidding me?" Anandur chuckled. "There will be riots."

There was something to that. As the only place that provided food in the village, people had grown to depend on it.

"I can call Jackson and have him take over for a week. After all, it's his business."

"He is not going to be happy about it. Last I heard, the kid opened another commercial kitchen. He is expanding his pastries and sandwiches empire."

"He will have to manage."

Anandur shrugged. "Good luck. When are we going, and who is coming?"

"Mey has just entered transition, but I hope that by Monday she will be well enough to travel. If not, some of us will go ahead and start the investigation, and she and Yamanu will arrive later. Syssi and I are probably going to stay only a couple of days. I can't stay away from the village for much longer."

"Why not?" Brundar asked. "You can work from anywhere, and

Onegus can handle security while you are gone. The village is not in danger."

"I don't know about that." Kian took another puff from his cigarillo. "After the botched mission, I sleep less peacefully at night. Some of the Doomers might have escaped and told the story of what happened. Navuh might be planning an attack as we speak."

Anandur arched a brow. "Wouldn't Lokan know about it? Or Areana? We are no longer flying blind as far as the Brotherhood's plans go."

"That is true."

31

ANNANI

*A*s Annani gazed at the beautiful table that her Odus had set up, a pang of sorrow pulsed through her heart.

Until the next visit, this was going to be her last Friday dinner with the family, and she was going to miss them.

In her Alaskan retreat, communal meals were the norm. Since no one had partners and everyone worked from home, it was a good way to alleviate the loneliness and connect with others three times a day.

It had been one of her better ideas to institute those.

But it wasn't the same as dining with her children and their spouses. She liked being just a mother for a change, not the Clan Mother.

As the knock on the door came, and Ogidu opened the way, she was surprised to see that the first to arrive were Kian and Syssi. Usually, Kian came in last, rushing in and apologizing for having been detained by this or that.

"Hello, Mother." He walked up to her and bent to kiss her cheek. "How was your day?"

"All my days in your village have been pleasant. But today, I was a little sad."

"Why is that?" Syssi asked as she gave her a warm hug.

"This is going to be the last Friday dinner I have with you before I leave."

Syssi patted her arm. "Then you should start planning your next visit and make sure that it's not months away from now."

"Or, you can stay," Kian said. "No one is forcing you to leave."

"I know." Annani sat down in her favorite armchair. She was going to miss that piece of furniture as well. "I have been away for too long already. The people in the sanctuary need me. Especially since Alena is gone as well. When she is there, I do not feel as bad for taking prolonged vacations. I know there is someone at the helm."

Sitting on the other armchair, Kian leaned forward and steepled his hands. "Who did you leave in charge?"

"Teresa. But before you say anything, she is not someone who can lead people. Teresa is just my assistant, and her job is to notify me if anything goes wrong, not to solve it."

"Then find someone who can lead. As you've told me countless times, we have plenty of capable people in the clan. You can find a person to promote."

Annani nodded. "The thought occurred to me. The problem is that my people are mostly artists. They are not interested in administrative or leadership positions."

Kian was about to come up with a retort when the door opened, and Amanda walked in with Dalhu.

"Hello, everyone." She walked up to Annani and bent to kiss her cheek, then moved to do the same to Kian and Syssi. "How come you are early? Usually, you are the last to arrive."

Kian shrugged. "It was a good day, and I wanted to share the news with my family. Mey started her transition."

When no one reacted with great surprise, he frowned. "You know about it already?"

"Of course." Annani leaned over and patted his thigh. "How long do you think it takes for news like that to travel through the village? I knew about it as soon as Yamanu was seen carrying Mey to the clinic."

"Same here," Amanda said. "The texts started to arrive from all over the place."

He threw his hands in the air. "How come I didn't get any? Is everyone keeping me out of the loop on purpose?"

Syssi chuckled. "No, my love." She rose to her feet and came over to sit in his lap. "They just assume that you are the first to know when something exciting is happening. Besides, everyone is well aware of your opinion on gossip."

He wrapped his arm around her. "The next news I'm going to share, I'm certain you haven't heard about yet." He scratched his stubble. "On second thought, I'm not so sure because I told Anandur about it, and he is the number one spreader of gossip in the village."

Amanda looked at Syssi. "The only exciting thing I heard about was Mey's transition. Did you hear about anything else?"

Syssi shook her head. "No, but I know what it is since Kian shared it with me."

"Now you've got me all excited." Amanda shifted her eyes to Kian. "Please tell us your news, brother of mine."

"Syssi and I, together with several Guardians and their mates, are going on a ski vacation. But that's just a cover for the real purpose of the trip. While Syssi and I are going to enjoy the slopes, the Guardians are going to question the resort's personnel about Ella's aunt, who we suspect has something to do with the para-normal division that recruited Mey's sister. Vivian says that her sister-in-law is an avid skier, and the ski resort in the Quiet Zone is one of the best in the country. If Eleanor is working somewhere in that area, which we have a strong reason to believe that she is, then she must have visited the resort quite frequently. Someone might remember her or even know where we can find her."

"When are you planning on going?" Amanda asked.

"Sometime next week. We need to wait for Mey to feel well enough to travel, and for Arwel to return. I want him there with us."

"He is coming back tomorrow night together with the rest of the team," Amanda said.

Annani stifled a smirk. The team was already on their way back, but she'd asked everyone to keep it quiet. Only Bridget and Shai knew about it, and they were cooperating. If everything went well, Alena and her team were going to arrive in time to join them for after-dinner coffee.

"He is," Kian said. "His empathic skills might come in handy."

Amanda glanced at Dalhu, and the two of them exchanged some silent communication, at the end of which Dalhu nodded.

"Who else are you taking with you?" Amanda asked.

"Anandur, Brundar, and their mates, and Mey and Yamanu. I promised Mey she could come with us when we went looking for her sister."

"Dalhu and I want to come too."

"That's awesome." Syssi clapped her hands. "But what about the lab?"

Amanda smirked. "I can schedule maintenance to repaint the lab during next week, and I'll have another professor take over my classes. Since I only have four, it's not a big deal to find a replacement."

"Dinner is ready, Clan Mother," Ogidu announced with a bow. "Should I start serving it?"

"Please do." Annani stood up. "Let us move this lovely conversation to the dinner table, shall we?"

KIAN

*A*fter dinner, Kian walked outside to smoke. It wasn't because he was craving nicotine, but because he hoped his mother would follow, so he could tell her the good news about Yamanu.

He wondered if there had been rumors about that as well. Anandur and William knew some of it because they'd helped Yamanu set up his experiment, but they didn't know the real reason. Still, Anandur might have kept his mouth shut if Yamanu asked him to keep quiet about it. William wasn't nearly as bad a gossip as Anandur, but his mouth sometimes ran ahead of him, and he blurted things he shouldn't have.

"It is a pleasant evening," Annani said from behind him.

He turned around. "The entire day was beautiful, and not only because of the favorable weather."

"Yes, indeed. It is a good day when a new Dormant transitions, and even a better one when her transition goes smoothly. I just spoke with Gertrude, and she said that Mey is doing splendidly."

Kian bent and kissed his mother's cheek. "You are a good leader, Mother. You really care about your people."

"Of course. But so do you."

"Yes, but it didn't occur to me to check on Mey. I assumed that someone would have notified me if anything was wrong with her."

She patted his arm. "You have a lot on your plate, Kian, and everyone knows it. People do not expect you to make phone calls inquiring about their well-being."

"I know. But it would have made me feel good to make that call."

"You are a perfectionist, and that is not good for your mental health. Give yourself permission not to be perfect." She stretched to her full height of five feet and half an inch. "And if you cannot do that, I will give you mine. You do not have to be perfect at everything, my son."

"Thank you, Mother." He offered her his arm, and when Annani threaded hers through it, he led her to the outdoor couch. "I have more good news for you."

He waited until she was seated before joining her. "Yamanu tested his powers yesterday evening, and the experiment was successful. His powers are fully functional. All it took was a short, thirty-six-hour abstinence. He should be able to shield us if given advance warning. It's not as good as having him ready at a moment's notice, but at least I know I have his ability when needed for missions."

Annani's smile was bright enough to illuminate the night. "You should always trust the Fates, Kian. They know what they are doing."

"I wish my faith was as strong as yours. I'm getting better at it, though." He chuckled. "I basically repeat what you keep saying even though I'm not as deeply convinced as you are that it is true. Syssi says that it is good to assume the win, and this is my way of doing it."

"Whatever works for you. The important thing is to have faith. It helps with the stress." Annani leaned forward and tilted her head. "I think I hear someone coming."

His mother's hearing was better than his, so it took a few moments before he heard the murmurs of a distant conversation.

Except, the speakers were still too far away for him to recognize their voices.

Annani rose to her feet. "Let us welcome whoever is coming."

He narrowed his eyes at her. "How do you know that they are heading this way?"

"Simple. Magnus and Vivian are in the Bay Area, Merlin is out on the town, and I do not have any other neighbors."

Kian had a feeling that his mother knew perfectly well who was coming and was playing one of her games.

The question was, what?

After dinner, she had started everyone on silly charades games that he had no patience for, and now he suspected that she might have done it to stall for time.

"Close the sliding door behind you," she told him as he entered the living room. "There is a draft."

Now he was sure that Annani was up to something. There was no draft, and the living room felt stuffy with the door closed. She just didn't want anyone to hear the new arrivals.

When the knock came, Annani pretended surprise. "I wonder who can it be?"

Watching Ogidu walk over to the door, her lips quivered with a barely stifled smile.

When the Odu opened it, Alena yelled surprise and barreled through Ogidu to catch her mother in a big hug.

Behind her, Arwel walked in with an apologetic expression on his face.

"I'm sorry." He walked up to Kian. "I had orders from the Clan Mother to keep our early arrival a surprise."

Laughing, Kian clapped the Guardian on his back. "I had a feeling Annani was plotting something. Where is the rest of the team?"

"Ethan was fussy, so Eva and Bhathian took him home. I only came because Alena dragged me along."

"I'm glad you're here. I have a new mission I want to discuss with you."

"Already?" Arwel cocked a brow.

"Not right now. Next week."

"Oh, well. That's plenty of time." His tone was more joking than sarcastic.

"Come, let us all sit down," Annani led Alena to the couch and sat with her, holding her hand as if she'd missed her terribly.

Given that the two were practically inseparable, she probably had.

"How did you make it here so soon?" Amanda asked. "Didn't you have a photoshoot this morning?"

"I did," Alena said. "But we packed everything beforehand, and half the team waited for us in the jet. I wrapped it up quickly and headed straight from the studio to the airport."

"When is your campaign going live?" Syssi asked.

"Two weeks." She plopped back against the pillows. "It was fun, but I'm glad it's over. I'm tickled silly that it was all for nothing, and that you found Kalugal right here under your noses."

"We didn't find him yet," Kian said. "And he still might take the bait and try finding you. The campaign is going to run nationwide."

"Are you excited?" Amanda asked.

Alena snorted. "Freaked out is more like it. I'm glad that I don't look like myself in those photos. I don't like the idea of my face being plastered over buses and billboards and magazines everywhere. I just hope that the company makes a lot of sales from those ads. I will feel terrible if we ruined it for them."

"They approved you without us having to thrall their executives," Arwel pointed out. "Besides, you are gorgeous, even when made to look like Areana."

"Thank you. That's sweet of you to say." She looked at Annani. "I guess we are going home soon?"

Annani nodded. "Monday. I'll give you the weekend to rest."

Alena let out a relieved breath. "Good. I need it."

Kian had a feeling she was reluctant to go back to Alaska. Alena had gotten a taste of freedom, and she was probably regretting that it was over.

"You can come with us to the ski resort," Syssi offered. "It's a part vacation and part mission. We are looking for Ella's aunt, who might be connected to Mey's sister, and who is an avid skier."

Alena's eyes sparkled for a moment, but then the light dimmed. "I wish I could, but it is time for Mother and me to return home. Count me in for your next vacation, though."

"Have you consulted Bridget?" Annani asked Kian.

"About Syssi? Do you think I should?"

Annani's smile was indulgent. "Syssi's pregnancy is not an issue, but Mey's transition might be. She might not be out of the woods, so to speak, by then, or her condition might worsen. You should at least have a doctor with you. Invite Bridget and Turner to join you."

"While we are looking for Eleanor, Mey can stay in the cabin and rest. But having a doctor with us is a good idea. Bridget has to stay in the village because she is heading the rescue operations, and she needs a longer advance notice than a couple of days. But I can take Julian, and Ella can come with him. She might prove useful with her aunt. I'm not sure how, but I'd rather have her there just in case we need her."

MEY

*M*ey was miserable. Yesterday it had seemed as if her transition was going to be a walk in the park. Today it seemed like a crawl through the desert with an empty water canteen. Everything hurt, from the muscles in her calves to the tendons in her shoulders and everything in between.

The worst were the gums.

Her fever had gone up, and as usually happened when she had a high temperature, her gums itched something awful. She kept rubbing her finger over them to ease the unbearable itch, but it didn't help.

"Can I get you something?" Yamanu asked.

"Yeah. Ask Bridget if she can knock me out. I'm way too miserable to be conscious."

Seeing the lost look in his eyes, she took pity on him. "I'm just joking. I'll survive."

"Are you sure? I can bring you painkillers. Bridget is not here yet, but Gertrude can give you some."

"That would be nice."

Gertrude was the nurse who looked like a witch. A pretty one, but still a witch. There was something about her expression that hinted at secrets. Perhaps after the transition, she could strike up a conversation with the witchy nurse and find out what her story was.

He rose to his feet and kissed her forehead. "I'll be right back."

Mey sighed. She didn't get sick often, which might have accounted for how whiny she had become on the rare occasions that she had. The feeling of helplessness was the worst. She liked feeling vital, capable, and the enforced convalescence depressed her.

Poor Yamanu had spent part of the night on a cot because she couldn't get comfortable with him sleeping in the narrow hospital bed with her. He was a big guy, and the thing was probably too small for him by himself, let alone the two of them together.

Nevertheless, she'd felt awful for practically kicking him out.

Yamanu returned with three little pills in a small paper cup. "Gertrude said that Motrin should be enough."

"She's probably right. I just wish that it could put me to sleep so I could wake up after this was all over. The Dormants who passed out were the lucky ones."

"Don't say that." He walked to the sink and filled a large cup with water. "Going through it without passing out means that you are doing well and that your body is strong. It can handle the transition without slowing down your other functions."

She snorted. "I'm lying in bed. Not running a marathon. I wouldn't call it functioning as normal." She waved a hand. "Ignore me. I'm just a lousy patient. I don't like being sick."

"You are not sick. You are on the road to immortality." He handed her the water and the Motrin.

"You are absolutely right. That's how I should think about it." She popped the pills into her mouth and washed them down with the water.

"So, what's new? Distract me with some interesting news."

"I've already told you about the ski vacation. Nothing new has come up since then."

"You said that Alena and the team are back home. Do you think she would come to visit me? I miss her."

"I'm sure she will. She's probably still sleeping."

It was early morning, but since Mey had spent most of yesterday sleeping, her schedule had gotten all out of whack.

Yamanu took her hand and lifted it to his lips. "Try to get a little sleep. You need as much rest as possible."

He was always so attuned to her that it was like he was reading her mind.

"I'll try." Mey turned on her side and tucked one of her hands under the pillow.

The other had a monitor attached to a finger, so doing the same was not going to work. Then there were all the wires attached to her chest. It would have been easier if she were a back sleeper, but Mey could only sleep on her side or on her tummy.

Thankfully, she didn't have a catheter or an IV drip and was allowed to get off the bed to go to the bathroom. That was the upside.

As the Motrin finally started working, her aches and pains subsided, and she was thankfully able to drift off.

Hours must have passed because when Mey opened her eyes next, everything hurt more than it had before. The Motrin must have worn off.

"Yamanu?" she rasped.

"I'm here." He took her hand.

"Can you get me more Motrin? And water?"

"Sure. I'll be right back."

He returned together with Bridget.

"I hear that you are in a lot of pain," the doctor said.

"It's not so bad." Mey turned on her back.

Bridget pressed the pedal and lifted the back of the bed. "From the way Yamanu described it, you were suffering."

"I am. Everything hurts, but it's more of a discomfort than severe pain. Except for my gums. I don't know what the deal with those is. I usually get tingly gums when I have a fever, but this is worse than ever."

Bridget frowned. "That's odd. You are the first female Dormant to complain of that."

"Why? Do the male Dormants suffer from tingly gums?"

"Of course, and sore throat. I told you that yesterday. They are growing fangs and venom glands."

"Oh, right, you did. The fever is messing with my brain."

"I checked your stats before I came in. Your fever is not that bad."

Mey pouted. "It feels bad."

The doctor smiled indulgently. "I bet it does." She pulled out a thermometer from her coat pocket, moved Mey's hair away from her ear, and touched the tip to it.

"A hundred and two," Bridget said after looking at the display.

"Let's look at those gums, shall we?" She walked over to the cabinet and pulled out a tongue depressor and a pair of gloves.

Snapping them on, she pulled a slim flashlight out of her coat pocket and turned it on. "Open wide."

"Ahh…"

Bridget looked, patted her gums, and frowned. "They are swollen over the canines." She pulled back and looked at Mey as if she was a strange creature. "I've never seen that happen before to a transitioning female."

Great. I'm a freak even among immortals.

"What can it mean?" Yamanu asked.

Yeah, Mey wanted to know that too.

Bridget rubbed her hand over her chin. "It might be similar to what happens to pubescent boys when their nipples swell up and hurt. They are not going to grow breasts, but the hormones affect them. Maybe your body is confused by all the changes and is mimicking the pubescent stage of growth because of the hormonal upheaval. I doubt that you are growing fangs. Once you stabilize, the swelling will probably go down. Let's wait a couple more days and see what happens."

"Does it happen to the girls born in the clan? Do they get phantom growing fangs pains in puberty?"

Bridget shook her head. "The clan girls transition as babies or toddlers by being with Annani. I don't know how it works, but it does. The mothers either travel to the sanctuary and give birth there or take their daughters there a little later. The girls spend time with the goddess and usually transition within a week or two."

"So, you don't have any experience with pubescent girls transitioning?"

"I don't. But in ancient times, the girls transitioned at the same age as boys, so they might have experienced your symptoms. I'll ask Annani about it."

"Maybe Wonder knows," Mey offered. "She transitioned as a pubescent girl."

"That's an even better idea."

"Can you hand me my phone?" Mey asked Yamanu. "I want to text Wonder."

Bridget smiled. "I like your attitude. Why wait when something can be done right away?"

Mey took the device. "Wouldn't you want to know if you were growing fangs?"

Bridget nodded. "Naturally."

Mey opened the phone and texted. *Did any of the girls you knew in your adolescence experience phantom growing fangs pains when they transitioned?*

Several minutes passed before her phone pinged with a return message. *No, why?*

Because I am.

The next text came right away. *If they did, they might have been embarrassed to admit it. No girl wanted to be thought of as manly.*

Mey answered. *Makes sense. Thank you.*

"What did she say?" Yamanu asked.

"She never heard of phantom growing fangs pains. Wonder thinks that girls might have been experiencing them but were embarrassed to mention it because they didn't want to appear masculine."

Bridget nodded. "That's a reasonable assumption."

It was, but Mey wasn't convinced.

What if she was a mutation?

After all, her and Jin's talents were very different from those of other clan members. But since Mey was transitioning, she had to have the godly genes. Except, they might have mutated somehow.

Mey and Jin the mutants.

As much as some things had changed, others had not.

YAMANU

*A*s Yamanu listened to the exchange between Bridget and Mey, he wondered whether he should say something.

Mey was distraught by the possibility of growing fangs, and Bridget seemed puzzled by it, but he found the idea super-hot.

Still, how was it even possible?

None of the other Dormants had grown new teeth, but the clan females had slightly elongated canines that could pass for human. Evidently, those who had been turned as young girls simply grew them from the get-go, but those who already had all their adult teeth hadn't gotten new ones.

How come no one ever wondered about that?

"Can I say something?"

Mey and the doctor looked his way. "Of course," Bridget said. "What's on your mind?"

"The clan females have tiny fangs. Only the Dormants who turn in adulthood don't. They just keep the teeth they already have. What Mey is experiencing might be just a slight deviation from that, not an anomaly."

Bridget nodded. "I haven't considered it, but you might be right." She smiled. "Phoenix's tiny fangs are adorable."

Mey slumped against the pillows and let out a relieved breath. "So, I'm just a little bit of a freak. Not a major one."

Bridget patted her arm. "You're not a freak in either case, but who knows? You might be the next step in our evolution."

Once the doctor had left, Yamanu sat on the edge of the bed and took Mey's hand. "I know you're not ecstatic about growing fangs, but I think it's hot as hell. I find the prospect of you biting me extremely erotic."

"Why? Even if I'm going to have fangs, which I hope I don't, I'm not going to grow venom glands, which means that my bite will deliver only pain and no pleasure."

He lifted her hand and kissed the back of it. "I don't know if it's an immortal thing or just a fetish of mine, but I find the idea arousing, and if you don't believe me, I can show you proof." He put her hand over the straining bulge in his pants.

That wrested a giggle out of her. "Stop it. Bridget could walk in at any moment."

"I'll hear her opening the door."

A mischievous gleam brightening her eyes, Mey caressed him through his pants. "Do you think we can lock the door?"

Laughing, he shook his head. "A moment ago, you were concerned about Bridget walking in on basically nothing."

"Yeah, but she can't walk in if the door is locked."

As if on cue, the door opened, and Bridget walked in.

Since his back was turned to her, she couldn't see where Mey's hand was, and he quickly snatched it back up and kissed it again.

"I brought you more meds. These are a little stronger than Motrin and will help you sleep." She handed Mey one paper cup with pills and another one with water.

Blushing, Mey took the two cups. "Thank you."

If Bridget guessed that they had been fooling around, she made a valiant effort not to show it. Still, Yamanu could see a ghost of a smile hovering over her lips.

"Try to get some sleep," she said before leaving the room.

"That was close." Mey puffed out a breath.

"I was blocking her view. She couldn't see anything. But your blush gave you away."

Mey shrugged. "I could've been flushed because of the fever." She popped the pills into her mouth and washed them down with the water.

Several minutes later, when Mey's eyes closed, Yamanu lowered the bed's back, tucked the blanket around her, and pressed a soft kiss to her forehead. "Sleep well."

"Don't leave me," she murmured.

"I'm not going anywhere. I'm right here next to you." He lifted the chair and brought it closer to the bed.

"Thank you." She drifted off.

With a sigh, Yamanu pulled out his phone and went through his emails and text messages.

There were many congratulations, with people wanting to know how Mey was feeling, and he answered all of them with a couple of short sentences.

The one response he needed to put more thought into was the one to Arwel's text.

He didn't want to bring up housing arrangements. Arwel had been his roommate since they'd moved into the village, and they'd become even closer friends than they'd been before that. How could he ask the guy to move out?

Simple. He wasn't going to. If Arwel decided to leave on his own, so be it, but Yamanu wasn't going to suggest it.

He must have typed and retyped the message five times before finally sending it. *Thank you. Mey is doing well. She has a fever and is aching all over, but she didn't pass out, so that's a good sign. She would probably like to see you and Alena, and perhaps Eva and Ethan too. She is sleeping now, so there is no rush, but try to pop in for a short visit later.*

The return text from Arwel arrived a moment later.

I'm moving my stuff to Ben's place. I'll come when I'm done.

Yamanu typed back. *Why are you moving? Mey and I want you to stay. It's your home as much as it is mine and now hers.*

It's not going to be comfortable for any of us, and Ben is lonely since

Carol moved in with Lokan. He's very happy about me rooming with him.

Clever guy. Making it about Ben ensured that Yamanu couldn't insist.

As you wish. I just don't want you to feel as if you have to.

Noted. Let me know when Mey wakes up. But first, ask her if she is in the mood to receive guests.

I will. Glad to have you back.

Same here. New York was tough.

Yamanu could imagine. For an empath, living in the center of a densely populated metropolis must have been hell.

MEY

*M*ey dreamt that she was at the dentist's, having her teeth cleaned. As the dental hygienist moved her soft drill thing back and forth over her teeth, Mey couldn't wait for it to be over. For some reason, it was painful this time, and not just tingly.

She wanted to tell the woman to stop and give her a breather, but she couldn't talk, and her arms felt too heavy to lift and tug on the hygienist's sleeve.

As it went on and on, Mey grew desperate. She groaned, hoping to get the woman's attention, but instead of stopping, she cast her an angry look and shook Mey's shoulder.

"Are you in pain?" the hygienist asked, but her voice came out sounding deep and masculine.

It was a voice that Mey recognized.

Slowly, as the cobwebs of sleep parted, she realized that she was dreaming and opened her eyes. Yamanu's face was hovering a few scant inches above hers.

"What's wrong? Do you need more pain meds?"

She nodded. "My mouth is on fire." It was only a slight exaggeration.

"I'll get Bridget." Yamanu rushed out of the room, returning a moment later with the doctor.

She sat on the bed next to Mey. "Let me see what's going on. Open wide." Bridget shined a flashlight into Mey's mouth and then gently touched her left canine with a gloved finger. "It's wiggling." She frowned and did the same to the other one. "This one wiggles as well."

Bridget leaned away and pulled the gloves off. "There is no more doubt. Your canines are about to fall out, and you are growing new ones. Rapidly. It's happening faster than it does for the men."

At this point, Mey didn't care if she were growing fangs the size of a saber-toothed tiger. All she wanted was for the pain to go away. "It hurts."

"I bet. I'll get you something stronger this time."

"Thank you."

Yamanu clasped her hand. "Everything is going to be okay. Fangs or no fangs, you will always be my beauty queen."

Mey tried to smile. "I can be a vampire on Halloween."

"The sexiest vampire ever."

Gertrude walked in and handed Mey the pills. "These should knock you out."

"Great. More sleep." Mey swallowed the pills.

"Those shouldn't make you as sleepy," the nurse said.

Mey waited for Gertrude to leave before turning to Yamanu. "I need your help to get up. I have to pee."

"I'm on it." He unclamped the finger monitor and then started removing the sticky pads holding the wires attached to her body.

She chuckled. "Once this is over, you can be a nurse."

"No, thank you. I'm very happy to still have my old job." He helped her out of bed.

The meds and the long sleep made her woozy, and Mey had to lean on Yamanu for support.

The medication Gertrude had given her was fast-acting, and by the time she was back in bed, the pain had subsided to a distant throb.

"Callie was here earlier, and she left soup for you." Yamanu pointed at the thermos. "Would you like some?"

She narrowed her eyes at him. "Did you tell her about the fangs?"

"I didn't. Bridget told her that you should only have clear liquids. She made you chicken soup."

Sinking into the pillows, Mey nodded. "I'm not hungry, but I guess I should have something to keep my strength up. Although ice cream would have been better."

"Ice cream is not a clear liquid, but I can get you popsicles."

"That would be awesome."

"After you eat the soup."

She had no idea where Yamanu was going to get popsicles from, but he sounded confident that he could. Perhaps Bridget stocked them for the transitioning guys.

Ugh. Why did she have to be the odd female who transitioned like a male?

Yamanu poured soup into the thermos's cover, which served as a bowl. "Open wide," he sing-songed.

"You have a beautiful voice. Did I tell you that?" She sipped from the spoon.

"Thank you. Would you like me to sing for you?" He offered her another spoonful.

"That would be wonderful. Your voice is so soothing."

He started a soft tune and kept feeding her soup until there was nothing left in the thermos.

When he was done, her eyelids started drooping again. "These meds are miracle workers. Almost nothing hurts. I just feel sleepy."

"Then sleep. That's what you are supposed to do during the first stage of your transition. Your body needs all of your energy to change."

She started drifting off when the door opened a crack, and she heard Alena whisper, "Is Mey sleeping?"

"Not yet. Come in and give me a hug."

Alena rushed in, then slowed down as she reached the bed. "How are you feeling?"

"Like crap."

Alena bent down and gave her the gentlest of hugs. "It's going to be over soon, and then you'll be immortal. I say it's worth it."

"It definitely is." Mey felt a tear slide down her cheek. "I'm growing freaking fangs."

Shock registering in her eyes, Alena pulled back. "What are you talking about?"

"You heard right. My canines are both loose and about to fall out, and new teeth are growing in their place. I was a freak as a human, and now I'm going to be a freak as an immortal too."

"Are you growing venom glands as well?"

"So far, no. But who knows? They might start growing soon."

Alena sat on the edge of the bed and folded her arms over her chest. "I'm jealous. How come I didn't get any? I'm the goddess's daughter. If any female should have gotten fangs, it should have been my sisters or me. Not fair."

Was Alena putting on an act? If she was, it was very convincing.

Mey tilted her head. "You really want to have fangs? Or are you saying that just to make me feel better?"

"Of course, I want fangs. That would have ended the delicate-flower perception everyone has of me. I could have been a badass." She smiled. "Especially if those fangs came together with venom glands. But even on their own, they are so cool."

Even though she sounded sincere, Alena was probably just trying to cheer her up. Surprisingly, it was working.

"You're weird."

"I am not. I've always fantasized about biting my lovers." She chuckled. "Naturally, I fantasized more about them biting me. Or rather him, not them. My fated mate hasn't shown up yet."

SYSSI

"*I*'m surprised that you want to be here on a Saturday," Syssi said as she joined Wonder and Callie at the table. "I would think that you'd had enough of this place."

Wonder shrugged. "As long as I don't have to serve anyone, I don't mind coming here on the weekend to meet my friends for coffee and gossip." She winked.

Amanda chuckled. "You are mated to the best gossip in the village. We are a bunch of amateurs compared to Anandur."

"Yeah, but you are girls. The gossip gets a different spin."

Callie nodded. "I went to see Mey earlier, but she was out of it."

Syssi gasped. "I thought she was doing okay. When did she slip into unconsciousness?"

"I meant that she was sleeping. Sorry for giving you a fright."

Letting out a breath, Syssi leaned back in her chair. "I should visit Mey as well. Do you think she'll be okay with that?"

"Why wouldn't she?" Amanda asked.

"When I transitioned, I didn't want anyone to see me. I looked bad and felt even worse."

Amanda lifted a brow. "I thought that you were unconscious for most of it."

"I was. I'm talking about when I woke up. I was a mess, and

then Annani wanted to see me, and I freaked out. I asked Kian to tell her that I needed time to freshen up. Graciously, she agreed."

"You see," Wonder waved a hand, "that's the kind of thing only a woman would understand. A guy would have gotten offended by that. Annani didn't because she is a female, and she understood that you wanted to look good for your first meeting with her."

"Perhaps you should text Yamanu and have him ask Mey if she is up to receiving visitors," Callie suggested. "She seemed fine yesterday, but I think she's gotten worse today."

"Why do you think so?" Amanda asked.

"Because Yamanu looked worried. He didn't say anything when I dropped the soup off, but I could see it on his face."

Syssi sighed. "I think Kian is deluding himself if he thinks that Mey will be okay to travel by Monday."

"Did he make the reservations already?" Wonder asked. "Because I was supposed to hear from Jackson about arrangements for next week, and I didn't yet. I can't just leave the café and go without having anyone fill in for me."

Syssi shook her head. "Turner is arranging everything. After what happened with the raid, Kian doesn't make a move without consulting him. Which is good because the guy has connections everywhere. He is arranging a cabin and transportation for us, all from private parties he knows. There will be no record of us arriving at the resort or leaving it."

"That's a good precaution," Callie said. "If Ella's aunt is working for the government, it's better that we don't leave a trace for them to follow."

Wonder nodded. "I don't know much about stuff like that, but I'm all for being extra cautious."

"Shouldn't we go shopping for ski attire?" Callie asked.

As the others discussed the latest ski fashions, and whether it was better to buy online or at the resort, Syssi texted Yamanu.

I'm in the café, and I was wondering if I can come to visit Mey. Is she in the mood for guests?

His answer came back momentarily. *Alena is here, and they are talking, but I don't know how long Mey is going to stay awake because she just took more meds. If you want to come, you should do it soon.*

She typed back. *I'll be there in under five minutes.*

Syssi put the phone back in her hoodie's pocket. "Yamanu says that Mey is awake and that Alena is with her, but since she just took her medication, she might fall asleep soon." She pushed her chair back. "Any of you want to come with me?"

"It's a small room, and I've already visited Mey," Callie said. "Bridget won't be happy about a crowd gathering in a patient's room."

Syssi looked at the other two. "What about you?"

Wonder stood up. "I'll come. Worst case scenario, Bridget will kick me out."

Amanda pushed to her feet. "I'll just say hello and leave."

"I'll be here, internet shopping." Callie waved them off.

YAMANU

*A*s Mey and Alena chatted, Yamanu watched Mey for signs of fatigue. If her eyelids started drooping, he was going to politely ask Alena to leave.

So far, Mey seemed fine. More than that, Alena had managed what he had failed to do. She'd lifted Mey's mood. Whether she'd been truthful about wanting fangs was beside the point, as long as Mey believed it.

"I should be going," Alena said. "You look tired."

"Stay a little longer. Syssi is on her way."

"Isn't it going to be a bit crowded in here?" Alena cast a glance at Yamanu as if seeking his approval.

"Don't be silly." Mey patted her hand. "One more person is not going to make a difference."

Except, Syssi brought Wonder and Amanda along.

"Hi, Mey, can we come in?"

"Of course."

"I'll bring chairs," Yamanu offered.

Mey waved a hand. "I'm okay with everyone hopping on the bed with me." She scooted back. "There is enough room."

Alena was already sitting next to Mey, and now Syssi joined her at the foot on one side and Wonder on the other.

Amanda leaned against the counter and folded her arms over her chest. "I'm just going to stay for a few minutes. How are you feeling?"

Mey cast a look at Alena and then shrugged, probably deciding that if she told one sister, she could tell the other and her friends as well.

"I'm growing fangs."

"So that's what the questions were about," Wonder said. "I should have guessed they were about you."

Syssi's eyes widened. "What do you mean?" Unlike Alena and Wonder, she sounded alarmed. "How can it be?"

Mey stiffened, and her smile turned into a scowl. "My gums hurt, so Bridget took a look. Both of my canines are coming loose, and she says that I'm growing new teeth. The only possible explanation for that is that I'm growing fangs like the transitioning guys."

"So, she is not sure those are fangs?"

"She'll need to take an X-ray, and she doesn't have a small one like the dentists use." Mey chuckled nervously. "Although at the rate they are growing, there is no need."

Syssi started twirling a strand of hair around her finger, and her scent acquired a tinge of anxiety. "Perhaps that was what my vision was all about. Mey growing fangs."

"The one about the Krall?" Amanda asked.

"Yeah, that's the one." She turned to Mey. "It wasn't like my other visions." She sighed. "To tell you about it, though, I need to backtrack a little. Kian and I own a virtual reality company called Perfect Match. It provides a safe and anonymous environment for people to experience their fantasies with a partner that the computer matches them with. For a hefty fee from both, of course. I helped develop a couple of those virtual environments, and one of them about vampire-like people called the Krall. It came from my imagination, and yet it somehow got mixed up in my vision with Odus and a spaceport. The Krall from my Perfect Match scenario were loading

Odus into shuttles, and their supervisor was a tall, majestic woman with fangs."

"Did she look like Mey?" Amanda asked.

"She had the same coloring, and she was tall and slim, but her facial features were different. She was just as beautiful, though, and as I mentioned before, majestic. So there is the beauty queen connection."

Mey smiled shyly. "Thank you, I guess. How big were her fangs? Were they small like Amanda's or big like Yamanu's when they are fully extended?"

Syssi twirled the strand again. "Bigger than Amanda's, but not as big as an immortal male's at full size. They were pretty big. Let's put it this way. If she were real, she couldn't open her mouth around humans without causing panic. Those were definitely vampire-sized fangs."

"Great." Mey groaned. "I just hope mine are not going to be bigger than Amanda's, or I can never leave the village."

"What's the deal with the Odus?" Wonder asked. "How are they connected to this?"

Yamanu remembered Mey telling him about the strange dream she'd had about the Odus, and he wondered whether she remembered it. Should he mention it?

It might have some significance.

"You dreamt about the Odus, remember?"

Mey's eyes widened. "That's right. I dreamt of thousands of Odus marching in formation like soldiers. What does it mean?"

For several long moments, no one said anything. Syssi looked as pale as a ghost, Alena played with the end of her braid, and Amanda tapped her finger over her pursed lips.

The only one who didn't seem perturbed was Wonder. Looking from one serious face to the next, she chuckled. "I think all of you are ascribing too much importance to dreams. The mind collects stuff all day long, storing it for later things we are not even aware of, and then makes a mashup of it at night." She turned to Mey. "You saw Alena's Odu and noticed that something was odd about him. You might have even thought that he looked like a cyborg but pushed that thought away. At night, your brain used that observation to create a scary army of cyborgs." She laughed. "Let me give you a visual that will make it less scary the next time you dream about the Odus. Imagine them all wearing suits with white aprons over them and holding a duster in one hand and furniture polish in the other."

That got everyone smiling except for Syssi, who shook her head. "What about my vision?"

Wonder shrugged. "No one doubts your foresight. But as you have said yourself, the Krall people were a product of your imagination. You might have had a premonition about Mey getting fangs with her transition, and your mind superimposed it on your Krall fantasy."

Syssi nodded. "That actually makes sense."

"What about the Odus, though?" Mey asked. "How can you explain them showing up in Syssi's vision? She has one living with her in her home, so it's not like they weird her out or scare her."

"I might have the answer for that," Syssi said. "Since his drowning accident, Okidu has been acting strangely, and I've noticed some peculiarities about Onidu as well."

"Like what?" Amanda asked.

Syssi shrugged. "It's subtle, but they seem more sentient, a little more human in their behavior."

Amanda pursed her lips. "I think that Onidu is and always was sentient. His imitation of human behavior is so good that sometimes I forget that he is not who he looks like." She glanced at Alena. "What about you? Do you get that feeling with Ovidu?"

"Don't forget that we grew up with them. To us, they are part of the family." Alena turned to Syssi. "That's probably what's happening to you now. It took a while, but you are finally starting to feel that Okidu is a member of your family and not just a servant."

Syssi let out a breath. "You might be right. I missed him when he was gone, and his accident gave me a scare."

MEY

"Ninety-nine," Bridget read from the thermometer's display.

"At least the fever is down," Mey said. "I'm toothless, but I'm not feverish."

Her canines fell out without much preamble when she bit down on a popsicle that wasn't even that hard.

"Let me check your glands." Bridget started patting her neck. "Nothing unusual on this side. Open up for me?" The doctor used a tongue depressor and turned on her flashlight. "I see no swelling. Not even redness. Everything looks normal." She turned the flashlight off.

"That's good news, right? Do the guys develop venom glands at the same time as the fangs?"

"They do, but it takes much longer for the glands to be fully operational."

"How long until their fangs are fully grown?"

Bridget patted her arm. "Don't worry. You are not going to have huge fangs like the guys."

Mey had a feeling that the doctor was saying that to ease her fears, and not based on any scientific knowledge. She hadn't taken

X-rays, so she had no way of knowing how big they were going to be.

"How do you know that?"

"Because even Annani's fangs are small, and she is the original."

"What if I am a mutation?"

Bridget chuckled. "Nature doesn't work in leaps. Things change gradually. Worst case, your fangs are going to be a little bigger than mine." She smiled, showing her pointy canines. "And if they end up too big for your taste, you can always have them filed down."

"Can I have them extracted and have implants instead?"

Bridget shook her head. "One of the advantages of being immortal is that we can regrow things that humans cannot. They will just grow back and push the implants out."

"If that's so, the filing down might not work either. They will grow back."

Bridget nodded. "There is a high likelihood of that. You might have to visit the dentist often. Just not the same one."

"Great." Mey slumped against the cushions. "What about the so-called ski vacation? Do you think I can go? I'm still weak."

"First, we need to do the famous cut test to determine that you are done with the first stage of your transition."

"Do we really need to?" Mey pulled the blanket up to her chin. "I think the fangs are proof enough of that."

Yamanu had told her about the test, and she wasn't looking forward to having a cut made in the palm of her hand. It wasn't a big deal, but she would rather avoid it if it wasn't necessary.

"The new teeth are not as conclusive as the cut test. But since it is usually a momentous event in a Dormant's life as well as her or his partner, I think we should wait for Yamanu to come back."

He'd spent the night with her and had only gone home to shower and change clothes. That had been nearly an hour ago, so he should be back soon.

"If you must."

He could hold her hand while the doctor cut into her other one.

Ouch.

Bridget smiled. "I can numb the area if you want, but it's really a tiny cut. It will barely sting."

"Right." Mey snorted. "When a doctor says a mild discomfort, I brace for intense pain."

"So, what do you do when the doctor says it's going to hurt?"

"I run the other away."

Bridget laughed. "At least you are honest."

"Did I miss a joke?" Yamanu walked in, his long hair still wet from the shower, and pulled back from his gorgeous face.

"Mey is scared of the cut."

He grimaced. "Do we really need to do that? Mey is growing fangs, isn't that proof enough?"

Mey nodded enthusiastically. "That's what I said."

Ignoring their concerns, Bridget started assembling her surgical tray. "I need to give Kian indisputable proof before he allows you out of the village, and what's happening with your teeth is not it. But a cut that heals in front of our eyes is." She cast Mey a stern look. "After getting bitten with fangs, are you afraid of a small pain that will last only seconds?"

"You have a point." Mey sighed and offered Bridget her hand. "Just do it quickly."

"I will."

The doctor cleaned the area with a small swab, then whipped out her tiny surgical knife so fast that Mey didn't have time to jerk her hand away.

It stung, but it wasn't as bad as she expected, and the amount of blood that welled on top of it wasn't much either.

"Are you okay?" Yamanu asked.

"I'm fine, it wasn't so bad."

Hovering over her hand from both sides of the bed, Yamanu and Bridget seemed to be holding their breath.

For some reason, Mey wasn't as anxious as they were. The

freaking fangs were all the proof she needed for her impending immortality. It would have been really mean of the Fates to give her fangs but not that.

Why wasn't she more excited, though?

After all, she was turning immortal. It was a big deal. Especially after the weeks of worry that it wouldn't happen. Perhaps it was because of how lousy and weak she felt. Once that was over, the full implications of what was happening to her would no doubt sink in.

"Look." Bridget wiped the blood away. "The cut is healing."

Even though Mey had been expecting to see just that, she stared at her palm, feeling awed and amazed. It wasn't going as fast as she'd anticipated, but it was a hundred times faster than human healing for sure.

When the skin was finally knitted back, and only a slight discoloration remained, Mey glanced up at Yamanu. "How long did it take?"

He seemed lost for words, and Bridget answered for him. "A little over five minutes."

"Is that good or bad?"

"It's good."

Mey frowned. "You don't sound sure."

"You healed much faster than a human, but a little slower than an immortal. Usually, it takes about a minute."

Mey closed her eyes. "Everything seems to be going differently with my transition. Any ideas why?"

Bridget shrugged. "I've given it some thought, and in my opinion, it probably has to do with the ancestor who transmitted the godly genes through your matriarchal line. She might have been a bit different. Perhaps the god who parented her had different attributes than the others. It's even possible that some of the gods played around with genetics and changed things. Up until now, we've only had Annani as a source of information about the gods, and hers was limited because she was very young when the others perished, and she wasn't overly studious in her youth. But now that we have contact with Areana, she might know a little more. She is several centuries older than Annani."

That sounded encouraging.

Mey was different because she was a descendant of another line, and the gods had not been all the same with the same powers. Perhaps the goddess hadn't heard about talents like Mey and Jin's because she hadn't been well-informed and not because none of the gods had them.

"I have another question," Yamanu said. "Kian wants us to leave tomorrow for the ski resort. Do you think that Mey is ready to travel?"

"Kian is taking Julian with him, so you will have medical help if you need it, but there is no reason that you will. Just take it easy and don't go skiing. You are not ready for that. If you get tired, Yamanu can carry you around."

Mey grimaced. "I'm toothless. I'm not going to leave the hotel room or cabin or whatever place Kian is arranging for us unless I absolutely have to. Hopefully, by the time we find Jin, I will have teeth that look normal."

39

KIAN

On his way to visit Mey, Kian decided to stop by Bridget's office in the clinic.

"Come in, Kian." She waved him in. "I see that I'm not the only one working on a Sunday. I'm not complaining, mind you. Any day that I can welcome a new immortal into the clan is a cause for celebration. I'm willing to sacrifice each one of my Sundays for that." She smirked. "I'll just take a day off on Monday."

"I'm not working." He closed the door behind him. "I was on my way to visit Mey, but I wanted to ask you what's the deal with the fangs."

"I guess you heard it from Syssi?" She motioned to a chair.

"She came home all shaken up."

Bridget arched a brow. "Why? I understand that it's unusual, but it's not a cause for concern. If they grow to be noticeably large, Mey can have cosmetic dentistry done on a regular basis." She chuckled. "It will be like going for a manicure, only instead of nails, she will get her fangs filed down. Vivian can finally make use of her skills as a dental esthetician again."

"It's not that. Syssi had a strange vision in which she saw a tall, beautiful woman with fangs as large as a male's, supervising the loading of Odus into space shuttles."

Bridget frowned. "That's strange indeed. What does she think it means?"

"No clue. What are your thoughts on the subject?" Kian asked. "How can it be possible? Are Mey's genes mutated?" He rubbed his chin. "Could it be a case of hermaphroditism?"

"The possibility occurred to me, but I didn't want to mention it to Mey. She is freaking out enough as it is. Another possibility is that the ancestor who started her line was different. Perhaps it went back to the god who fathered or gave birth to the immortal female who passed her genes through the generations to Mey and Jin."

"Is there a genetic test you can run?"

"I don't have the equipment or the time to do extensive genetic research, and we can't send it out either." She smiled. "Unless you want a Guardian to deliver the sample in person, thrall everyone in that lab to forget what they discovered, and then erase all the data. Just make sure that he is prepared to spend months there."

"Perhaps we can get the equipment. What's involved?"

"It's not something we can do here. Most labs can't do it either. Gene sequencing takes a lot of time and resources. There are approximately six billion base pairs in each human diploid genome. Ours probably have more."

Kian had no idea what she was talking about, and he didn't have the patience to hear a long lecture either. Besides, it didn't really matter. As long as Mey transitioned and gained immortality, he was good. His curiosity would have to remain unsatisfied.

"Did you conduct the rate of healing test?"

Bridget nodded. "It took her a little longer than average, but it was still rapid compared to a human's."

"That is what's important." He rose to his feet. "Thanks for the update. I'm going to congratulate the happy couple now."

Bridget smiled and nodded.

"One more question before I leave. Will Mey be okay to travel tomorrow?"

"I don't see why not. She is going to be low on energy, though, so it would be best for her to rest as much as possible. But other than feeling weak, she's doing great. The first stage of her transition has gone smoothly, aside from the fangs, that is. She is not happy about the prospect of a toothless vacation."

"Yeah, I can see how that could be a problem." He opened the door. "Which room is she in?"

"Second one on the right."

"Thanks." He stepped out and was about to close the door when Bridget stopped him.

"Leave it open. I like knowing who is coming or going."

"As you wish."

On the way to Mey's room, Kian decided it would be best if he didn't mention the fangs. Mey was upset about it, and she didn't know why it was happening to her either, so there was no point in bringing it up.

He smiled as he knocked on the door. Syssi would be proud of him for being sensitive about Mey's feelings.

Yamanu opened up. "Kian, I didn't expect you to come."

Damn, he should have texted or called instead of just showing up. Evidently, his emotional intelligence still sucked. "Is it a bad time? I just came to congratulate you two."

"No, it's good." Yamanu looked over his shoulder. "Kian is here."

"Don't let him just stand there," Mey said. "Invite him in."

Yamanu opened the door all the way. "You heard the lady. Come in."

Propped up on several pillows, Mey held her hand over her mouth. "Hi, Kian. Excuse the hand, but I have an embarrassing problem that I prefer for you not to see."

"That's okay. I just came to say congratulations and ask how you are feeling."

"Thank you. I'm better today, except for the missing teeth, that is. I don't know how I'm going to travel like that."

"You have nothing to worry about. We are flying in a private jet, and Turner found us a private cabin that can accommodate all of us. No one is going to see you."

167

"Except for our group," she said.

"Except for us. But we are family now. Besides, your new teeth might grow in a couple of days. The first stage of transition is marked by rapid growth."

Mey's eyes widened. "Oh, my God. I need a measuring tape. What if I grew even taller?"

"I don't think you did," Yamanu said. "In fact, other than the teeth, nothing about you has changed, and I thank the merciful Fates for that."

Bridget must have heard her question and walked in. "I'm going to take your measurements before you go home, and Julian is going to take more during the trip."

Looking down at her toes, Mey wiggled them under the thin blanket. "I don't seem to be longer."

Yamanu took her hand and brought it to his lips. "Even if you gained an inch, I'm still seven inches taller than you. You can wear heels, and we can go dancing. Once your teeth grow in, that is."

Bridget lifted a finger. "I have a solution for that. You can wear one of those masks that filter germs. No one will think that's odd."

Mey chuckled behind her hand. "Because I'm Asian?"

Bridget shrugged. "You can use the stereotype to your advantage."

40

YAMANU

"It's good to be home." Mey walked out of the shower with a towel wrapped around her lithe body and another one around her head.

"You'd better get dressed. Arwel is on his way to pick up more of his stuff."

Mey grimaced. "I feel bad about him moving out. And I also feel bad about him seeing me without teeth."

Yamanu took her hand and pulled her down to sit on his lap. "He is coming with us to West Virginia, so he is going to see your cute toothless smile anyway." He kissed her lips.

She'd lost weight during her transition that she couldn't afford to lose, and he was determined to fatten her up as soon as Julian said it was okay for her to eat solids again.

"Only you could think that I look cute like that. Others will think that I got my teeth knocked out by an abusive partner."

"No one is going to think that. They know better."

"In our group, sure. I'm talking about humans." She shook her head. "I can't believe that I'm talking like that. I was a human up until two days ago, and now I'm suddenly something else."

"You are still my lady Mey. The one and only." He lifted her up and placed her on the bed. "What do you want to wear? I'll bring it to you." He walked over to the closet and opened the door.

"I can dress myself." She started to get up.

"Sit." He pointed with a finger. "Just tell me what to get you."

"The grey sweatpants, the red T-shirt and the red hoodie. Can I at least pick up my panties? They are right here in the dresser drawer."

"I'll get them." He opened the drawer and pulled out a pair of black ones. "These okay?"

When she nodded, he tossed them to her.

She caught them effortlessly, her reflexes already faster than what they had been as a human.

He smirked. "Did you see that? You are starting to move in immortal speed."

"You are right, I am. That's awesome." She dropped the towel and pulled the panties on.

Yamanu salivated, but he swallowed it quickly. Mey was in no shape for bed sports. Instead, he ducked into the closet and pulled out the items she'd requested.

Handing them to her, he tried not to stare at her breasts. "Don't you need a bra?"

"Nope." She pulled the T-shirt over her head. "I'm going to wear the hoodie over it so there'll be no nipples showing. I'm too tired for a bra."

He didn't know a woman needed to feel energized to wear one, but he wasn't going to say anything and appear insensitive.

When Mey was dressed, he lifted her up in his arms and carried her to the living room.

She chuckled. "Is this how it's going to be from now on? You are going to carry me everywhere?"

He put her down on the couch. "Just for the next day or two until you feel better. Do you want something to eat?"

"Do we have ice cream?"

He smiled. "In fact, we do, thanks to Callie. She filled the fridge with ready meals and the freezer with an assortment of ice cream."

Mey's eyes brightened. "Did she bring cookies and cream?"

"I believe so." He headed to the kitchen and opened the freezer.

There were about twenty small containers of ice cream in different flavors, each one an individual serving. He found the one Mey craved and brought it to the living room. "It has a little spoon under the lid."

"Oh, I know." She opened the container. "This is my favorite brand, and Callie is my new favorite person." She smiled at him sheepishly. "After you, of course. But seriously. How awesome is she?"

"Incredibly so."

"Once we are back from the trip, I'm going to invite her and Brundar and Wonder and Anandur to dinner." A wistful look flitted through her eyes. "And maybe my sister will be here to help me prepare it. Jin is a better cook than I am."

Yamanu sat next to Mey on the couch. "I hope so. But if not, you can count on me for help. I don't know much about cooking, but I can cut and peel and clean."

"You are the best." She leaned her head against his shoulder.

The front door's buzzer going off ended their cozy moment, and Yamanu got up to open the door for Arwel.

"Congratulations!" His friend walked in with a bouquet of flowers in one hand and champagne in the other.

Yamanu pulled him into a bro hug and slapped his back. "Thank you."

"Hi, Arwel." Mey started to get up, holding her hand in front of her mouth. "I'm so happy that you are coming with us to search for my sister."

"Don't." Arwel handed the flowers and the bottle to Yamanu and rushed to intercept her. "You should take it easy." He gave her a gentle hug. "Welcome to the clan, Mey. I'm so glad that your transition was uneventful."

Mey cast Yamanu a questioning glance. "I guess you haven't heard about the fangs."

Arwel frowned. "What fangs?"

She lowered her hand and smiled. "My canines fell out. Evidently, I'm growing fangs."

"That's definitely not uneventful." Arwel sat next to her on the couch. "Any idea why this is happening?"

"Bridget thinks it's something that I inherited from my original ancestor." She sighed. "I was freaked out at the beginning, but I'm starting to get used to the idea."

"I think a female with fangs is sexy."

"That's what I said." Yamanu put the flowers on the counter. "But Mey doesn't believe me." He pulled out a pot and filled it with water. "I really need to order a few vases for the house. We are running out of pots."

Arwel chuckled. "I'll get them for you as a housewarming gift."

Mey reached for his hand. "Why are you moving out? I want you to stay."

Arwel patted her hand. "You and Yamanu are a mated couple. You need your privacy, and with me around, you are not going to have any even with your door closed. Besides, the guy I'm moving in with is Carol's old roommate Ben, and he is lonely now that she has left. He is looking forward to rooming with me."

The same argument that had worked on Yamanu seemed to be working on Mey as well.

She smiled. "Then, you have to visit often."

"I will." Arwel pushed to his feet and turned to Yamanu. "If you help me schlep things over to Ben's, I can be done faster and get out of your hair."

"We are in no hurry to get rid of you, but I'll help you." Yamanu started following Arwel to his bedroom when his phone buzzed on the counter.

Snatching it, he was surprised to see it was from Alena. Did she want to visit Mey?

Frowning, he read the text. "I have bad news for you, Mey."

She tensed. "What?"

"You'll have to put a bra on after all. The Clan Mother is leaving tomorrow, and she wants to see you and congratulate you on your transition beforehand. Alena is asking if you are well enough to come over and say goodbye."

Mey groaned. "I can't say no to the Clan Mother. If not for the freaking missing teeth, I would have loved to go over and say goodbye to her."

"Let me help you." He bent, attempting to lift her into his arms.

"Stop it. I can walk." Her tone left no room for argument.

"Would you at least lean on me?"

Mey sighed. "Fine." She turned to Arwel. "I'm sorry that I can't stay and that Yamanu can't help you schlep things."

He waved a hand. "I'll manage. When the Clan Mother issues a summons, you don't say no. I'll see you both tomorrow."

41

ANNANI

"*I* wish you the best of luck on finding your sister and your life with Yamanu." Annani pulled Mey into her arms.

The girl was stiff as a broomstick, evidently shocked by the contact. Taking pity on her, Annani let go.

Mey bowed. "Thank you, Clan Mother."

Annani shifted her gaze to Yamanu. "Take care of her. Mey is still recuperating from the change and reeling from the new reality that you have brought her into."

He dipped his head. "I will do my best." He smiled. "If she lets me."

Annani cast a stern look at Mey. "You should not exert yourself, and you should not worry your mate by refusing his help."

Stifling a smile, Mey bowed again. "Yes, Clan Mother."

Annani patted her arm. "When you have your sister back, and you and Yamanu decide on a wedding date, let me know. I will do my best to preside over it."

Mey nodded. "It will be a great honor, Clan Mother."

When Yamanu and Mey left, and Ovidu closed the door behind them, Annani glanced at Alena. "What do you make of that?"

"The fangs?"

"The fangs and the Odus. I find it most unsettling." She walked over to the armchair, sat down, and lifted her feet onto the ottoman.

"I don't see why. Bridget's theory sounds logical."

"It does, but contrary to what she assumes, I knew most of the gods and what their special talents were. I was not running around and having fun. I was being groomed to become the next ruler, and my father had me sit in the throne room every day and listen to the proceedings."

Alena walked into the kitchen and pulled a bottle of water out of the fridge. "Even so, I'm sure you didn't meet everyone. There might have been some minor gods that your father didn't bother with, and one of them might have produced an offspring with a slight mutation." She chuckled. "Perhaps that's how the veil became a thing. A female who wanted to hide her fangs might have started that fashion."

Annani waved a dismissive hand. "That was not how the use of veils started. Did you not read the Bible? There is a story which demonstrates who wore veils and why."

"If I did, I don't remember it."

Annani smiled. "Let me refresh your memory. It is in the story of Juda and Tamar. When Tamar's husband dies, leaving no heir, Juda is bound by tradition to give her his second son, but when he dies as well, he hesitates to give her his third son, thinking that she is bad luck. Tamar wants to preserve the family line, so she takes off her mourning garb and puts on a veil, disguising herself as a prostitute. She seduces Juda while he is on the road to supervise the shearing of his sheep. Naturally, Juda does not recognize his daughter-in-law, for she has her face covered in the manner of prostitutes."

Alena laughed. "That's the exact opposite of what the veil came to symbolize."

Annani nodded. "It is not the first or last thing that humans somehow managed to turn on its head. But I digress. I would like to speak with Syssi about her vision. Could you please call her and Kian and invite them over?"

They were leaving for West Virginia the next day, while she and Alena were going home. For some reason, this time around, Annani found it harder than ever to part with her family. Syssi's strange vision was a good excuse to spend a little more time with them.

Alena pulled her phone out. "Do you want me to call Amanda and Dalhu too?"

Her daughter knew her well.

"I do not have a good excuse for inviting them."

Alena smirked. "You are the Clan Mother. You do not need an excuse. You issue a summons, and that's it."

"That may be true, but I need to keep up appearances. I do not wish to be thought of as a dictator."

"Fates forbid." Alena put a dramatic hand over her heart. "Not a dictator, just a diva. I'm calling Amanda."

Annani shook her head. Alena probably wanted to see her sister and brother one more time before leaving too, and she was using Annani as an excuse.

When her children and their spouses arrived, she hugged each one a little longer, memorizing their scents and the feel of their arms around her. Except for Dalhu, who seemed so shocked by her embrace that she let go of him quickly.

He bowed nearly to the floor. "Thank you, Clan Mother."

"No need to thank me, Dalhu. We are a family now. Although, I would have loved for you two to have an official ceremony, so I could call you my son by marriage."

The huge man swayed on his legs, and she had a feeling he would have toppled over if not for Amanda's supporting arm.

"Stop pestering Dalhu, Mother. We don't need a ceremony."

"I know that you do not need it, but it would be nice to have a party and celebrate your union with the people who care about you."

"Are Mey and Yamanu getting married anytime soon?" Syssi

asked, diverting attention from poor Dalhu, who looked like he wished for the floor to swallow him up.

"They do not have a set date yet, but as soon as they locate Mey's sister, they will start planning their wedding."

As Ogidu entered the living room with a tray of appetizers, Annani motioned for everyone to sit down.

"I want to ask you about your vision, Syssi. Alena tells me that you have predicted a woman with fangs and something about the Odus.

Syssi shifted her eyes to Ogidu, then back to Annani. "It wasn't exactly a vision. It was more like a dream. I think I just fainted."

Kian wrapped his arm around his wife and pulled her closer to him. "You need to take better care of yourself now that you are growing another person in your tummy. Eating regular meals and not skipping any is important."

She smiled at him and cupped his cheek. "I know, my love. And since that fainting spell, I always carry a snack or two in my purse."

He let out a breath. "I'm glad."

"You are married to a very sensible woman."

"I know, and I thank the Fates for that every day."

Annani had a feeling that Syssi was stalling, waiting for Ogidu to leave. Except, there were three more Odus in the house, and no one knew for sure how good their hearing was. They might be able to hear her despite the excellent sound-proofing.

As if to prove Annani's suspicion, Syssi looked in the direction of the kitchen before continuing.

"The woman in my dream looked a lot like Mey. She didn't have her exact features, but she had similar height, coloring, beauty, and also very distinctive fangs. What makes me think that it was a dream and not a vision is that I invented a species of people called the Krall for the virtual company that Kian and I have bought, and those were the people in the dream. What I don't understand is how the Odus got mixed up with the Krall in my head. Alena suggested that since Okidu's accident, I might have been thinking about him more like family, and that's why the Odus were on my mind."

"What were they doing in your dream?" Annani asked.

"Not much. The Krall, the vampire-like people who I made up, were loading them into space shuttles, and everyone looked kind of depressed except for the queenly woman."

"Interesting." Annani pursed her lips. "What did those Krall people look like?"

"Very tall, dark-haired, dark-eyed, olive-skinned, and with fangs that didn't retract all the way like our males' do. They were the size of about a quarter of fully extended fangs, but that was enough to make them look vampiric. They all had long hair, the males too, and they wore it in different styles. Some wore it loose, some had it in long ponytails, and others had it braided either in one or two braids or more. The only female in the entire spaceport was the majestic one, and her fangs looked the same size as the males'."

"Anything else that you remember from that dream?"

Syssi twirled a strand of hair round her finger. "The sky was dark with a reddish tint to it, it was very windy, and everyone's eyes were glowing."

Annani nodded. "Fascinating. Your dream could have been made into a *Star Trek* episode."

As everyone started commenting about the show, Annani took a moment to digest the information.

Had Kian told Syssi about the Odus having been used in battle and then decommissioned?

What Syssi had described could have been a scene from when the Odus had been ejected into space. Except, the gods had been pale, light-haired, light-eyed. They had not looked like vampires either unless they had been fighting or having sex, which would have caused the males' fangs to elongate. Syssi's explanation made sense. Part of what she had seen might have been indeed a vision, but the rest was probably conjured up by her own mind.

42

MEY

"We are about to land," the pilot announced. "Please fasten your seatbelts."

Mey did as he asked, as did Syssi, Callie, and Ella. In short, all the former humans who were programmed to respond to the pilot's command.

The others ignored him.

Wonder was asleep, her head resting on Anandur's lap. Amanda was reading a magazine with Dalhu's head resting on her shoulder. He was snoring softly. Kian was on his laptop, Julian was talking with Ella, and Brundar was imitating a statue, staring into the void and not moving a muscle.

Arwel, who was the only one without a mate, was reading something on his phone. Probably a book.

A total of thirteen immortals were being flown by a human crew who had no idea how unusual their passengers were. Mey smiled. It was good that thirteen was a lucky number in Judaism, or she would have been worried.

A lot of thought had gone into making their presence in West Virginia not only anonymous but also untraceable.

Instead of using one of the clan's jets, Turner had arranged their transport with a buddy of his from his days in the military so they could fly incognito. They were leaving no trail that could lead back to their home base.

Turner had also used another contact to secure a cabin for them, again, totally incognito.

Mey still hadn't met Bridget's fascinating mate, and she was really curious about him. He was also a former human who had transitioned not too long ago, and yet he appeared to be one of Kian's right-hand men.

It was good to know that the clan didn't have a hierarchy in which newcomers were thought of as lesser members. That would have sucked.

Shifting in her seat, she tried to rest her cheek on Yamanu's shoulder, but the sharp pain that followed reminded her of why that wasn't a good idea.

"Do you need more meds?" Yamanu asked.

"No, I'm good. I just forgot that I shouldn't put any pressure on the area."

When she'd woken up in the morning and patted her sensitive gums with a gentle finger, Mey had discovered that two tiny but very sharp tips had broken the surface.

Perhaps by the end of the day, she was going to have teeth instead of gaps, and hopefully, they could pass for sharp canines. She wouldn't mind tiny fangs like Amanda and Wonder's. They were kind of cute, and she could see why Yamanu found them sexy. If hers grew to be as big as his, she doubted he would still think that.

In the meantime, Mey had decided against wearing a dust mask. Instead, she was going to open her mouth as little as possible, and when she absolutely had to talk, she was going to cover it with her hand.

Problem solved.

Besides, once they arrived at the resort, it would be cold enough to justify a scarf covering her entire face except for the eyes.

The weather in Lewisburg, the tiny town where they were

about to land, was mild. But they were going straight into the vehicles waiting for them near the runway, and an hour and a half later, they were going to arrive at the resort where it was going to be cold.

The private runway in Lewisburg was used primarily by crop dusters and the occasional delivery of supplies to the nearby farms, so the plane's arrival would not be something out of the ordinary.

Its passengers hadn't been registered.

"Touch down," Anandur called out as the wheels made contact with the ground.

Mey started clapping, but when everyone regarded her quizzically, she stopped. "Where I come from, it's customary to applaud the pilot for landing the plane safely. After all, our lives are in his or her hands, so I think that showing gratitude is a nice sentiment."

"It is." Yamanu started clapping and then leaned and kissed her forehead.

The others reluctantly joined in.

Mey laughed. "You don't have to do it if you don't want to."

A burgundy Suburban and two gray minivans waited for them next to the strip. None was new, or clean, and Mey wondered where Turner had found them. Was there a special rental place for nondescript cars that aroused no suspicion?

Anandur wrinkled his nose when Kian handed him the keys to the Suburban. "Do you want me to drive that?"

Kian cocked a brow. "Do you prefer one of the minivans?"

The Guardian let out a tortured breath. "I'll take the Suburban."

Nearly two hours later, when they arrived at the chalet, Anandur's mood improved dramatically. "Now, that's what I call a cabin."

It was as big as a mansion and looked luxurious.

"The place has eight bedrooms and ten bathrooms, and the couches in the living room and the loft open into beds." Kian helped Syssi out of the SUV. "It can sleep twenty people, has all the amenities and even internet, which is a big deal in this area. It's not

Wi-Fi, but there are ports all over the cabin so everyone can hook up their devices."

The only cellular reception that worked in the area was AT&T's, and they had all gotten simple phones that they could use in the resort. The satellite ones were prohibited in the Quiet Zone.

After Anandur put in the code to open the door, they all scattered to choose their bedrooms. Syssi and Kian naturally got the master.

"Hey, there is even food in the fridge!" Callie called from the kitchen. "Who wants to help me start dinner?"

43

ELLA

*T*he next morning, Ella woke up early and padded to the kitchen, lured by the smell of coffee.

Callie turned around and cast her a smile. "Want to help?"

"Sure. What do you want me to do?"

"Set up the table. Breakfast is almost ready."

Ella opened a cabinet and pulled out a stack of plates. "How long have you been awake?"

"An hour. I wanted to surprise everyone and have breakfast ready when they woke up."

"That's so sweet of you."

Callie was awesome.

Ten minutes later, the table was set, and more people started drifting down, lured either by the smell of coffee or the mountain of hash browns Callie had made. There were also pancakes and eggs and toast, enough to feed an army.

"Thank you for making breakfast," Kian told Callie.

"It was a joint effort, right, Ella?" Callie winked at her.

"I just set the table. Callie did everything else."

Syssi waved her fork. "Thank you both. Tomorrow, though, it should be someone else's turn."

Callie shrugged. "I don't mind doing it every morning."

When they were done eating, Kian lifted his phone and waved it from side to side to get their attention. "Does everyone have Eleanor's picture on their phones?" When people nodded, he opened his. "Please double-check before we go out."

Ella lifted her new phone and opened the photo application that had only one picture in it. Her aunt's. It wasn't a good one, driver's license photographs were usually the worst, but she could imagine how her aunt looked in a better light.

She was dark-haired, like Ella's father, and she had the same striking eyes that were a beautiful shade of greenish-blue. But hers lacked the mirth that Ella remembered her father's always held.

Or perhaps what she remembered was the photograph of him in uniform that her mother still kept on the fireplace mantel.

It was nice of Magnus not to object to the prominent place his mate's first husband's portrait took in their house. He probably did it for Parker's sake. That picture was what kept his father's memory alive in his heart, and that was important.

Joshua Takala was not going to be forgotten by his children. Ella just wished that his sister was more of a family person. She had disappeared from their lives long before joining the paranormal talent collection program.

Not that they knew for sure that she was part of it.

They were basing their assumptions on circumstantial evidence. All they had was a fake West Virginia driver's license with the name Marisol Ortega on it, and Ella's suspicion that her father had been a Dormant, which meant that his sister must be one too.

That, combined with Mey finding a West Virginia travel guide with an earmarked page about the Quiet Zone, was what had brought them here.

It was flimsy, but that was all they had. And as Julian had pointed out, if they didn't find Eleanor or Jin, at least they could enjoy a ski vacation and a fun time with friends and family.

Except, Ella didn't know how to ski, while Julian was an experienced skier. He would be tackling the intermediate and advanced slopes, while Ella was going to take a beginner's class.

"Remember," Kian continued. "She is not going by Eleanor. She might be going by Marisol, or she might have another alias."

"What do we tell the people we question?" Anandur asked.

"That you are looking for a girl's long-lost aunt. The girl's father was killed in the war, and the aunt is the only family she has left. Last she heard, her aunt worked in a ski resort."

Except for the part about working in the resort, the rest was true.

Several eyes turned her way, making her uncomfortable. But when Kian kept going, their attention returned to him.

"Those of us who are experienced skiers will take the red and black runs and question the people operating them. After you do that, thrall the memory away."

"I have another question," Anandur said. "Brundar and I are supposed to be glued to you. Do you suggest that we spread out?"

Kian cast a quick look at Dalhu and smiled. "I'm nominating Dalhu as my temporary bodyguard. He and Amanda are going to join Syssi and me on the reds."

"I can go on a black," Syssi protested.

Kian reached for her hand. "I know that you can, and after the baby is born and is old enough to travel, we can go skiing down any run you wish. But until then, I want you to take it easy."

Amanda leaned toward Syssi from the other side. "I can do the black, but I prefer the red. I don't like the intensity of the black."

That seemed to placate Syssi. "Okay. I'll do it for you." She winked.

Anandur shook his head. "I'm not happy with Dalhu taking our place. He is only one man."

The former Doomer folded his muscular arms over his chest and grinned. "Are you questioning my abilities?"

Anandur waved dismissively. "Don't get your panties in a wad. Other than in the safety of the village, Kian is supposed to have two bodyguards at all times. You are big, but you are not two men."

Amanda scowled at Anandur. "Dalhu can take on an entire unit of Guardians on his own. Give it a break, Anandur. Since when are you such a stickler for the rules?"

"Kian can do as he pleases, but if Annani finds out about this, I'm going to blame him for breaking her rules."

"Fine with me," Kian said. "Here is a map of the runs." He held it up for everyone to see. "Syssi, Amanda, Dalhu and I are going to take this one. Anandur and Wonder, you take this one." He pointed.

"I can't ski," Wonder said.

Ella perked up. She wasn't the only one. "I can't either. Do you want to take a class with me?"

"I would love to." Wonder turned to Callie. "How about you? Can you ski?"

"I'm a beginner, but I'm just going to stay here, keep Mey company, and prepare lunch."

Kian shook his head. "We are going to dine out, and not together. There is a small chance we will stumble upon Eleanor in one of the resort's restaurants or coffee shops. We will meet back here at two in the afternoon and go check out the town." He looked at Mey. "Do you think you can manage an easy stroll?"

"I'm sure. I feel much better." She opened her mouth and pointed at her new teeth, or rather small fangs. "I'm not toothless anymore."

"Let me see." Amanda rounded the table. "Oh, they are so adorable."

"Yeah." Mey grimaced. "I hope they will stop growing by the end of the day or tomorrow morning. Otherwise, I'll have the opposite problem. From the toothless lady, I'll turn into the fanged lady."

44

YAMANU

"*A*re you going to be okay here by yourself?"

Yamanu couldn't bring himself to leave Mey. She was still weak, still took a lot of pain medications, and Julian was not staying in the cabin to take care of her. He was going on the slopes because he was a strong skier.

"I'm not going to be alone. Callie is staying with me. She brought a bunch of DVDs for us to watch, and she found popcorn in the pantry." Mey grimaced. "Except, I can't have any. Can you get me ice cream on the way back?"

"I will. Arwel and I are not going to stay for long. I plan on doing the questioning, going up and down the run three or four times just so I look like any other Joe Schmo on vacation, and that is it. What flavors do you want?"

"Cookies and cream, chocolate chip, vanilla, coffee, basically anything you can find except for mint. I don't like it. Until these damn teeth stop growing, I'll be eating mainly ice cream."

"I hope I can find some in the resort. They are supposed to have a mini market."

He kissed her again, and then followed Arwel outside. "Who are we riding with?"

"Julian, Ella, and Wonder."

Everyone was bundled up, a little more than was called for, but just enough to obscure their features. Ski masks and ski goggles were perfect for that.

Yamanu pulled his over his head and tucked his long hair inside his jacket. The goggles went up next.

Arwel chuckled. "In your case, the camouflage is not going to work. There aren't many guys who are six foot eight."

"There are enough. And without my eyes and my hair showing, I'm good."

Julian got behind the wheel. "Everyone ready to have some fun?"

"Yes!" Ella and Wonder cheered.

"Then let's get this baby on the road."

45

SYSSI

*T*he lift operator shook his head. "I don't remember seeing her. She doesn't work here, that I'm sure of. Maybe she used to, though. I just started this season. You might want to check with HR."

Kian put his phone away. "That's a good idea. Thank you. Maybe we will have better luck there."

As Kian erased the memory of the conversation, Syssi eyed Dalhu from the corner of her eye. The guy was observing everyone and doing what they did, but she could tell he had never skied before.

She sidled up to him and motioned for him to bend down. "Have you ever been on the slopes?"

He chuckled behind his ski mask. "Sand dune slopes, yes. Snow slopes, no."

"You shouldn't go on a red run without training. You'll break something."

He shook his head. "Don't worry. I'm a quick learner, and anything that has to do with sports has never been a problem for me. I'm a natural."

Amanda nodded her agreement. "I'll stay close to him. Dalhu will watch what I do and follow my lead. It's going to be all right."

They were both nuts, but they were adults, and she couldn't tell them what to do. Maybe Kian could talk sense into Dalhu?

The problem was that their turn had arrived to get on the lift, and Amanda and Dalhu went first, and then she and Kian.

"Dalhu doesn't know how to ski."

"How do you know?"

"I asked him when you were busy thralling the operator. He confirmed it, claiming that he can learn it on the go. Your crazy sister knows it, but instead of talking sense into Dalhu, she's encouraging him."

Kian shrugged. "I can't tell them what to do."

"Yes, you can. You are the boss."

He snorted. "Amanda doesn't acknowledge anyone as boss. Besides, when it's not clan business, I have no say."

"How about as her brother?"

He shook his head. "Even less."

As their turn came to disembark, Syssi glided down unhurriedly, enjoying the beautiful scenery and the crisp air. Kian skied next to her, probably bristling with impatience to go fast.

"Go ahead. I'll catch up."

"I'm not leaving you."

Knowing that there was no use arguing, Syssi dropped it. Besides, she enjoyed having him near her, and it was safer. She hadn't skied in a while, but her body remembered all the moves, and she didn't have to put any thought into it. The only thing that was casting a shadow over her pleasure was the fear of finding Dalhu splattered against a tree on her way down.

Except, Dalhu made it in one piece. When she and Kian stopped next to him and Amanda, the guy was the picture of satisfaction even with the mask and the ski goggles covering his face. It was in the way he stood, his shoulders back and his chin held high.

Amanda pulled her ski mask down to show them her smile. "My guy is invincible. His first day on the slopes, and he made it down in one piece."

"I'm ready to go up again," Dalhu said.

Kian looked at Syssi. "Do you want to go again, or do you want to take a break and rest?"

She rolled her eyes, but he couldn't see it behind the goggles. "I'm not even tired yet. Let's go."

After the third round, though, Syssi was ready for some hot cocoa.

"I'll come with you," Amanda offered. "The guys can do a couple of more rounds, and then we can head back to the cabin."

As Kian and Dalhu headed for the lift, Syssi leaned closer to her sister-in-law. "Are you sure it's safe to leave the boys alone? Without us to keep an eye on them, they will start showing off and could get injured." She was referring to Dalhu, who was getting dangerously cocky.

Amanda waved a gloved hand. "They are both too old for that. They know better."

"I wouldn't count on it."

She threaded her arm through Syssi's. "I'm not going to worry about that. Let's go for that cocoa and discuss birthday party plans for Kian. He's going to be two thousand soon. That calls for a big-time celebration."

"I've been meaning to talk to you about that. Should it be a surprise? Because I was trying to think how we can pull it off and still have the entire clan attend."

46

KIAN

"One more time," Dalhu said as they reached the bottom.

"No problem."

Kian was enjoying himself. Dalhu was learning at a rapid speed, his progress impressive even for an immortal. The guy was a natural. So much so that he was getting cocky and trying to compete with Kian.

That wasn't smart.

Nothing could beat experience, and Kian had lots of it. Not recent, but skiing was like bike riding. Once learned, the skill didn't go away.

"Whoever gets down first buys coffee," Dalhu said as they were about to get off the lift.

"Isn't it supposed to be the other way around?"

"Nah. If I beat you, it will put me in a generous mood."

"Don't do anything stupid."

"I won't." Dalhu pushed off and went bombing down like an idiot.

Kian pushed off hard and followed. If the moron hit a tree, he wanted to get to him fast. Amanda was never going to forgive him if her mate came to some harm while Kian was with him.

When Dalhu chose to enter a chute, Kian's heart started

pounding in earnest. Two rock walls enclosed a narrow path of snow between them, but Dalhu could have avoided the obstacle by going around it. Instead, he was showing off his newbie skills, which were not enough to traverse the narrow space. He was going to get hurt.

Somehow, though, he emerged on the other side without incident and kept going.

Kian let out a relieved breath and slowed his descent to a more reasonable pace. He'd planned on beating Dalhu and buying the guy coffee, but it seemed that Dalhu was going to be the one to pull out his wallet.

Except Fate had other ideas.

For no apparent reason, Dalhu went flying, and Kian's breath caught in his throat.

He'd either hit a rock or tried to make a turn and accidentally dug his ski into the snow. The result was a most ungracious fall with Dalhu's long limbs getting all tangled up.

He landed in a heap.

Kian was by his side in seconds, making a sharp turn to slow his descent to a stop.

Releasing his skis, he dropped his poles and trudged through the snow to Dalhu. "Tell me that you didn't break your stupid neck because my sister is going to break mine if you did."

Dalhu groaned, which was a huge relief. "Just my leg. Can you snap it back in place for me?"

Kian shook his head. "Not out here. I'm calling Julian."

Except, Julian was not going to make it in time. Someone must have seen the fall and called it in because a ski patroller with a toboggan was rushing their way.

"Don't let them touch me," Dalhu hissed.

The pain activated his flight or fight response, and his eyes were glowing. In seconds, his fangs were going to punch over his lower lip.

Kian stood up and shielded Dalhu with his body. When the paramedic arrived, he lifted his hand and smiled. "Everything is okay. Nothing is broken. My brother-in-law just took a nasty fall, and he is resting."

He used only a gentle thrall to validate what he was telling the guy, but the paramedic was one of those stubborn and suspicious humans who were not easy to thrall.

"I'd better take a look." He tried to push past Kian.

Kian stopped him with a hand to his chest and got close in his face. "Everything is okay. But we could use a lift down. I'll help you load him into your toboggan. And if you have something for the pain, that would help a lot."

The guy shook his head, trying to shake the thrall off, but Kian had gone deeper this time, and it was taking effect. "So, nothing is broken?"

"Nothing is broken." Kian pushed the thrall even further.

The patroller whipped out his two-way radio and made a quick report.

"I'll get him on."

Dalhu was a mountain of a man, and the patrol guy would have sweated bullets trying to get him onto the sled.

"Okay, buddy," Kian whispered. "This is going to hurt, so bite on something." He threaded his arms under Dalhu, hefted him up as gently as he could, and deposited him on the sled.

"Do you have morphine with you?" Kian asked the patroller.

"No morphine," Dalhu hissed from the toboggan. "I'm fine."

Whatever. If the idiot wanted to suffer, it was his choice. "I'll meet you down the slope," Kian told the patroller.

When the guy started downhill, Kian put his skis back on and called Julian. "Dalhu has a broken leg, and the ski patrol is taking him down. Meet us at the bottom."

"I'm on my way."

MEY

*M*ey happened to glance out the window when the Suburban pulled into the driveway.

She turned to Callie. "They are back."

"I thought I heard a car." Callie came out of the kitchen and joined Mey at the window. "They are early. They were supposed to return at two, and it's not even noon yet."

It wasn't snowing or raining either. The sky was clear, and it seemed like a perfect day to be on the slopes. As Mey wondered what had made them cut it short, the reason became apparent when Kian hopped out of the vehicle, reached inside, and hefted Dalhu out.

"Oh my gosh." Callie dropped the dishtowel on the counter and beat Mey to the door, throwing it open. "What happened?"

"Dalhu broke his leg." Kian brushed by her and bee-lined for the couch with the passed-out Dalhu in his arms.

Amanda and Syssi followed behind.

"Julian did what he could to immobilize the leg," Amanda said. "And he even managed to convince the stubborn oaf to get a morphine shot so we could transport him."

"Where is Julian?" Mey asked.

"He went to get a brace from the paramedic station," Syssi said.

"It wasn't part of the medical supplies that he thought would be needed on this trip. He should get here soon."

Poor Dalhu.

"How did it happen?"

"Stupidity," Kian grumbled. "I didn't know he was such a fucking show-off, or I would have never invited him on this trip. Especially since the idiot had never skied before and didn't tell anyone."

"He told me." Amanda cast her brother an angry look. "And I would appreciate it if you didn't call my mate stupid."

Kian shook his head. "You both are. Him for thinking he could wing it, and you for encouraging him."

Her hands on her hips, Amanda was ready to tear into Kian, but her impending tirade was stopped by his phone going off.

"It's Arwel," Kian said as he pulled it out. "I guess you heard?" He put the phone on speaker.

"Heard what?"

"About Dalhu's fucking leg."

Arwel chuckled. "No, but I get now why you are barking into the phone. Yamanu and I have good news that might cheer you up. We found someone who knows our girl. We are on our way to the cabin, and I called to ask you to meet us there."

"I'm here. We brought him back to the cabin. Julian is also on his way with a brace."

"Do you need us to turn around and bring the others?"

"I'll do it," Callie volunteered. "After I hear the good news, that is."

The phones weren't secure, and they all knew not to say anything revealing. Mey worried that Kian shouldn't have mentioned Dalhu's injury over that line.

Looking in a much better mood, Kian ended the call and put the phone back in his pocket. "I can't wait to hear what they have learned."

"I wish everyone were here to hear it," Syssi said. "Ella will be disappointed that she wasn't told right away."

"I could go get Ella and Wonder now," Callie offered. "But Anandur and Brundar are on the slopes, and I'll have to wait to catch them at the bottom."

"I'll call them and have them wait for you," Kian said. "You can bring everyone at once." He pulled out the keys to the Suburban and handed them to her. "I'll have Arwel and Yamanu wait with their news until everyone gets back."

Callie took the keys and pulled Kian into a quick hug. "You're awesome. Thank you."

He waved a dismissive hand. "Let's just hope that they have reception up there."

As Callie rushed upstairs to get her coat and the rest of the snow paraphernalia, the door opened, and Julian came in.

"He is still out. That's good." He walked over to the couch and pulled out a new brace from the packaging. "I just hope this is large enough for him." He turned to Amanda and Mey. "I suggest that you go upstairs. I'll probably need to re-break the leg."

"But he is out," Amanda said. "He's not going to feel it, right?"

"I'm going to give him another dose before I do that, but I would still prefer it if you didn't see it. People get nauseous." He looked up at Kian. "I need you to stay in case I need help to hold him down."

Kian nodded.

Amanda put her hands on her hips. "Dalhu is my mate. I'm not leaving."

"I am." Mey headed for the stairs. "I don't want to add stress to the situation by puking all over the floor."

"Yeah, same here." Syssi followed. "I'm nauseous enough as it is."

48

YAMANU

*A*s Yamanu followed Arwel through the door, the first thing he saw was Dalhu sprawled over the living room couch with his head cradled on Amanda's lap.

"Is he knocked out?" Arwel asked.

Julian nodded. "I gave him a dose large enough to put a horse to sleep. By the time he wakes up, he should be fine to hobble around. The pain will be gone."

Yamanu chuckled. "Thank the merciful Fates for modern medicine. I still remember the times when we had to bite on a leather strap or knock ourselves out with a gallon of alcohol."

"Or both," Arwel added.

"Where are the other ladies?" Yamanu asked.

"Syssi and Mey are upstairs, and Callie went to pick up the rest of the team." Kian walked toward the kitchen. "I promised her that you will wait with your news for their return." He pulled out a bottle of Snake Venom from the fridge.

Yamanu was glad of Arwel's foresight to bring two cases of their favorite beer as well as a full case of good scotch on the trip. None of it could be obtained in the area.

"Anyone want a beer?" Kian asked.

As Arwel lifted his hand, Kian tossed him one.

"I'll have one too," Yamanu said. "But I want to check on Mey first."

A door opened upstairs, and Mey peeked at him over the banister. "Is it safe for us to come down?"

"It's all over," Amanda said.

As Syssi and Mey came downstairs, Julian walked over to the fridge, pulled out a beer for himself, and sat next to Kian at the dining table.

Aside from Amanda and Dalhu, who remained on the couch, the rest of them joined him and Kian.

When pulled to its full length, the table could accommodate twenty people, so their entire group could have meals at the same time. Which reminded Yamanu that he was starting to get hungry. "I guess that our plan for an afternoon stroll through the resort's village is canceled. What are we going to do for food? Order pizza?"

"I don't know if they deliver," Syssi said. "We can whip something up. Turner's guy stocked this place with enough food to last us a week." She chuckled. "Well, maybe not us, but a similarly sized group of humans."

Mey pushed to her feet. "I'm going to take a look at what we have to work with."

"Wait for Callie to return," Syssi said. "She will organize it."

"I'll bring snacks to tide us over until everyone comes back."

"I'll help you look for them." Syssi followed Mey into the kitchen.

"In the olden days, we would open a can of Spam," Arwel reminisced.

Yamanu clapped him on the back. "Maybe in *your* olden days. In my youth, we hunted or fished for our food."

Syssi dropped two bags of potato chips on the table. "That's all I found as snacks go."

"It will do." Kian tore open the bag, took a handful, and passed it back to Syssi.

She handed it to Yamanu. "I'm not feeding my baby this junk. Do you have any idea how much sodium is in this stuff?"

As they killed time with chitchat about what an expectant mother should and shouldn't eat, Yamanu was keenly aware of Amanda's silence.

Since losing her child, she did her best to stay out of conversations that had to do with pregnancy and babies. The only reason she hadn't left the room yet or changed the topic was that Dalhu's head was cradled in her lap.

When the door opened, and the rest of the team poured in, the air of anticipation in the room became electrified.

"Callie said that you have news," Anandur said. "Brundar and I have news as well. But Yamanu and Arwel should go first."

"What news?" Dalhu croaked from the couch and tried to sit up.

Amanda pulled him back down. "Take it easy. Can someone bring Dalhu a bottle of water?"

"I'll get it," Anandur said.

Wonder took her coat off and hung it on a peg by the door. "How are you feeling, Dalhu?"

"Groggy." He looked at Julian. "How much morphine did you give me?"

"Enough to make you sleep through the worst of it. How is your pain level, do you need me to give you another shot?"

Dalhu groaned. "No more. The headache is worse than the pain in my leg."

Julian grinned. "You are welcome. You would have been singing a different tune if I hadn't knocked you out."

"Appreciated."

Anandur came back with the water. "Here you go."

Kian looked around the room, impatience written all over his face. "Can we get down to business now? I want to hear what you've found out."

"The guy operating the lift recognized Eleanor," Arwel started.

"He says that she comes often, usually in the middle of the week when there aren't as many people on the slopes, and there is practically no wait for the lifts. She comes around noontime, skis for a couple of hours and leaves."

Syssi snorted. "Her job must allow for a lot of free time."

"Maybe she is an independent contractor," Amanda suggested. "She gets paid per assignment and has free time whenever she wants."

"I don't think so." Kian rose to his feet and started pacing. "If lodging and transportation are provided by her employer, it's more likely that she is salaried."

"She might be using another alias for her car and housing," Julian said.

"She doesn't have another driver's license, and she would need one to rent an apartment and register the car."

"The driver's license could be totally fake," Ella said. "Like the ones kids use to get alcohol before they are twenty-one. You can get one for fifty bucks online."

"That's a possibility," Kian agreed. "Has the guy seen her recently?"

"He said that the last time was two weeks ago, but she might have been using a different run. He suggested that I check the other lift operators."

Anandur lifted his finger. "Already done. Our guy saw her yesterday and says that she'll probably come back tomorrow. He says she is a regular on the black run. She goes by Marisol."

"Wow." Ella put her hand over her heart. "I can't believe that we actually found her and that I might see her tomorrow."

"We are getting near, but we don't have her yet." Kian walked over to Ella and squeezed her shoulder. "I don't want you to get your hopes up."

"That's okay. I'm keeping my expectations low. The impression I got from what my mother has told me about Eleanor is that she is not the type of aunt who would be overjoyed to see me."

Kian nodded. "I'm glad that you are mentally prepared for her rejecting you. When we find her, I don't want anyone other than Arwel talking to her." He turned to the Guardian. "I want you to send your feelers out and check what kind of person we are dealing with. Also, before we approach her with questions, we need to determine whether she is susceptible to thralling or not."

49

MAGNUS

"*D*id I tell you already how stunning you look tonight?" Magnus offered Vivian his hand.

"Once or twice." Extending one shapely leg clad in a sexy high-heeled pump, Vivian took his hand and let him pull her up from the Porsche.

Standing a couple feet away, the valet waited patiently to close the door behind her.

"Thank you." She smiled at him.

Magnus put his hand on the small of her back. "Are you ready to dance the night away, my love?"

Vivian cast him a lopsided smirk. "If the music were not so loud, I might have enjoyed these outings." She shook her head. "God, I sound like my mother."

He leaned to whisper in her ear, "Imagine how I feel."

"You are amazingly adaptive. Much more so than I am."

"I have plenty of practice adapting to new situations. In time, you will too."

"I can pretend just as well as you do, but that doesn't mean I like it. I've never enjoyed this kind of music, not even when I was a teenager."

"That's why we have these." He handed her a pair of disposable earplugs and then put his in before entering the club.

It had been fun in the beginning, the restaurants, the clubs, but Magnus was tired of it. He missed his home in the village, and he missed Parker and Scarlet, and so did Vivian.

With Ella and Julian gone, Parker and Scarlet were enjoying Merlin's hospitality. The kid was having such a blast that he'd practically begged them not to come home. Supposedly, Merlin was supervising Parker's schooling, but Magnus had a feeling said schooling was more about teaching Parker to brew potions and having him read ancient texts. He doubted that Merlin insisted on Parker sitting in front of the computer and doing his schoolwork.

As someone who had never been overly studious, Magnus could empathize with Parker for wanting a break from boring math problems and science lessons. They must have paled in comparison to what Merlin could teach him.

Heck, maybe the kid would get inspired to pursue medicine. That would make his mother happy.

"I see a table." Vivian pointed. "We need to hurry before someone snatches it."

"There are plenty more." Magnus pointed in the other direction. "That's why we came early."

Since they were out to look for Kalugal's men and not to enjoy themselves, they had to spend long hours in each place. Finding a table that was as far as possible from the loudspeakers and the dance floor was a must.

"I'm going to order drinks. Your usual?"

She smiled. "A strawberry margarita this time."

"You got it." Leaving Vivian at the table, he headed to the bar.

His crew of Guardians was doing much of the same, each one hanging around different bars, clubs, restaurants and cafés, hoping to spot an immortal.

Except, a week had passed, and none had been encountered.

Kri and Michael had arrived the day before, and they were

doing the same thing. But unlike him and Vivian, the young couple was enjoying the clubbing and the bar hopping.

He wondered how long Kian was going to have them do that. In his opinion, lying in wait near the mansion would have been a much better strategy. They could have just followed anyone leaving its gates to wherever they went and brush by them to confirm or disprove whether they were immortal.

But after the near failure of the raid, Kian had become too cautious.

According to him, the mansion was too well-guarded, and Kalugal was too smart to ignore any kind of public works getting done on his street without checking them out.

On second thought, perhaps Kian was right. It was crucial not to alert Kalugal to their investigation.

A drink in each hand, Magnus was making his way back to Vivian when his phone vibrated in his pocket.

"Here you go, sweetheart." He handed her the margarita she'd asked for.

Putting his own drink down, he pulled out his phone and read the message from Oidhche. *I got one. He just entered the bar, and the hairs on my neck stood on alert. He looked around, probably feeling it too, but I managed to sneak out back using the storage room. Instructions?*

Magnus typed back. *Did you get a good look at him?*

Oidhche responded. *If you're asking if I can recognize him, the answer is yes. Typical nothing-special Doomer, but he still moves with immortal grace and holds himself like a warrior. The ladies were all over him the moment he entered. Good for me. They distracted him so I could make my escape.*

Magnus chuckled. *Text me the address and then go wait in your car while watching the entrance. If he goes out, follow him. Vivian and I are on our way to take over.*

Understood.

"What's going on?" Vivian asked once Magnus had put the phone away.

He bent to whisper in her ear. "We have confirmation. Oidhche spotted an immortal male in a bar. He's going to wait outside until we arrive or the guy goes out. If we are not there by the time the man leaves, Oidhche is going to follow him until we take over, and if needed, another Guardian will take over for us. I want to keep switching cars so he won't notice the tail."

Magnus lifted the shot glass and emptied it down his throat. It would have been a shame to waste the whiskey.

"Do you think I can take my drink to go?" Vivian asked.

"Sure. We will pretend to be going out to smoke."

She shook her head. "I meant in a to-go disposable cup."

"No time." He pulled out his wallet and dropped two twenties on the table. "That should cover the cost of the glass, including the trip to the store to get it."

50

KIAN

"What's the plan for tomorrow?" Arwel came down the stairs wearing sweats and a pair of worn-out fuzzy slippers.

It was late, and Kian was ready to call it a day and take Syssi up to the master bedroom. Regrettably, the soundproofing in the chalet was standard, which meant that everyone could hear everyone else. But he'd thought of a solution. Provided they kept it quiet, turning on the jacuzzi tub's jets in the master bathroom was going to drown out the sounds of their activity.

Anandur chuckled. "You brought those old things on the trip? You should have tossed them in the garbage a long time ago."

Arwel looked down. "These are my favorite. I'm not throwing them out until they have holes in them."

"I can help with that," Anandur teased.

"No, you can't. I don't live with you anymore."

"I'll come to visit and get you new ones as a housewarming present."

Arwel shrugged. "I'm going to hide them."

Kian was about to suggest pink bunny slippers with a matching robe when his phone buzzed.

"What's up, Magnus?"

207

"We've spotted one of those fellows we were looking for."

"Did you talk to him?"

"Not yet. Oidhche spotted him in a bar and called me. I told him to wait in the car until the guy leaves the bar and see where he was heading. Well, the dude left the bar with a woman and took her to a hotel. I hope he is going to treat her right. You know the kind of reputation those fellows have. Anyway, I'm parked in front of it, waiting for another buddy to join me. Just making sure that the lady is okay..." he trailed off. "And see where he goes from there."

Magnus didn't need to elaborate. He was going to have one of the Guardians follow the guy, hopefully to the mansion. That, along with checking the woman's memories for gaps, should be confirmation enough.

"Good job. Keep me informed."

When he hung up, Kian lifted his head and looked at the hopeful faces of his friends and family. "It looks like things are moving nicely along. Magnus is following a suspect, and so are we."

"What did we miss?" Amanda and Dalhu appeared at the top of the stairs.

"Magnus called. They are following a suspected immortal."

"Yes!" She pumped her fist in the air. "Both teams are making progress."

Using his powerful arms to brace his weight on the banister on one side and the wall on the other, Dalhu hobbled down on his good leg.

"How are you feeling?" Syssi asked. "Is your headache better?"

"It is. Thank you for asking." Jumping on one foot and leaning on Amanda's shoulder, he made his way to the couch.

"I'll get you coffee," Amanda said after he plopped down.

As Kian waited for her to return from the kitchen, he thought about the plan for tomorrow. Dalhu's injury had cost them half a day, but they had gotten the information they needed, so it was all good. Especially since Eleanor was expected to show up on the slopes sometime around noon the next day.

"How long do I need to keep the brace on?" Dalhu asked.

"You should be good in a couple of days." Julian smiled. "Just don't put pressure on that leg, and once the brace comes off, stay away from the reds and blacks. And you should probably take some lessons."

Dalhu shook his head. "I'm not going back. Tomorrow, I'm going to pull out my easel, my canvas, and my paints, and find a nice spot to paint."

Kian felt bad for the guy. He'd been doing great up until he fell, and one accident shouldn't deter him from doing something he obviously enjoyed.

"You should go back. Just be aware of your limitations and don't push yourself so hard. You are so damn competitive."

"I don't know how to be any other way," Dalhu admitted. "That's why I'd better stick to painting. No one here can compete with me in that."

"That's true." Kian nodded. "So how about you get it into your stubborn head that you don't have to be the winner in all things? I'm competitive as well, but I know my limits. The stick figures I can draw will not win any awards."

Amanda cast him a look that said he should give it up. "Anyone want coffee? I brewed a fresh pot." She handed Dalhu a steaming mug.

Once the coffee was served and everyone was sitting in one spot or another, Kian rose to his feet. "So, this is what we are going to do tomorrow. At noontime, which is when Eleanor usually makes it to the slopes, Arwel is going to wait for her to show up at the bottom of the hill and follow her to the lift. Anandur and Brundar, you are going to follow them up." He turned to Julian. "You as well."

"What are we going to do in the morning?" Mey asked.

"Stroll around the village center like we had planned to do this afternoon." He cast a mock stern glance at Dalhu.

51

SYSSI

*S*yssi sank into the bubble-filled tub and sighed in pleasure. "I feel bad about us having the only hot tub."

Sliding behind her, Kian wrapped his arms around her middle. "We can let them have turns in it." He cupped her breasts.

She stifled a moan.

The chalet was lovely, but it hadn't been built with immortals in mind, and everyone could hear what was going on in the other rooms.

"I'll turn on the jets," Kian whispered in her ear. "The noise will drown out the lovely sounds you make."

"Not really, but I'll try to be quiet."

He nuzzled her neck. "I like hearing you."

As his phone buzzed on the vanity counter, Kian ignored it.

"Aren't you going to get it?"

"Let it ring." He tweaked her nipples.

This time the moan escaped her throat before she had the chance to stifle it. "It could be from the village, and if they are calling you here, it must be important."

With a groan, he got out of the tub and snatched the phone, his perfect nude body glistening from the moisture.

Her man was a god.

"It'd better be important, Magnus." He put the Guardian on speaker.

"If you are busy, I can call later," Magnus said.

"You've already got me out of the tub, so talk."

"We have what we came for. After he dropped the woman off, we checked on her, and she was fine, but like we suspected, she didn't remember much from the encounter."

"What about the guy? Did he go home?"

"He lives where we thought he does."

"Excellent."

"What do you want us to do now? Should we go home as well?"

"Stay a few more days. Maybe you can discover more interesting things."

"We will head home on Sunday. Is that okay?"

"That should do it. Say hi to the missus for me."

"I will."

As Kian ended the call, he brought the phone with him and put it on the ledge between the tub and the wall.

He got back in and slid behind Syssi. "Kalugal made a mistake by building his base in a small city. It's much easier for immortals to hide in a big place like Los Angeles. What Magnus and his team have done would have never worked in New York, for example. With countless places for the men to go to, the chances of us stumbling upon one of them would have been minuscule."

Syssi turned around and planted a kiss on Kian's lips. "That's why my guy is smarter and chose to build the clan's base in Los Angeles. What about Sari and her people, though? Aren't they making the same mistake as Kalugal?"

Kian cupped her butt cheeks and gave them a gentle squeeze. "They are careful, and they are shrouding their castle. The area has many small towns and villages, and they know not to visit the same places too often."

"Good. I was worried for a moment."

"Kalugal's other mistake was pulling permits for the underground complex in his backyard. He was practically begging to be

211

found out. It's like marking a huge X on his location. Even without Lokan's cooperation, we could have discovered Kalugal's address by checking the permits." He chuckled. "That is where I have another advantage over him. As a developer, I can get away with not getting permits for some of the things I build, like the keep's underground, because I do it in house."

"Maybe he didn't pull permits? If an inspector walked onto the property, Kalugal or his men could have thralled him to think that they had them."

"For a project like that, he needed to hire a top-notch contractor with a large crew and office personnel. It would have been difficult to thrall everyone to do work without permits. Especially since he probably didn't think it was a big deal."

"Did you check the records?"

"I didn't have to. Lokan found out the address from the description his contact had provided, and he gave it to me."

"You see? Lokan is a good guy, and he is trustworthy. He is sharing information with you."

"When it's beneficial to him. Lokan does what's good for Lokan. He has little regard for others, aside from Carol, that is. I know that he would do anything for her, and conversely, he wouldn't do anything to deliberately hurt her family. But that's the extent of it."

Kian could be so stubborn sometimes, and trust was difficult for him, especially when Doomers were involved. It had taken him long months to stop suspecting Dalhu, and now the two were almost buddies, which made Syssi and Amanda really happy.

Perhaps in time, he would start trusting Lokan as well. The two were cousins after all, and Kian could use a friend outside the clan.

"If Lokan were a bad person, Arwel wouldn't have befriended him. He can sense who is good and who is bad."

"True, but I didn't say that Lokan was bad. He's neither good nor bad, just selfish. I don't have Arwel's talent, so I don't know how selfish feels, but my guess is that it feels neutral."

MEY

*M*ey stood in front of the mirror and opened her mouth. The tips of her fangs had grown overnight, reaching one-third the length of her other teeth. She still looked ridiculous, and eating anything solid was out of the question because it hurt too much. So, the outing wasn't going to be fun, but she was sick of being cooped up in the cabin.

Besides, after weeks in the village, she just wanted to be among humans again, to go shopping and do the things she used to do before this bizarre turn of events had changed her life forever.

Her mind and her body were in turmoil, much worse than what she'd experienced during puberty. Back then, it had been bouts of sadness and inexplicable anger, and her breasts had hurt, but it had been nothing compared to what she was going through now.

The anxiety was the worst.

Mostly, it was about Jin and whether they were going to find her and whether she would want to come with them if they did. Mey was going to feel terrible if after all the insane effort that had gone into the search, Jin refused to leave.

Then it was her future and what she was going to do with it. Working at the café was fun, but it was a temporary thing, not a career. Her modeling days were obviously over unless she modeled Halloween vampire costumes, and Mey doubted there was much demand for that.

If Jin decided to stay and finish her contract, Mey would have to find something to do for the next five years because she wasn't going to launch their dream business without her sister.

Maybe she could use the time to make babies?

She smiled at her reflection in the mirror and then grimaced. Would her daughters have fangs as well?

Since her transition had started, Yamanu hadn't made love to her yet, and frankly, she hadn't felt well enough for it. The pain medication was making her nauseous, and as many meds as she was taking, the throbbing pain in her gums never subsided sufficiently for her to forget that it was there.

Poor Yamanu could probably shroud the entire ski resort if needed. But he wasn't complaining, which she really appreciated. Oliver used to get nasty whenever she'd got her period. She'd usually gotten moody and bloated and hadn't been in the mood for sex.

Perhaps that should have clued her in that he wasn't the guy for her.

Hey, no periods was another benefit of immortality, and getting rid of those was worth the price of having fangs.

Almost.

Yamanu knocked on the bathroom door. "Are you okay in there?"

"Yeah." She turned around and opened it. "I was just staring at my wee little fangs."

"Let me see."

She opened her mouth.

"They've grown since last night."

"Tell me about it. But they are still too small to fill the gaps. I'll have to cover my face with a scarf."

"You should let Julian check them before we go out."

"Why? It's not like I'm sick."

"Just do it. It can't hurt."

As they got downstairs, everyone was already seated around the dining table, eating breakfast.

"Good morning, everyone," Mey said without smiling.

Julian wiped his mouth with a napkin and pushed away from the table. "Let me have a look at your teeth. I want to see how much they have grown overnight."

He whipped a small flashlight out of his pocket and one surgical glove. It seemed that he'd been prepared for her. "Say cheese."

To hide her embarrassment, Mey struck a pose, tilting her body slightly to the left and flipping her hair back. "Cheese…"

He shined his flashlight into her mouth and then patted her gums and new teeth with a gloved finger. "Looks good."

"What does it mean?"

"That the rate of growth is steady, and they are still relatively small. From what I've read up in my mother's notes about the growth rate of fangs in male Dormants, yours is much slower, which leads me to believe that they will not be as long as the males'."

She let out a breath. "That's a relief."

"On the other hand, the swelling and the amount of pain you are in indicate that more is going on. I suspect that your fangs will elongate on demand."

"That's so freaking cool," Amanda said. "I want fangs like that."

Bless her heart, the woman knew the right thing to say. If a gorgeous creature like her thought that elongating fangs were cool, then Mey could live with that.

"As long as they look normal most of the time, I'm okay with that. The question is, why would they elongate if I can do nothing with them?" She eyed Julian suspiciously. "I'm not growing venom glands, right?"

"You are not."

"So, what would they elongate in response to?"

Julian shrugged. "I don't know. They might elongate in

response to the same triggers that males' fangs do, just without the ability to inject venom. But even without the venom, fangs can do a lot of damage in a fight."

The Guardians, including Kian, all nodded in agreement.

"You can tear an enemy's throat out," Brundar said.

Mey shivered. "No offense, but that's just gross."

ARWEL

*M*ey stopped next to a store's window display. "They have cute things here."

"Do you want to go inside?" Yamanu asked.

She looked at him over her shoulder. "What are you and Arwel going to do while I'm trying things on?"

"We will guard the entry from the outside. Go, have fun."

"Are you sure you don't mind waiting?" She turned to look at Arwel.

How could he say no?

She'd been so miserable for the past several days and putting a brave face on it, that he couldn't deny her anything that might lift her spirits.

"I don't mind. I can sit on that bench over there and look at the hotties passing by."

Mey put a gloved hand on his arm. "Thank you."

"Nothing to thank me for." He leaned closer to whisper in her ear. "It will look strange for you to walk around the store with your snow goggles on, but don't take them off. Not even in the changing room. They might have cameras in there."

She nodded.

As Mey entered the store, he and Yamanu walked over to the bench and sat down.

"Mey is in constant pain," Arwel said.

"I know. She refuses to take stronger pain meds because they make her nauseous." Yamanu sighed. "The fangs are really bothering her."

"I think they are cute."

"I do too, but how they look doesn't bother Mey as much as being different does. Bridget came up with a couple of hypotheses for why this is happening to her, but no one knows for sure."

"Yeah, as someone who has always been different, I get how that might be troubling."

"You have a talent. That's not the same as having a divergent physical attribute, especially if that attribute is gender-specific and it's not your gender."

As Arwel tried to imagine how he would have felt if his fangs were small, static, and feminine, his phone went off in his breast pocket.

Pulling it out, he saw Brundar's new number on the display and clicked it open.

"What's up?"

"Come to the Starbucks across the street. We need to show you something."

The urgency in Brundar's tone made it clear that he should get moving fast. "I'm coming." He closed the phone.

Yamanu nodded. "I'll stay here."

As Arwel crossed the road and headed for the Starbucks that was further down the street, he saw Brundar and Anandur coming out and walking in the opposite direction.

Jogging to catch up, he fell into step with them. "What's going on?"

Brundar motioned with his head at a woman holding a paper cup and walking briskly. "That's her, and she is immune to thralling. I tried to get into her head and encountered a wall."

The guy was a strong thraller. If he couldn't get into Eleanor's head, no one could. It was up to Arwel and his empathic ability to try to assess the risk involved in approaching Ella's aunt.

"I got her."

Elongating his strides, Arwel caught up to Eleanor in seconds and kept pace a few steps behind her.

The woman must be an extremely guarded person because she broadcast very little, but it was enough for Arwel to recoil.

Eleanor's vibe was one of the most unpleasant he had encountered, and given that he had dealt with plenty of vicious Doomers as well as humans, that was saying something.

What could have made an average middle-class woman so bitter and hateful?

From what Ella had told them about her father, he had been a swell fellow, a good husband to Vivian, and an awesome father to Ella and Parker. How could his sister, who had grown up in the same house, turn out so rotten?

Had something terrible happened to her that Ella and Vivian weren't aware of?

Whatever the reason was, though, Eleanor shouldn't be approached with questions about Jin. Without being able to thrall her to forget them, it was a no go. And that was a big problem. What were they going to do?

Beat the information out of her?

Kian was not going to like it.

Slowing his steps, he waited until the brothers caught up to him. "Keep following her but do not engage. Aunt Eleanor is one hell of a rotten apple. I need to call Kian. Hopefully, he is still here so we can talk face to face." This wasn't something he could discuss with the boss over an unsecured line.

Brundar nodded.

As the brothers followed Eleanor, Arwel made the call.

KIAN

*I*t was a rare occasion for Kian to just stroll down the street, holding his wife's hand, not hurrying anywhere, and he was enjoying himself immensely. For the past hour or so, he hadn't thought about reading emails, solving the various problems that popped up every day and required his attention, or even the mission they were on.

Syssi stopped in front of a clothing store. "I'm going to take a look. Do you want to come in with me?"

"Sure, why not." He looked back at Amanda and Dalhu. "I'm sure Amanda would want to join you, but Dalhu needs to sit down."

"He can join Yamanu on the bench." Syssi pointed. "I guess Mey is inside."

Kian hadn't noticed the Guardian before Syssi had pointed. Huddled inside his coat, his head covered with a hat and his eyes behind a pair of ski goggles, Yamanu looked like any other guy in the resort. Just taller.

"On second thought, I'll join Yamanu and wait for you outside."

His phone went off before Syssi had a chance to respond. "Hold on. It's from Arwel."

"Where are you?" he asked.

"I'm heading toward the Starbucks. Brundar spotted the aunt, but she seemed in a bad mood. I need to discuss it with you."

"Got it."

Arwel had conveyed the meaning clearly enough. Brundar had seen Eleanor, but when he'd probed her mind, he'd either discovered information that made it problematic to approach her, or worse, that her mind was impenetrable.

"I need to call the rest of the team. Can you go inside and get Mey? We are meeting in front of Starbucks."

Syssi nodded and pushed the door open.

Anandur and Brundar were probably following Eleanor, Yamanu was right there, and Amanda and Dalhu had just caught up to him. That left Julian and Ella.

"What's going on?" Amanda asked.

"The aunt has been spotted. Go to the Starbucks across the street. The entire team is meeting there."

Amanda nodded, and she and Yamanu headed that way.

Hopefully, Roni was systematically erasing the records from the team's calls like Kian had told him to and not waiting for the end of the day. It might have been somewhat paranoid to do that, but he was following Turner's advice, and the guy knew what he was doing.

When everyone made it to the front of the coffee shop, Kian signaled for them to stand in three separate groups. They could hear each other fine without huddling all together.

Arwel joined Kian and Syssi. "Brundar tried to thrall her, but she seems to be immune. Although it is possible that she just has strong walls up. What I sensed from her wasn't pleasant. She is bitter, hateful, and highly suspicious. Anandur and Brundar are trailing her, but we need to decide how to proceed."

"Fuck." That one word that Syssi was trying to make him stop using so much had summed it up nicely.

To his left, he heard Ella sigh, and Julian whisper encouraging words to her.

That must have been difficult for the girl to hear, but Kian had no time to consider her feelings at the moment. He had to come up with a new plan on the spot.

If Eleanor was an immune, they would have to kidnap her and interrogate her the old-fashioned way. Aside from having an issue with forcibly extracting information from a woman, the problem was that they couldn't erase the memory of the interrogation after they were done with her.

Unless she wasn't immune to compulsion.

They weren't far from Washington, and he might be able to get Lokan to help.

After all, if Eleanor talked, they would hopefully find Jin, and Jin could be instrumental in finding out what Kalugal was up to, which Lokan no doubt wanted to know as well.

Looking over his shoulder, Kian signaled for Julian to join their group. "Do you have something that can knock her out instantly?"

Julian shook his head. "I used up what I had on Dalhu, but I can get whatever is needed from the ski-patrol station."

"Go and get it. Come back here when you have it."

After making sure Ella was with Mey and Yamanu, Julian left.

"So, here is the plan." Kian leaned closer to Arwel. "As the only unattached male here, you will have to be the one to follow Eleanor and flirt with her."

Arwel grimaced. "Lucky me."

"When she gets on the lift, make sure to be the one sitting next to her and strike up a conversation. After she is done skiing, lure her into having dinner with you and then escort her to her car. Julian is going to be there with a tranquilizer and will knock her out. One of the brothers will come with a vehicle and help you load her inside."

"Where are we going to take her? The cabin?"

Kian shook his head. "I'll drive to where I can use a clan issue phone and call Turner. I'll ask him to find us a safe house out of the Quiet Zone."

He turned so the others could hear him better. "We need to get back to the cabin. Arwel needs to get suited up for the slopes, and someone needs to pack his stuff and load it into the vehicle."

"I'll pack Arwel's stuff and also Anandur and Brundar's," Amanda offered. "I assume that you want to take them with you."

"Yes. Good thinking." He looked at his watch. "If Eleanor is a creature of habit, she will get suited up and hit the slopes in an hour, ski for two, and then hopefully spend another hour with Arwel over dinner. Four hours is plenty of time to get organized."

"Are we all leaving?" Ella asked.

"I didn't figure out all the details yet. I will need Julian, Arwel, and the brothers with me. The rest should stay here and keep up appearances but be ready to leave on a moment's notice."

If they needed to use force to get information out of Eleanor, he preferred that no civilians be present. And especially not Syssi. She was too soft-hearted for that.

"I can help question my aunt," Ella tried.

Kian shook his head. "She can't even see you because you are supposed to be dead, and we can't thrall away her memory of you being alive and well."

It was good that he had a valid excuse for refusing her. The last thing he needed was for Ella to witness the interrogation.

55

ARWEL

*S*uited and ready to go, Arwel called Anandur. "Which one?"

"West mountain," Anandur answered. "She's already gone up. You can wait for her next ride up."

"Got it."

With everyone covered from head to toe, it wasn't easy to spot Eleanor. It had been incredibly lucky that they had seen and followed her before she suited.

She hadn't put her hair up though, leaving it loose under the hat, and since it was long and dark, it was what he used as a beacon.

Moving people out of the way wasn't a problem when he was allowed to thrall whomever he wanted, and soon Arwel was right next to her, waiting for their turn on the lift.

Breaking protocol, he lowered his scarf and pulled his goggles over his head. If he wanted the woman to respond to him, she needed to see him smile at her, and since his eyes were his best feature, she needed to see those as well.

"Hi, I'm Arwel," he started. "It's my first time in this resort, and you look like you know your way around here. Any particular run that you would recommend?"

She pursed her lips. "What's your level?"

"Expert."

"Then you can take the one I'm taking." She smirked. "I hope you are not exaggerating your ability because this one is difficult."

"I've been skiing since I was a wee little lad." He let his Scottish accent come through, which usually worked on the ladies.

"Okay, then." She nodded, and that was the end of the conversation.

Eleanor was indeed a strange bird. She hadn't been rude, but she hadn't told him her name when he'd offered his. She had smiled, but on the inside, she'd remained cold.

Maybe she wasn't into guys?

That would ruin the entire thing. Maybe Amanda could put on an act and lure Eleanor into having dinner with her. She could pull it off, no problem.

And the best part would be that he wouldn't have to do it. The vibe Eleanor was emitting was so negative that it was difficult for him to remain at her side and act flirty.

As their turn arrived, and he hopped onto the lift, he caught her looking at him. Perhaps she appreciated athleticism. If so, she would be much more amiable after he showed her what he could do on the slopes.

"When we get off, follow me," she said. "Just try not to bump into me."

Arwel smiled. "No worries. Just point the way, and I'll take it from there." He decided to take a gamble. "How about a little competition? The loser buys the winner dinner?"

She smirked. "Is that how you save money on your vacation? Trick unsuspecting ladies into buying you dinner?"

Unsuspecting my ass.

"Let's switch it around then. The winner buys the loser dinner."

"I'm going to win."

"Okay. Whoever wins or loses, I buy you dinner. How about that?"

"Why?"

Damn, she wasn't giving him an inch.

He shrugged. "I came here with my best friend and his fiancée, and I feel like a third wheel. I don't want to have dinner with them every evening."

"Let me think about it." She pushed off the lift and headed toward her chosen trail.

He followed, and as he got to where she stopped and waited for him, Eleanor waved goodbye and took off.

That was nice of her. She wasn't a complete jerk. Just jaded, selfish, and suspicious. If he wanted to impress her, though, he needed to win, and from the looks of it, she was very good.

Except, he was an immortal with superior physicality that no human could hope to attain. He was going to win this little competition without breaking sweat.

When he got to the bottom, Arwel pushed his goggles up and waited for Eleanor, who took only several seconds longer.

"You are good," she said, this time with a genuine smile. "I'm Marisol." She offered him a gloved hand.

Well, that was progress. He shook it. "Ready for another one?"

"Of course."

"Then let's go."

She didn't say much on the way up, but she seemed more relaxed around him. He had a feeling she was a loner and that talking to people was an effort for her. Even her name implied solitude, and he wondered whether she'd chosen it for that reason.

Perhaps now that her shields were lowered, he could attempt to thrall her. Everything would be so much easier if she weren't an immune.

But not yet.

Maybe on the next ride up.

56

KIAN

"You know that this is ridiculous, right?" Dalhu asked as Kian pulled out of the chalet's driveway. "I can't do shit for you with my busted leg."

Kian cast him an amused glance. "Per my mother's orders, two bodyguards must accompany me whenever I'm away from the village. Anandur and Brundar are busy, Arwel is trying to seduce a lady, and I need Yamanu to guard my wife and everyone else in the cabin. So, it has to be you. I don't expect any trouble on the round trip out of the Quiet Zone and back."

Dalhu pushed the passenger chair even further back to make room for his leg. "You said that you need two bodyguards. I'm just one man, and I'm unarmed."

Kian chuckled. "You are big enough to count as two, and even unarmed and injured, you are a better fighter than most."

That brought a ghost of a smile to Dalhu's lips. "I appreciate your confidence, but it's highly unmerited."

"Just take the compliment and shut up. I need to think."

"Yes, boss."

"Thank you."

That was the other reason he'd taken Dalhu with him. The guy didn't feel the need to chitchat idly to fill the silence, and Kian needed to form a plan.

An hour later, when they were safely out of the zone, he pulled out the clan's phone and called Turner.

"Kian, how is the vacation going?"

"We've got the woman, but there is a complication."

"That's indeed a problem," Turner said when Kian was done. "I like your idea of bringing in Lokan to try to compel her, but if that doesn't work, there are drugs that can make her forget the interrogation."

That was something that Kian hadn't considered. "Would Julian know what to do?"

"If he doesn't, I can have someone explain it to him. Better yet, I can have the drugs delivered. First, though, I need to find you a safe house in a large enough urban center, and the nearest one is Harrisonburg. Let me make a few phone calls, and I'll get back to you."

"I'm in a bit of a time crunch. I drove an hour out to clear the zone to call you, and it will take me an hour to get back. That leaves about another hour to put everything in motion."

"I understand. Park somewhere and wait. It shouldn't take me long." Turner ended the call.

"He's a real asset," Dalhu said. "How does he do it?"

"He has connections from his days in special ops, old buddies of his who turned private operators after leaving the service. And I guess many people feel indebted to him after he rescued their loved ones. I would assume that kidnappings for ransom usually involve family members of either the very rich or the politically powerful."

Dalhu nodded. "He is very good at what he does."

"Incomparable."

"How are you dealing with that? I mean, he seems better than you at planning and executing complicated operations. That must be hard on your ego."

"It is, but I'm not so full of myself that I don't realize it. The mark of a good leader is not only what he's capable of doing himself but also how good of a team he assembles to assist him. I just need to keep reminding myself of that."

For the next ten minutes or so, they waited in silence, and Kian tried to come up with interrogating techniques that didn't involve violence.

Perhaps there was a drug that made people talk?

He'd heard about a truth serum, but as far as he remembered, its effect was dubious.

His phone rang.

"That was fast," Dalhu murmured.

"I got a place for you. I'm sending you the address. By the time you get there, it's going to be fully stocked. There is a lock pad, and I'm sending you the combination to open it as well."

"Is it big enough for the entire team? Not that I want them all there during the questioning, but if it takes longer than expected, they might want to join me."

The mated couples were going to start to chafe, and he didn't need to add extra stress to a situation that was already stressful.

"It's a duplex, and I rented both sides for you through a friend. For an additional fee, the owner will stock both kitchens."

"You are the best."

A duplex was a great solution. He could have the civilians in one, and Eleanor and the Guardians in the other.

"I know. So here is how you are going to do it. I'm going to make room reservations in one of the hotels in the area. Once you have the lady, knock her out and send her with one of your guys and Julian to the duplex. Have one of your other guys drive her car to the hotel's parking lot and check in. He will have to thrall those working in the reception counter to remember him coming in with Eleanor. While he is doing that, another Guardian will need to get into the control room and make sure that those several minutes of recording are erased. You have to ensure that no record will be left to dispute what the people working at the counter will remember. Do you need a moment to write it down?"

Kian shook his head. "No, I'm good. I'm just impressed with the level of detail. Please continue."

"Once that is done, you and your bodyguards can follow the first team to Harrisonburg. The others should stay behind. I secured the other side of the duplex, but hopefully, it's not going to be needed because Lokan will compel Eleanor to talk. Unless the interrogation takes longer than expected or if other complications necessitate the others joining you, it's better if they stay behind. You don't want everyone leaving at once and possibly attracting attention."

"I agree. If we get her to talk and she knows where Jin is, we will have to go back to get Jin anyway, so it's better if the others stay. In fact, I'm going to join Arwel and the others and leave the two vans for the rest."

"Let's leave that part of the plan for when we have more information, but you will have to go back in any case to deliver Eleanor to the hotel."

"One more thing. If Lokan's compulsion doesn't do the trick, is there a truth serum that actually works?"

Turner chuckled. "What's known as the truth serum, or rather something that is based on it, is what Julian is going to give her to forget. It's quite effective for that. Unfortunately, it's not as good at getting the truth out of people. It lets the imagination take over, and she might tell you fantastic tales, which will be completely false. She might tell you the truth as well, but you won't know the difference, and neither will she. Even Andrew wouldn't be able to separate facts from fiction."

"That's a shame. I don't want to get rough with her."

"Oftentimes, the threat of pain is enough. Once Julian is out of the Quiet Zone, I want him to call me with more information about Eleanor's weight and medical condition. I'll send him what's needed to take care of her memory because I doubt that he can find it locally. When she wakes up in the hotel, she will not remember anything from the past twenty-four hours or so."

"Are those drugs always effective?"

"On a regular human they should work pretty well."

"What if we have to detain her for longer than twenty-four hours? Not that I expect to, but just in case it is necessary."

"I'm not sure. I'll have to check with my guy."

Kian sighed. "I really hope that Lokan can compel her to talk as well as to silence afterward, and the drugs won't be necessary."

"That would be best, but it's always good to have a plan B."

E L L A

"*J*can't believe that my aunt is an immune," Ella murmured. "I'm not, or rather I wasn't before I transitioned. And Parker wasn't immune either before his."

Mey wrapped her arm around her shoulders. "Turner is an immune too, and I heard that he is a brilliant guy. Perhaps that's a trait of very smart people."

It was nice of Mey to try to cheer her up, and if Eleanor were at least a decent person, it probably would have helped, even though it implied that Ella and Parker weren't overly smart. Well, compared to Turner, they weren't.

"Maybe she is an immortal?" Wonder suggested. "She might have been accidentally turned like Eva."

Amanda shook her head. "I doubt it. The chances of that happening twice are so small that it's practically nonexistent."

"Unless the Fates had something to do with that," Syssi said, but she didn't sound as if she really believed it. She'd said it out of kindness, not conviction.

Arwel's unique talent enabled him to feel people's emotions, and according to him, Eleanor was up to no good. Still, if not for Vivian's impression of her sister-in-law, Ella could have hoped that her aunt had been having a bad day, and that was why Arwel had sensed darkness in her. But when two independent sources reported the same thing, it was likely true.

Could Eleanor be redeemable, though?

Every person had some good in them. Even Gorchenco, who by most standards was a bad man, and who had greatly wronged her, had some goodness in him. He sincerely cared for his people and looked after their well-being.

Eleanor must have some good in her as well. The question was whether it would be enough to bring her into the clan.

"I hear a car," Syssi said. "I hope it's Kian." She walked up to the front door and opened it. "It's him."

The air sizzled with anticipation as everyone waited for Kian to fill them in. The phone situation meant that very little could be reported over the cellular connection. All the important stuff had to be done in person.

As he walked in with Dalhu hobbling behind him, Ella bit her lower lip to stop herself from attacking him with questions.

"Do you guys want something to eat?" Callie asked. "I made lunch."

"That would be greatly appreciated." Kian shrugged his coat off and hung it on a peg by the door.

The rest of them had already eaten, but everyone joined Kian and Dalhu at the table, eager to hear the news.

"Turner got us a duplex in Harrisonburg. That's where we are going to take Eleanor. I also spoke with Lokan, and he is going to meet us there. If he manages to compel her, it will save us a lot of trouble."

Callie came out of the kitchen with two plates and put them in front of Kian and Dalhu. "There is plenty more, so don't hesitate to ask for refills."

"Thank you," Kian said. "I probably will." He dug into the spaghetti.

For several long minutes, everyone waited for him to sate his initial hunger and continue his report. When he was half done, he put the fork down.

"If Eleanor is susceptible to compulsion, it will not only make the interrogation easy but also letting her go after she spills the beans. If she is not, we will have to give her drugs that affect memory." He looked around. "Where is Julian?"

"He is upstairs, preparing what he needs to knock Eleanor out," Ella said.

"Do you need me?" Julian asked from the top of the stairs.

"Turner asked that you call him once you are out of the Quiet Zone. He needs information on Eleanor's approximate weight and medical condition for his guy to formulate the correct dose. Did you know that what's called the truth serum can be used to make people forget things?"

"Only while it is administered. I don't know of a drug that does it after the fact. I'm curious to find out what he uses."

"I guess you are going to find out."

"Who is going?" Amanda asked. "I mean aside from Arwel and Julian."

"I'm going with Brundar and Anandur. Everyone else stays. But in case the interrogation takes longer than anticipated, or something else comes up, Turner's secured the other side of the duplex for us as well. There is room for everyone."

"You should take me too," Ella said. "Five men traveling with one unconscious woman would look suspicious. What if you get pulled over?"

Kian shook his head. "We are going to drive carefully, and if we are stopped for some reason, we can thrall the police officers."

Well, it was worth a try. But if she wasn't going, she needed to argue on her aunt's behalf before Kian left.

"We assume that Eleanor is a Dormant. Don't you want her to join the clan?"

Kian cast her an apologetic look. "I'm sorry, Ella. But if Arwel is right, and he usually is, we can't. One rotten apple could bring ruin to the clan, especially since she will feel no loyalty to us."

Crossing her arms over her chest, Ella huffed. "I'm sure that not every clan member is a saint."

"That's true, but even Doomers know that it's in their best interest to keep the existence of immortals secret. Your aunt's connection with the government spells trouble because her loyalty or her self-interest is with them. From what we've learned about her, chances are that she would not hesitate to expose us despite her connection to you and your family. Nothing in her behavior over the years indicates that she cares about what happens to you."

Ouch, that hurt. But he was right. Still, there might be another option. Things were seldom black and white, and perhaps the solution was somewhere in the gray area.

"I get what you're saying, but why give up on a sure Dormant? Eleanor might be someone's mate. Perhaps after the mission is over, and she remembers nothing of it, we can watch her and reevaluate? Maybe even send someone to befriend her? I'm a great believer in redemption. People can change."

He nodded. "That's a possibility. We will address it after this is all over, and we either find Jin or find out that we've been on the wrong trail."

ARWEL

*E*leanor, or rather Marisol as Arwel had been calling her for the past two hours or so, was warming to him.

He'd been careful, not laying on the charm too heavily, just friendly banter with a bit of competition, which she seemed to appreciate. He'd let her win a couple of times, trying to not make it too obvious that he'd held back.

As it was, the woman was suspicious of every word and motive, proving once again that everyone saw the world through the prism of their own beliefs and convictions. A crook thought that everyone was dishonest, and an honest person believed the opposite.

In Arwel's experience, people were mostly honest about things they attached moral value to, and sometimes dishonest about those they didn't.

The classification of what was okay or not okay to do depended on the culture around them.

Some societies viewed lying in general as morally wrong, while for others, it was a way of life, and everyone expected everyone else to lie. Some societies valued the work ethic, and their members wouldn't think of making personal phone calls or playing games on their computers during work hours, while others thought nothing of it.

Marisol believed that everyone was out to get her, and in his case, her instincts were correct.

Arwel didn't like being the bad guy in the story. He had a hard time convincing himself that he was the good guy catching the bad one, even though his opinion of Eleanor, aka Marisol, hadn't changed despite her somewhat warmer attitude.

Making sure that he made it down only a few seconds ahead of her, he pulled down his scarf and smiled. "I don't know about you, but I'm hungry. How about we find a restaurant and I buy you dinner? Any place you want."

She arched a brow. "Any place? There are some pricy ones in the hotels."

He nodded. "Any place."

"I wish I could, but I need to get back to work."

He glanced at his watch. "Isn't it a bit late to start your workday?"

She shrugged. "I have flexible hours."

"What do you do?"

"I'm a part-time bookkeeper," she said without hesitation, and if he hadn't known better, he would have believed her.

"So you don't have to clock in. Whenever you put in the hours is fine, right?"

After painting herself into a corner, she had no choice but to nod. "Still, I don't want to work until midnight."

"We'll make it short and share a pizza in the village."

"Okay."

Thank the merciful Fates.

Half an hour later, they were sitting across from each other in the pizzeria.

When she was done with the first slice, Marisol lifted her cola, took a few sips, and put it down. "So, I told you what I do for a living. But you didn't tell me what you do."

"I'm a therapist. People pay me to listen to their troubles."

She cracked a smile. "Do you actually help them or just take their money?"

He shrugged. "Talking about what's troubling them is therapeutic in itself. Usually, I can't offer solutions, but I can help them develop better tools to deal with whatever they are facing."

"Do you enjoy it?"

"Not really."

His answer seemed to surprise her. "So, why do you do it?"

"Because I know I can help, so I feel obligated to do it. But I'm not the type who can leave work at the office. I carry the things I hear with me, and they weigh me down."

She eyed him like he was a strange creature. "That's the trouble with being empathic. I'm glad that I'm not."

No, she wasn't.

But her problem was not the lack of emotions or even empathy. Eleanor was too angry and suspicious to allow herself to feel anything for anyone.

Arwel forced a smile. "I envy you. One day I'm going to switch professions and become an accountant. It'll be heaven for me."

"You should do it then. Don't wait." She took another sip from her coke. "I should be going, but I would like to see you again. How long are you going to stay in the resort?"

"I'm leaving Sunday afternoon."

"Perfect. I have Saturday off, and we can meet on the slopes." She pulled out her phone. "Can you give me your number?"

"Sure." He gave her the burner phone's.

"What's your last name?"

"Maddox." Arwel blurted the first one that popped into his mind. "Can I have your phone number?"

"I'll call you." She smirked. "After I check up on you and make sure that you are not on America's most wanted list."

He had no doubt that given the chance she would do precisely what she'd said.

"In that case, do you want my social security number as well? It will make your background check easier."

She chuckled. "It would be nice, along with your driver's license number. I'm cautious about the guys I date."

If he were a regular guy going after an ordinary girl, that was where he would have made a mental fist pump. Still, he had to keep up the act.

"Is that your covert way of inviting me on a date?"

"Only after I run you through my security check."

"I like how careful you are. That's very smart of you."

She liked his compliment. "Next time, dinner is on me. If there is a next time." She rose to her feet. "I had fun, but I really need to go."

He stood up as well. "I'll escort you to your car."

She eyed the tray with the half-eaten pizza. "Don't you want to stay and finish it?"

He threaded his arm through hers and leaned to whisper in her ear. "It's not that good."

At least he wasn't lying about that.

She shrugged. "If you are already being such a gentleman, you can carry my equipment."

"Gladly." He hefted her bag over his shoulder.

From across the street, Brundar nodded, giving Arwel the sign that everything was ready.

When they arrived at the parking lot, he saw Yamanu leaning against the Suburban.

Arwel released a relieved breath. What they were about to do would go unnoticed no matter who else was at the parking lot. Yamanu was going to shroud the entire area. Even if Eleanor screamed, no one was going to hear her.

As they reached her car, Eleanor popped the trunk, and he casually dropped her equipment bag inside. Watching Julian approach her from behind, Arwel closed the trunk and walked up to her.

Taking her gloved hand in his, he smiled. "I guess I'll have to wait to see you on the slopes on Saturday. Is there a chance you can make it sooner?" He pulled her against his body and wrapped his arm around her middle.

Surprised by the move, Eleanor pushed on his chest and was about to say something when Julian plunged the syringe into her arm.

As the extremely long needle went through all the layers of her clothing, Arwel held her tightly against him, muffling her scream. It was an instinctual response, and only later he remembered that Yamanu was shrouding the scene.

Or maybe he just didn't want to hear Eleanor scream.

It seemed to take forever until she stopped struggling and slumped against him.

In the next moment, Anandur pulled up with the Suburban. Julian opened the door, and Arwel climbed in with the unconscious woman in his arms.

After laying her over the back seat, he allowed himself a moment, closing his eyes and puffing out a breath.

"Check her phone," Kian told Anandur. "She might have useful information stored in it."

"What are we going to do with her car?" Arwel asked.

"Yamanu is going to take it to one of the lodge's parking lots. I'll tell you the rest of the plan on the way."

"All I see is Arwel's number," Anandur said. "It must be a burner phone because she has nothing on it. Not even a record of incoming calls. No email, no contacts, nada."

Kian nodded. "Erase Arwel's number, put the phone in her purse, and leave it in her car."

After that was done, Julian went back to watch over Eleanor, Brundar hopped inside, and Anandur took the wheel.

As he pulled out of the parking lot, Arwel asked, "Where are we taking her?"

"Harrisonburg." Kian locked his seatbelt in place. "Lokan is meeting us there."

Arwel nodded and closed his eyes again. Hopefully, Lokan would be able to compel Eleanor, and the interrogation would be effortless. He really wasn't looking forward to seeing the woman suffer.

59

LOKAN

"*How* much further?" Carol asked.

"Not much." Lokan checked the map on the navigation system. "We should get there well ahead of the others."

Naturally, Carol had jumped at the opportunity to see her family and friends, refusing to stay behind. When he'd tried to point out that witnessing an interrogation might be unpleasant, he'd gotten an earful from her about forgetting who she was and what she was capable of.

"I'm so excited for some action." Carol shifted in her seat. "Your car is nice, but I don't like long drives."

"It's not long. In fact, Harrisonburg is smack in the middle between Washington and the Quiet Zone. It's a two-hour drive from each direction."

"So how come we are early?"

"When I talked to Kian, he estimated that they would be heading out in three hours. So, if his estimate was correct, we would arrive nearly an hour before them."

"You have the code to the door, right?"

He smiled. "Why, were you hoping to see me break it?"

Lifting her arms, she flexed her muscles. "Seeing my manly man in action would have made me all hot and bothered."

"You are going to see your man in action, hopefully, compelling a human to talk."

They arrived at the duplex just as it began drizzling, the dark clouds that had been gathering ominously over the city, fulfilling their promise of a rainy night.

"The weather is cooperating. It's appropriate for the occasion," Carol said as he opened the door for her.

Holding an umbrella over her head, Lokan walked her to the front porch and opened the door. "Make yourself comfortable. Kian said that the place would be fully stocked. I'm going to get our things."

Stretching on her tiptoes, she kissed his cheek. "I'm going to choose our bedroom. Since we are the first to arrive, we can call dibs on the best one."

"Shouldn't you leave the master for Kian?"

Carol scrunched her nose. "First, I'm going to see what's available. After all, we are the only couple here, so we deserve the master."

"Yeah, but Kian doesn't even know that you are coming. Maybe it's not the best idea to antagonize him."

"You've got a point."

Since they weren't expecting to stay for more than one night, he and Carol had brought along only two small carry-ons.

"There is one bedroom downstairs and three upstairs." Carol leaned over the railing at the top of the stairs. "The bottom one should be the interrogation room."

"What about the upstairs?"

"Two have queen beds, and one has two singles. I think we will be sleeping on the other side of the duplex. There aren't enough bedrooms for everyone."

"Works for me." He left the two rollers next to the front door and went to check out the downstairs bedroom.

It was small, with one twin-sized bed, a compact desk, and a chair. The best part was that it had only one window, and it faced the back yard. There was also a three-quarter bath attached to it.

Carol peered inside over his arm. "We should take the bed and the desk out and leave only the chair. It's a shame that we didn't think to bring handcuffs. I'm going to search for something to tie Eleanor up with."

"Do we really need to? She's just one human female. She can't escape five immortal males. Six, if you count me as well."

"It's for the psychological effect. Don't underestimate it."

"She's going to be scared enough as it is."

Carol shook her head. "It would be better if she wakes up tied to a chair. It will send a clear message that this is about getting information out of her and not sex. She will be more willing to cooperate when she realizes no one is going to rape her. That's why we need to take out the bed."

"Interesting. I guess it takes a female to think like one. I'll take out the bed."

"I'll help you."

"I can manage by myself."

"I know you can, my love, but you are going to bang the walls if you do it alone. Together, we can maneuver it without causing damage."

Lokan leaned and kissed the top of Carol's head. "You are so wise."

She eyed him suspiciously. "I hope you are not mocking me."

"Mortdh forbid." The invocation had left his lips before he thought better of it.

Carol ignored it. "I'll take this end, and you take the other. We are just going to put it in the living room for now."

When they were done, Carol rearranged the bedding that had gotten messed up. "We need to find a rope and some masking tape. I'm going to tape towels over the windows in the bedroom and the bathroom. We don't want dear Aunt Eleanor to know where she is."

"You can just close the curtains."

"I meant tape on the outside. Kian is not going to leave her tied up the entire time. She will need to use the bathroom at some point, and if left alone, she would peek outside. Not that there is much to see, but it's the psychological effect."

"Have you done interrogations before?" He followed her to the kitchen. "You seem to know a lot about it."

She shrugged. "I didn't interrogate anyone, but I've been interrogated. Did you forget?"

He wanted to slap himself. "Right."

"Not that this is the same. No one is going to torture Eleanor, I hope. The idea is to scare her into talking." She opened the laundry room door and looked at the supply cabinet. "Here we go." She pulled out a spool of coarse rope. "They will have to wrap washcloths around her wrists and ankles. Otherwise, it will be torture for real."

"I'm truly impressed. You think of everything, and you are very compassionate."

She smiled sadly. "I know how it feels to be on the receiving end of it."

60

KIAN

They were about twenty minutes away from the duplex when Lokan called.

"We have the downstairs bedroom ready for Eleanor. We took everything out except for one sturdy chair. Carol prepared a rope to tie her to the chair with."

"Good thinking. Fear alone might make her talk."

"That's what Carol thought. How far away are you?"

"Twenty minutes or so. How is the place, passable?"

"Basic, but okay. Except, there are only four bedrooms on this side of the duplex, and we turned one of them into an interrogation room. I suggest that Carol and I sleep on the other side."

"No problem. But maybe no one will have to spend the night here. If your compulsion works, we can all go home once we get what we need out of her."

"I hope so. Compared to this place, the cell you had me locked in was luxurious."

Kian chuckled. "It was luxurious period. You were treated like royalty."

"I'm not complaining."

"Right. See you shortly." Kian ended the call and turned to look back at Julian. "How is she doing?"

"Stable."

"Good."

After Julian had checked Eleanor and sent Turner her stats, he'd been put in touch with Turner's guy who'd explained how to use the drugs he was sending over.

Hopefully, they would arrive tonight. If not, they would have to stay and wait for the delivery to arrive before they could leave the place.

"Home sweet home," Anandur said as he pulled up in front of the duplex. "Is there a garage?"

"It should be in the back."

"Lokan's car is blocking the driveway."

"I'll get him." Kian opened the door. "I don't want the neighbors to see us bringing an unconscious woman inside."

"I can shroud her," Brundar offered. "In fact, I should shroud us getting in."

"Good thinking."

Brundar's shrouding wasn't anywhere near Yamanu's caliber, but he could cast a decent shroud around a small area, blocking sights and sounds. It should suffice.

Kian put in the code and opened the door. "I need you to put your car in the garage."

"Oh, right. I should have thought about that."

As Lokan left to move the car, Carol took Kian to see the interrogation room they had prepared.

"Nice work."

The curtains were drawn closed, and the one in the bathroom had something taped over the glass on the other side. When he parted the drapes in the bedroom, he found that window had gotten a similar treatment to the one in the bathroom.

It was a bit of an overkill, but he couldn't fault Lokan and Carol for being extra careful.

A small lamp was tucked in the corner, the shade covered with a pillowcase to reduce the amount of light. Eleanor would be able to see their silhouettes, but not much more.

Not that it was important. They were going to either compel her to silence or drug her to forget everything that had happened today. When she woke up the next day in a hotel room, she would assume someone had slipped her a roofie.

Not a bad plan, provided it worked.

As Arwel walked in with Eleanor slumped in his arms, he stopped and looked around the bare room. "Are you kidding me? You want her tied to the chair?"

"You have a better idea?"

"Yeah. Put her on a bed. She is not going anywhere with all of us here."

"If she wakes up on a bed, she is going to panic way worse than if she wakes up in a chair," Carol said. "She's a woman. If she opens her eyes and sees six men watching her, she will assume that you intend to rape her."

Arwel sighed. "I'm not sure that you are right, but I trust your instincts on this. I will need help tying her up, though."

"I'll help you." Carol lifted the stack of washcloths off the chair. "Just hold her, so she doesn't slide off while I do the tying."

61

LOKAN

*T*he screaming and thrashing started the moment the woman opened her eyes and realized her predicament.

Lokan walked in with the bottle of water Julian had thrust into his hand and tried to calm her down first.

"Relax. Nothing is going to happen to you. All we want is information."

She squinted. "Who are you? What do you want?"

He walked closer and showed her the bottle of water. "You must be thirsty. Would you like a drink?"

Up close, she could see that it was a sealed plastic bottle, but it still took her several seconds of indecision before she nodded.

He broke the seal and brought the bottle to her lips. She gulped it up until there was nothing left and then tried to wipe her mouth on her shoulder, succeeding only partially.

"What do you want?" Her voice shook.

She was still terrified.

"As I said, we only want information. Who do you work for?" He imbued his voice with compulsion.

"I'm a bookkeeper. I have many clients."

Damn, she was lying, and it didn't even require effort. Evidently, his compulsion wasn't working on her.

He tried again, more forcibly this time. "Don't lie to me. Who are you working for?"

Pulling on her restraints, she shook her head. "I'm not lying. You must have the wrong person. I'm a nobody." She started crying.

Damn, a woman's tears were a weapon he had no defense against.

He turned to look at Kian, who had been leaning against the door and invisible to Eleanor.

Kian pushed away from the door and motioned for Lokan to follow him into the hallway. They'd turned the lights off in the entire downstairs, so none would spill into the room when the door was open.

"Where are you going?" As her panic rose, so did her voice. "Let me go! You have the wrong person!"

If Brundar wasn't shrouding that portion of the house, the neighbors would have called the police by now.

"I'll be right back." He closed the door behind him.

"It seems that she is immune to your compulsion," Kian said.

Lokan nodded.

"Could her panic do that?"

"I doubt it. In my experience, humans are either susceptible to compulsion or immune to it. Their state of mind at the moment doesn't matter." He smiled sheepishly. "If that were the case, Vivian and Ella would have not responded to my compulsion either. They were both terrified of me."

Sighing, Kian dragged his hand through his hair. "Ella suspects that her aunt might be a compeller like her younger brother, and it would seem that a compeller can't be compelled."

"I think that's true. That's why my father's compulsion doesn't work on me. Then again, it might be because he is my father, and my talent comes from him. We don't know enough about that to make assumptions."

"That's true. Give it another try. Maybe when she calms down a little, she will respond to you better."

Given Eleanor's ongoing screams to let her go, that was unlikely.

"Perhaps it would be better for Arwel to talk to her first. Maybe he can calm her down before I try again." He tilted his head toward the door. "In the state she is in, she is not going to respond to anything."

"I agree. Let's get Arwel."

62

ARWEL

"*S*he is not going to respond to me either." Arwel pushed his hair back. "I'm the asshole who kidnapped her."

Why the hell did he feel so guilty? And why were Eleanor's shrieks affecting him like that?

She wasn't a good person, and there was a reason why she was tied to a chair and being interrogated.

Except, he couldn't be sure. She might be a jaded grouch and harbor some dark thoughts, but that was not a crime. She might have never wronged anyone, might've known nothing about Jin and her whereabouts, and he might have just helped kidnap and torment an innocent woman.

Kian put a hand on his shoulder. "Look, I'm really not looking forward to interrogating her the traditional way. If Lokan manages to compel her, it will go much easier for her and for us."

"She is most likely immune to his compulsion, just as she's immune to thralling. I'll be wasting my time with her. Worse, she might get even angrier and become completely unresponsive."

Kian nodded. "I'm willing to risk it. Go in there and do your best. If it doesn't work, so be it. But at least we gave it a try."

Taking a deep breath, Arwel let it out slowly through his mouth. "Fine." He depressed the handle and walked in.

"Hello, Marisol."

She recognized his voice right away. "You son of a bitch, how dare you show your face?"

"I know you are angry, and rightfully so, but this can be over very quickly if you cooperate and tell us what we need to know."

"Fuck you, Arwel. If that is even your real name. I'm not telling you anything."

She'd slipped without realizing it.

"So, you admit to having secrets and being unwilling to share them."

Her eyes widened for a moment, but she recovered quickly. "I don't. But your interrogator didn't believe me when I told him the truth, so there is no point in me saying anything at all."

He got closer and crouched in front of her. "We know that you are not a bookkeeper. You can drop the charade."

Hatred dripping from her eyes, she stared into his and hissed, "Let. Me. Go!"

"I can't do that."

Looking surprised, she tried again, more clearly this time as well as forcefully. "Release me, right now!"

Had she been trying to compel him, or was she just acting illogically?

Underneath the sludge of darkness that was wafting from her in spades, he could feel her hopelessness and despair, and it affected him even worse than the oppressive negativity.

"Look, Marisol, we really mean you no harm. We don't even mean your employer harm. In fact, once you answer our questions, we will let you go, and no one will know that you told anyone anything. We are just searching for a young woman that we think you have information on. That's all."

Heaving out a sigh, Eleanor stopped struggling against her restraints, and he could feel her panic subsiding. "Who are you looking for?"

"First, I need to ask you a few questions about your employer."

"You said that you are looking for a woman."

"I did, but we want to know why your employer needs her, how much money she was offered for her services, etc."

It was a spur-of-the-moment inspiration to make it seem as if they were after Jin's ability. The story that was taking shape in his head was that they were another spy organization. They wanted to lure Jin from her current job by offering her a better deal. Someone like Eleanor, who believed that everyone was as self-serving as she was, would buy this story more readily than anything with a humanitarian twist.

Eleanor shifted in the chair as much as her restraints allowed. "I need to pee."

"Tell me who your employer is, and I'll take you to the bathroom."

"I don't have an employer. I'm an independent contractor."

She hadn't said a bookkeeper. An independent contractor could be doing anything, including spying.

Could she be telling the truth?

"Let's assume that I believe you. Are you providing services for more than one client?"

"I'm not going to answer until you let me pee."

It was progress.

Perhaps this was a good time to bring Lokan to try again. Also, he needed to consult with Kian and ask Carol to take Eleanor to the bathroom.

Having a woman do that would help Eleanor calm down even more.

63

KIAN

On the other side of the door, Kian and Lokan listened to the exchange between Arwel and Eleanor.

"I think she is ready for you," Kian said. "She sounds much less frightened."

"Her defenses are just as solid, though. I don't think it will work. But I'll give it another try just because you are asking me to."

Arwel opened the door and stepped out, closing it behind him. "She needs to visit the bathroom."

"We heard," Kian said. "I think it's the perfect opportunity to press her into revealing more. She's stubborn and proud, and she won't allow herself to pee in her pants. We can torment the information out of her without laying a finger on her."

Arwel waved a hand. "Be my guest."

The guy was too soft-hearted for a Guardian, but that was the flip side of his empathic nature. Then again, even Anandur would have had a problem with letting a woman suffer. Brundar, on the other hand, would have thought nothing of it. After all, he was a part-owner of a BDSM club and a practitioner. He had no qualms about inflicting pain as long as it didn't cause long-term harm.

If it came down to it, Kian was going to send him to talk to

Eleanor. Hearing Brundar's robotic, emotionless voice, she might start talking.

"Ready?" Kian asked Lokan.

"After you."

Eleanor narrowed her eyes, trying to see who was there, but they stayed near the door where she couldn't see their faces.

"Tell me your real name," Lokan commanded.

"Marisol Ortega. Now let me go pee."

Lokan shook his head.

Well, it was worth a try. Kian opened the door to let Lokan out and waved Arwel in.

Leaning against the door, Kian motioned for the Guardian to stay next to him.

"We know who you are," Kian said. "Your real name is Eleanor Takala, you used to work in pharmaceutical sales, you had a brother who died in a helicopter crash. His wife and two children also died in another accident not too long ago."

A wave of sadness washed over Eleanor, proving that she wasn't an entirely emotionless sociopath. But she shook it off quickly. "Who are you?"

"You can call me Kevin."

"I meant you as in you people. Who are you, and what do you want from me?"

"My friend explained that already. We are looking for someone, and we believe that you know where she is."

"I don't know what you are talking about. I'm an avid skier who finances her hobby working as a part-time bookkeeper."

He chuckled. "With the amount of money that you have in the bank, you can ski for the rest of your life without working."

She narrowed her eyes, trying to see his face. "You really did your homework. But what does it prove? The money in the bank is my retirement fund. I'm a single woman with no family. I need to take care of myself."

"Why did you change your name?"

"A stalker ex-boyfriend."

The woman was an excellent dissembler. She didn't hesitate even a moment before spouting her lies.

"I know that you are lying, Eleanor. What do you know about the paranormal talent our government is collecting?"

It was a gamble, but it paid off as he felt a wave of fear wash over her. If she knew nothing about it, she would have no reason to be scared.

"I don't know what you've been smoking, but what you're asking is absurd."

Kian was impressed. Despite her fear, Eleanor managed to sound believable.

"We are not after everyone in that program. We need to find just one person. Jin Levine." Even without his supernatural senses, Kian could tell that she recognized the name, and pressed forward. "Tell us where to find her, and we will let you go, not just to the bathroom but back to your life. We will put you to sleep once again, deliver you to your car, and you will wake up there in a couple of hours free and unharmed."

He could see the indecision in her eyes.

"What if I don't know the person you are talking about? How can I tell you where to find her? Are you going to kill me?"

"We are not going to kill you, but we will leave you tied to this chair, and days might pass until someone finds you. But if you die, it's not going to be by our hands."

Heaving a sigh, Eleanor hung her head. "Even if I tell you where you can find her, she is not going to accept anything that you offer. You're wasting your efforts and tangling with forces that you shouldn't."

Evidently, Eleanor believed what Arwel had implied. Which was good. Kian could work with that, pretending that he was after Jin's talent and willing to pay for it.

"Whatever your employer is paying her, we will double it."

"It's not about the money. No one is forcing her to be there. She is doing it because she wants to and because she is a patriot."

Eleanor sounded sincere, but Kian wasn't as good at detecting lies as Andrew, or even Arwel. He glanced at the Guardian and lifted his brow in question.

Arwel leaned to whisper in his ear. "Truth mingled with lies."

Kian nodded. It made sense. Some form of coercion might be involved, either monetary or extortion, but Jin hadn't been abducted, and she probably wasn't imprisoned either.

"If she is there voluntarily, then why hasn't she called her parents since she joined the program?" He avoided mentioning Mey on purpose.

"They are not allowed to make phone calls during the training period, but she will be free to do so once it's over. Can I go to the bathroom now?"

"Just a few more questions. Where is that training taking place?"

"I can't tell you that, and even if I could, you would have no chance of getting in there. It's heavily guarded. Your best chance to make contact with her is to wait until the trainees get a day off and are bussed into town. If you wanted proof that everyone in that training program is there voluntarily, that is it."

"When is that?"

"Saturday."

Damn. That was three days from now. It could be a clever ploy on Eleanor's part to stall until help arrived.

He looked at Arwel, who shrugged.

"I'll send a lady to take you to the bathroom."

Eleanor huffed out a breath. "Thank God."

LOKAN

*A*s Lokan listened from the other side of the door, a picture started forming in his mind.

When Eleanor had said that she was an independent contractor, she'd sounded truthful. He wasn't the best at detecting lies, especially when so many other intense emotions were present, but he'd believed her. Her story was collaborated by her flexible schedule. An employee didn't get to spend half days on the slopes two to three days a week.

Then there was Ella's suspicion that her aunt might be a compeller, and Eleanor's confidence in Jin's refusal to accept a better offer.

Eleanor must be the recruiter for the program.

If money and patriotism didn't do the trick to lure potential candidates, she used her compulsion ability to bring them in. Just as she had done in the pharmaceutical field. She must have had nearly a hundred percent success rate, which explained the hefty amount in her bank account.

Shifting from foot to foot, Carol huffed out a breath. "How long are they going to keep that poor woman from going to the bathroom? She is probably about to explode."

"That poor woman is the recruiter for the program. She probably used her compulsion power to get Jin to sign the contract."

"How do you know that?"

He touched his nose. "A strong hunch supported by a lot of circumstantial evidence."

When the door opened, and Kian stepped out together with Arwel, Carol rolled her eyes. "Finally. Can I go in now and take her to pee?"

Kian nodded. "Do you need someone with you?"

"Oh, please." She rolled her eyes again. "Do I have to tie her up after she is done?"

"Yes. She can use that lamp in the corner as a weapon, and if we take it out, it's going to be pitch black in there."

"Got it." Carol walked in and closed the door behind her. "Okay, girl. I'm going to untie you and take you to the bathroom. Don't try anything, or you will quickly learn that I'm much stronger than I look. Besides, there is a bunch of burly men on the other side of that door."

"Just take me to the bathroom, and I'll kiss your little feet."

Kian chuckled. "It seems that Eleanor is in a much better mood now that salvation is near." He turned to Arwel. "So, what do you think? Was she telling the truth?"

"She was," Lokan answered instead. "I have a strong feeling that she is indeed a compeller, and that's why she is confident that Jin will refuse to leave."

Kian nodded. "It occurred to me. The question is, what are we going to do until Saturday? We have to hold her here until we get Jin, and we can't keep her tied to a chair. What's more, Brundar can't go on shrouding indefinitely. Eventually, he will need to sleep, and she might decide to start screaming for help again."

"We will have to keep her drugged," Arwel said. "I'll go ask Julian if he can do it."

"I can," came the answer from the living room. "But I'll need to get more supplies."

"Go now," Kian said.

"Yes, boss."

"I'm debating whether we should bring the rest of the team here," Kian said. "By now, Yamanu should be done with erasing every piece of footage that has Arwel's face on it, and the hotel room for Eleanor's return is reserved. The problem is that no one is going to believe a roofie put her out of commission for four days."

"I don't think you should worry about it," Lokan said. "If she is indeed an independent contractor, she doesn't need to show up on schedule."

Arwel scratched his stubble. "Yeah, but since she doesn't have a place of her own, we assume that she lives in the facility. She is going to be missed."

"Plant drugs in that hotel room," Lokan suggested. "Eleanor is going to be so scared that she'd been using that she is going to invent a cover story for her absence."

"I like it." Kian clapped him on the back.

A moment later, Carol opened the door and stepped out. "Poor thing peed for five minutes straight."

Lokan wrapped his arm around her waist. "Did she give you any trouble?"

"Except for a few snide remarks, not really."

"I'm going back in," Kian said. "Now that she doesn't need to empty her bladder, she might get stubborn again. Check out what's in the fridge that's easy to make and produces an appetizing smell. We are going to torment her with that."

Lokan snorted. "That's not going to work. Instead, bring in the blond and have him sharpen his throwing knives in front of her. If she has any pee left in her, she is going to wet herself."

"Not a bad idea," Arwel said.

Kian put his hand on the door handle. "First, the food."

"I'm on it." Carol pulled out of Lokan's arm. "You can come help if Kian doesn't need you here."

"Gladly."

65

KIAN

"Feeling better?" Kian asked as he entered the room.

Next to him, Arwel leaned against the wall and crossed his arms over his chest.

"Much, but I'm still tied to a chair."

"Unfortunately, this is necessary for now."

"Where am I?"

He smiled, even though she couldn't see him. "Do you really expect me to answer that?"

She shrugged. "Can't blame a girl for trying."

"Where are the trainees dropped off?"

"The Outlet Mall in Harrisonburg. They get there around ten in the morning and are picked up at six."

And wasn't that a stroke of good luck. Then again, this was the nearest urban center, so it made sense. The question was why Jin hadn't used the opportunity to call Mey while on those outings.

"Do they have phones with them?"

She shook her head. "Radios, so they can communicate with each other and the group supervisor."

"If they are free to go, why the restricted communications?"

"It's done to encourage bonding within the group and wean them from outside attachments. It's like the military."

"Is it military?"

"No. It's like it. But you are not going to achieve anything by approaching her. I'm only telling you all this so you will let me go like you promised."

He wasn't going to mention that they were keeping her locked up until they made contact with Jin, but she was smart enough to figure it out on her own.

"What do they do in that training camp?"

"I can't tell you that because I don't know. I only bring the recruits in."

That confirmed Lokan's suspicion that Eleanor was the recruiter for the program. But it wasn't all she did or she wouldn't have lodging on the premises. Which meant that she was lying again.

"If you are just the recruiter, what reason do you have to live right next to the training camp?"

"I don't. I'm here because of the skiing."

He lifted a brow. "You don't have an apartment, and the car you drive is not registered under your name. Where do you live?"

"Sometimes the new recruits need a pep talk and hand-holding. I stay on the premises in case I'm needed."

So her compulsion power wasn't as strong as Lokan's, and she needed to reinforce it from time to time. That also made sense. Eleanor was a Dormant, while Lokan was an immortal. Not only that, he was the son of the most powerful compeller in the world.

They would need Lokan to remove the compulsion from Jin. Otherwise, she wasn't going to come with them.

"Are you going to let me go now?"

"Not yet. Are you like a headhunter who finds new recruits for the program, or are you given names and addresses and give them an offer they can't refuse?"

"I get the names."

"Do you know why these people are recruited?"

"No clue. I don't ask questions. I just get paid for each one I bring in."

Next to him, Arwel shook his head. Kian didn't need the confirmation. It was such a blatant lie that even he sensed the deceit. It was tricky with her because Eleanor was an accomplished liar and felt no guilt or remorse. But he had learned her tells.

What gave her away was that Eleanor was conceited and prideful, probably because she could fool the best of human detectives. Whenever she thought she was getting away with a lie, those two emotions showed on her face and in her scent.

"Okay, let's assume that you really don't know why they are brought in. You should know how many, though. You are the recruiter."

"I'm probably not the only one."

"How many did you bring in?"

"Fourteen."

"And how many are in the program?"

"I don't know. You can count heads when they get off the bus."

"That's true only if everyone gets the day off."

"They do. Are you going to let me go now?"

"I can't. Not until we verify the information you gave us and make contact with Jin."

She let out a breath. "I figured as much. Am I going to spend the entire time tied to this fucking chair?"

"We will find a different solution."

Kian opened the door and motioned for Arwel to follow him.

Out in the corridor, the smells of cooking reminded him that it had been hours since he had eaten anything. But he wasn't going to take a break until he had the Eleanor situation figured out.

He found Lokan and Carol in the kitchen.

"It looks like you will need to stay until Saturday to remove the compulsion from Jin. Assuming that this is what we are dealing with."

Lokan shook his head. "I can't. I have meetings scheduled for tomorrow afternoon and for Friday. But I can move things around and come back on Saturday." He rubbed a hand over his jaw. "I've never attempted to remove someone else's compulsion. It might be a gift unique to Ella's brother."

"He said that he didn't remove it. He overrode it." Kian smiled. "Which means that he's a stronger compeller than you are."

Lokan puffed out his chest. "That's not possible. I'm my father's son, and I have centuries of experience. There is no way a teenage boy is more powerful than I am."

"Well, you can prove how talented you are on Saturday when you override Eleanor's compulsion."

A smirk lifted one corner of Lokan's mouth. "I'm always glad to assist. In exchange for future favors, of course."

Kian clapped him on the back. "Each time you prove yourself helpful, you are adding another stone to the foundation of your future home. When there are enough stones for me to trust you, I'll let you build it in the village."

Next to Lokan, Carol beamed a smile at Kian.

Lokan arched a brow. "What makes you think that I want in?"

"In case you do, cousin. I know you like to keep your options open."

66

ARWEL

"What's next?" Arwel asked. "I want her out of those restraints already. She's been tied up for hours."

Kian raked his fingers through his hair. "Perhaps you should get her into the shower. I'm sure she will appreciate that. And while she is in there, we will get the bed and desk back in. I don't want to tape towels over all the windows in the house, and I don't want her to know where she is. With all due respect to Turner's guy, I'm not at all sure that drugs can eliminate four days of memories. The less she knows, the better."

Lokan nodded.

"She will need a change of clothes," Carol said. "But I'm much shorter than she is. Then again, I'm sure she will be fine with a big T-shirt if any of you guys can spare one."

"I can give her a T-shirt and a pair of sweatpants," Arwel offered. "And she can wear one of my flannel shirts as a robe."

"That's awfully nice of you," Carol said. "Are you experiencing Stockholm syndrome in reverse?"

"No, I just feel guilty even though it makes no sense. If she were a guy, I would have had no problem with any of it."

As Kian and Lokan nodded, Carol shook her head. "You guys are such chauvinists, but in a good way."

"I'd rather think of it as being gentlemen," Arwel said. "I'm going to get her clothes." He headed for the stairs.

Passing through the living room, he glanced at Brundar and Anandur, who were sitting on a couch and watching a soccer game.

Slackers.

"When you hear the water going in Eleanor's shower, bring in the bed and the desk."

"Yes, boss," Anandur saluted.

"Is Julian back?" Arwel asked.

Brundar shook his head.

"I wonder what's taking him so long. I hope he didn't get arrested for trying to buy drugs."

It was a joke, of course, but just in case, he called Julian. "What's keeping you?"

"I went grocery shopping. If we are going to be stuck here until Saturday, we need supplies. Why? Is our girl misbehaving?"

"No. I was just worried."

"I'm okay, Mommy."

"Up yours." Arwel disconnected.

After pulling the clothing items from his duffel bag, he went into Eleanor's room and turned on the light. She'd already seen his face, so that didn't really matter.

Squinting, she looked at the bundle of clothes in his arms. "Are you going to disguise me?"

He put the bundle in the bathroom and returned to crouch next to her chair. "I figured that you would want clean clothes after your shower." He started untying her ankles. "Carol's are too small for you, so I brought you some of mine."

"That's so kind of you," she said sarcastically, then moaned when he started massaging her calf. "I'm willing to forgive you your sins for this."

"That's so magnanimous of you." He smiled up at her while untying her other calf.

She moaned again when he massaged that one as well.

"Why are you doing this?" Arwel asked.

"Moaning? Because I was in so much pain, and this feels so good."

"Why are you doing the recruiting? You were making good money as a pharma rep. Getting these young people to sign their lives away is not a good thing."

She shrugged. "First of all, not all of them are young. And secondly, this is better money for much less work."

There wasn't even a smidgen of remorse in her tone. She really didn't care what happened to the people she brought into the program.

He untied her wrists, massaging each until her circulation returned, then helped her up and led her to the bathroom.

"I hope you don't plan on staying here and watching me shower. You can bring Carol back if you want."

He glanced at the window. It was too small for her to try to escape through, but she could open it and scream murder. Not that it was going to help her. Brundar was still shrouding the place.

"I'm going to be right outside the door. If you as much as whistle in there, I'm going to get in and haul you back to the chair. So, unless you want to spend the next three days tied up, I suggest that you don't try anything."

Looking at the small window, she shrugged. "I can't fit through there anyway."

"You have five minutes. So you better hurry." He stepped outside and closed the door behind him.

67

KIAN

*J*ulian opened the front door and walked in with three shopping bags in each hand. "I have more groceries in the trunk."

"Good thinking. The rest of the team is arriving later tonight," Kian said. He'd called Syssi and asked her if she was all packed and ready to go.

That had been as much as he'd dared to say over the unsecured line. But it was enough for his smart mate.

"I hope you brought steaks." Anandur pushed off the couch and stretched.

The guy was a total carnivore.

"And vegetables too," Kian said. "You guys can survive on meat, but the ladies like to have some greens on their plates."

"I got veggie burgers for you. The new kind that you like that taste like the real thing." Julian put the bags on the kitchen counter.

"They don't come even close, but they are good." Several new brands had come on the market and were even served in fast food places. "Did you get the drugs?"

"That was my first stop. I went into an urgent care clinic and thralled a bunch of people."

He could have probably used his doctor's credentials to get what he needed, but it was better not to leave a trail. "What did you get for her?"

"Opiates. I'm going to give her just enough to make her loopy but not knock her out. We want her to be able to eat and use the bathroom."

"Good thinking."

He chuckled. "I'm a doctor."

Brundar snorted. "That doesn't prove that you are smart. Just that you can study your ass off."

Julian flipped him off, then looked around the living room. "Where is the bed?"

"We took it back into the room," Kian said. "Eleanor showered, and she is eating dinner now with Arwel watching over her. You should prepare to give her the first dose." Kian pushed to his feet. "I'm going to check on them."

Before entering the room, he debated whether he should turn the light off. Eleanor had already seen Arwel's face, so there was no point in him hiding in the shadows, but she hadn't seen his.

Maybe it would be better if she didn't.

Inside, he heard the two talking and decided to stay in the corridor and listen instead of going in.

"You're making a mistake by holding me until Saturday. I'm going to be missed, and someone might come looking for me."

"No one is going to find you, and you know it," Arwel said. "We searched you for tracking devices, and you had none on you."

"That's good to know," she murmured. "I never know with these people."

"You don't trust them."

"I don't trust anyone. But that doesn't always help. I didn't trust you, and I still ended up here."

"You should start thinking about a good story to tell your superiors. If they believe that you've been captured and talked, they might decide to eliminate you."

Smart. In case the drugs Turner's guy had sent didn't work, putting fear into Eleanor's heart was a good thing.

She snorted. "They need me. I'm the best they've got, and they are not going to find anyone as good."

"Don't fool yourself. Everyone is replaceable. Are you done?"

He was probably referring to the food.

"Yes. Thank you for feeding me."

"You should get in bed."

"I'm not sleepy."

"Nevertheless, I want you in bed. I'm going to turn the lights off."

He must have sensed Kian standing outside.

"Are you going to tuck me in?" she teased.

"I'll put the dishes in the kitchen, and I'll come back."

"I was joking."

Arwel opened the door and walked out with a tray in his hands. "Is Julian back?"

"I'm here." Julian joined them in the hallway.

"It would be best if she went to sleep now. She is exhausted but too agitated to let herself drift off."

"I can give her sleeping pills instead of drugging her."

Arwel nodded. "Let's keep the drugs to the bare minimum."

"I'll get the pills for you. It's best that you give them to her."

"I figured you would make me do it."

As Arwel headed toward the kitchen, Kian followed. "You seem very sympathetic toward Eleanor. Did you change your mind about her?"

"No. She is just as hateful and bitter and selfish as I initially thought she was, and she had no qualms about bringing in the recruits, knowing that it's probably a one-way ticket. Still, I feel sorry for her. It's not fun being her."

Kian chuckled. "She is her own worst punishment."

Arwel put the tray down and leaned against the counter. "I wouldn't go that far. What bothers me about our plan is that once this is over and we dump Eleanor in the hotel, she will go back to recruiting."

Lokan walked over to where they were standing and leaned against the counter next to Arwel. "I've been thinking about that as well. Since she is an independent contractor, getting paid by the head, what if you offer her a better deal? If she brings the recruits to you instead of the program, she'll get paid double."

Kian shook his head. "She is getting the names from her client. If she fails to bring the recruits in, they will stop using her."

Lokan waved a hand. "That's what you want, right?"

"They will get someone else to do their dirty work for them. Coercion works almost as well as compulsion."

"How do they know who to send her after?" Carol asked.

"We think that they are using their Big Brother spying network to listen to people's phone conversations. The bots are programmed to flag certain trigger words. The same way that the mention of bombs and explosives flags possible terrorist activity, mentioning precognition or telepathy or any other paranormal ability might flag paranormal talent. Once the bot flags a conversation, a human probably checks it out. If it sounds credible and seems worth pursuing, it goes up to another department, and eventually Eleanor or someone like her is sent to recruit the talent."

Lokan rubbed his jaw. "She is not going to remember any of this, right?"

Kian nodded. "We hope."

"Then put a tracker on her or have a Guardian follow her when she goes on her recruiting trips. Snag the talent from under her nose."

Arwel shook his head. "Someone is going to connect the dots. In fact, she will probably get kicked out after Jin is gone. It won't take a genius to make a connection between Eleanor's so-called vacation and Jin's disappearance."

"Right." Lokan nodded. "Is there a way to make Jin's escape seem like a random act? Or even better, fake her death?"

Kian chuckled. "I have no idea how to pull something like that off. I need to contact the expert."

"Turner?" Julian came down the stairs.

"Who else?"

M E Y

"I'm exhausted," Ella said as they neared the van. "It was fun learning to ski, and it has taken my mind off what's happening with my aunt."

Mey wrapped her arm around the girl's shoulders. "We will find out soon. I'm sure they are treating her well." Or as well as they could under the circumstances.

Extracting information from an unwilling subject could never be pleasant, but hopefully, Carol's mate had been able to compel Eleanor.

It was frustrating not to know what was going on, especially for Ella, which was why Yamanu had offered to take them to a beginners' slope and teach them to ski. But they were both tired and hungry, and it was time to return to the chalet.

"How are you feeling?" Yamanu asked as he helped her into the passenger seat.

"Good. I'm tired, and I can't wait to make us some hot cocoa."

He turned on the ignition. "That tells me that you are feeling better. This morning you were still cringing when you drank coffee that wasn't even that hot."

"Yeah, you are right." Mey took her glove off and patted her gums. "It doesn't hurt as much." She pulled down the shade and flipped the mirror open. "Look at that. They are almost normal."

He turned to her. "Let me see."

Mey cracked a wide smile.

"Adorable. They are just a little more pointy than Amanda's, but they could pass for human."

"Why didn't I get any?" Ella complained from the backseat. "Nothing about me changed after the transition. Even my hearing and eyesight are only slightly better than they used to be. It's such a bummer."

Mey turned around and smiled. "You shouldn't complain. I think your superpowers are all channeled into your telepathic ability. You told me that it improved after your transition."

"Only a little. I managed to communicate with Michael, who is also a telepath. It doesn't sound like a big deal, but it is. Before my transition, I could only do that with my mother."

"We should have brought him along," Yamanu said. "That would have solved the communication problem. He could have gone with Kian and transmitted to you what was going on over there."

"Yeah, but we didn't anticipate having to kidnap my aunt. This was supposed to be easy. Find her, thrall the information out of her, find Jin, and go home. Besides, Michael can't transmit verbal communication, only pictures and feelings."

Mey nodded. "It's impossible to plan for everything. Improvisation is a necessary part of nearly every mission."

Yamanu cast her a questioning glance. "You sound as if you speak from experience."

She hated keeping things from him, but she had no choice. Still, she could at least admit to having secrets. "I do, but I'm not allowed to talk about it, so please don't ask me. It's really not my choice."

He reached over the center console and took her hand. "Thank you for telling me that. And I will never pressure you into revealing things that are not yours to reveal."

Was he the best or what?

"I love you so much, Yamanu. I don't know what I've done to deserve such a perfect mate."

He smiled and lifted their conjoined hands to wipe off the tear that slid down her cheek. "That's no reason to cry, my love."

"I know. I think this transition is affecting my hormonal balance. I'm much more emotional than usual."

"It's the stress," Ella said from the backseat. "You are anxious about your sister and about what's going on with your body. It's no wonder that you get emotional."

"Anyone want pizza?" Yamanu said. "We can get a couple to go and bring them home."

"I'm sure they have already eaten dinner," Ella said. "But I'll check."

Her nails made clicking sounds on the phone's screen as she typed. A moment later, her phone pinged with a return message. "Syssi says that they have already eaten and that they saved some for us." She leaned forward, sticking her head between Yamanu and Mey's seats. "I don't know about you, but I'm really in the mood for pizza. Carbs covered with cheese are the best mood picker upper."

Mey glanced at Yamanu. "We are in no hurry. We can stop for pizza and even a little shopping." If that was what it took to lift Ella's spirits, then why not.

Yamanu nodded. "Pizza it is."

After dinner they checked out the stores, and Ella's mood had improved after buying herself and Julian matching sweaters.

"What do you think?" Yamanu wrapped a scarf around his neck and handed her its twin. "We can do matching too."

She smiled. "Why not. Let's get them."

It was dark when they left the store, and as they got back to the chalet, they found a stack of suitcases by the door.

"What's going on?" Yamanu asked.

"Kian called," Syssi said. "We are leaving here and heading to Harrisonburg to join them." She chuckled. "Of course, that wasn't what he said over the phone, so I might be wrong. We will find out once we leave the Quiet Zone."

"What exactly did he say?" Mey asked.

"He asked me if I'm all packed and ready to go."

"That's good enough of a clue," Ella said. "Did he hint anything about my aunt?"

Syssi shook her head. "Pack your things. The sooner we are out of the zone, the sooner we will find out what's going on."

"Do I have time for hot cocoa?" Mey asked.

Syssi smiled. "There is always time for that. But you'll have to take it to go."

69

KIAN

$\mathcal{U}$p in his bedroom, Kian called Turner and gave him a short version of what he'd discussed with Arwel and Lokan.

"What do you think?" he asked when he was done.

"Tough call. I understand your desire to go after the recruits before Eleanor gets to them, but I agree with Arwel. After you get Jin, Eleanor will probably be out of a job. And as for staging something that will take the suspicion elsewhere, it's too ambitious even for me. You are talking about the US government, not a Russian mobster. I don't see how we could possibly pull it off."

If Turner couldn't come up with a plan, no one could.

"What if they keep Eleanor? I doubt they have another compeller they can use for recruiting. They will assume that she'd been compromised, drugged into revealing things she shouldn't have, but not due to any wrongdoing on her part."

"It's possible. They might give her a new identity but keep her. She is a valuable asset."

"But even then, if we follow her, we might get away with snagging one or two Dormants from under their noses, but no more than that. They will fire her or get rid of her."

"No doubt. But that's a worry for another day. Right now, you have only one objective, and that's to get Jin. Don't try to kill two birds with one stone because you might get none."

"What if we ambush that bus and get everyone on board? We could set the thing on fire and make it look like an accident."

"You would need to collide it with a nitrogen tanker. Anything less than that would not incinerate the bodies into ash. And even if you can get cadavers to replace the talent, they will not match the dental records they have on file. Again, you are dealing with the US government. You don't want to mess with them, and you don't want them to start investigating. One girl disappearing may not justify a full-on investigation, but an entire bunch of new recruits gone missing will."

Dragging an agitated hand through his hair, Kian leaned back against the headboard. "I don't like it. The thought of leaving a group of Dormants behind frustrates the hell out of me."

For a long moment, Turner didn't respond, and his silence gave Kian renewed hope. Perhaps he was thinking about another twist. Something they could do to get those Dormants.

"I wonder how many they have recruited before this last batch, and what they have done with them. At some point, the recruits are put to work, and maybe we can get to them then."

Excited, Kian pushed up on the pillows. "You are brilliant, my friend. We follow Eleanor, find out who the recruits are, but we don't approach them until they are done with the training. We get them later. The connection to her would be much less clear."

"They will probably get new identities, but we can find them using William's facial recognition program."

"Imagine the possibilities. Not only will the government find possible Dormants for us, but we can also find out what their talents are used for."

Turner chuckled. "What good is it going to do you? It's not like you want to sabotage the US spying activities."

"Entertainment. It will satisfy my curiosity. Do you have any suggestions for Jin's Saturday extraction?"

"I'll give it some thought and get back to you. I also need to arrange your transport out of Harrisonburg. As far as anonymity, the best thing would be for you to drive all the way to Washington and fly from there. But once Jin is reported missing, they might put up roadblocks. Not that it's a big problem for you and your team. You can just thrall the officers."

"I'll leave it up to you. We have three days to come up with a plan. That's plenty of time." He chuckled. "For you."

"Indeed."

70

MEY

"*I*s it safe to turn on the clan phones now?" Mey asked an hour into the drive.

She was worried. At first, she'd been excited about joining the team in Harrisonburg, thinking that Kian's instructions to leave earlier than planned meant that he'd found out where Jin was, and they were heading there. It had taken some time for the gears in her brain to process the other possibilities.

There were several possible reasons for Kian to have them leave earlier than planned. One was that Eleanor didn't know anything about Jin, and he was folding the operation. Another was that what he'd learned had made him decide to abort the mission for some reason. A third possibility was that he'd found out Jin's whereabouts, and it wasn't where they'd thought she was.

Yamanu checked the GPS. "I think it is."

They had split into two groups. Dalhu, Amanda, Syssi, and Callie had left in the first van, while Yamanu, Mey, Wonder, and Ella had closed up the place, leaving twenty minutes later. The idea was not to have the two vans leave at the same time, but she didn't see the logic. If they were really a group of people on vacation, sharing a chalet, it made sense for them to arrive and leave together.

Pulling the clan issue phone out of her purse, Mey turned it on. "There is a message from Kian." Her heart started beating faster as she read through it.

"Eleanor told them where we can find Jin. She is getting a day off on Saturday and gets dropped off at a mall in Harrisonburg." She looked at Yamanu. "How lucky is that?"

"It's certainly good news."

"I've got the same message," Wonder said. "It seems that Kian sent it to everyone in our group."

Ella sighed. "My poor aunt. They will have to keep her prisoner for three more days."

That was probably the least of Eleanor's problems.

Kian hadn't specified how they had gotten the information out of her, and Mey hoped it had been with Lokan's compulsion and not torture.

Not that she really minded how they'd done it. Eleanor wasn't a good person. And although Mey would have preferred to avoid brute-force measures, finding out what was going on with Jin as well as with the other possible Dormants in the program justified any means. Well, maybe save for killing the woman.

Closing her eyes, Mey let her head drop against the headrest.

She was so incredibly grateful for the clan's help, and for Lokan's. Without them, she wouldn't have been able to locate her sister, and none of this would have been possible.

Until meeting Yamanu, Mey had considered herself lucky on account of two major events. One was her and Jin's adoption by the Levines, and the other one was winning the beauty queen title that had opened up so many opportunities for her.

But even though her chance meeting with Yamanu would not have happened without the first two lucky events, it was the most important one. The others were necessary milestones in the journey that had brought Mey to her mate and to an entire clan of people who she could now call family.

Her army.

Mey was going to be forever grateful to this tight-knit community of people for mobilizing their best to help her save her sister.

71

YAMANU

*I*t was close to midnight when Yamanu pulled up next to the duplex and killed the engine.

The door on the right opened, and Amanda waved them in. "You are on this side."

Ella opened the back door and jumped down. "Where is my aunt?"

Amanda pointed to the left door. "In the other one, sleeping."

"Is she okay?" Ella whispered.

Amanda nodded and motioned for her to get inside.

Yamanu collected several pieces of luggage and carried them up the front porch's steps. Behind him, Mey and Wonder brought in the rest.

He put everything down just inside the door. "I'm going to find a parking spot down the street."

The others must have done the same with their vehicles because none were parked in front of the house.

"Leave it for now," Kian said. "I've been waiting for you to arrive so I can update everyone in one go."

"I'll just lock it then." He jogged out, closed the van's doors, and jogged back in.

"I'm making drip coffee and hot cocoa for everyone," Syssi said. "What would you like?"

"Coffee, please." He joined Mey at the dining table, where most of their team was congregated.

Arwel wasn't there, and Yamanu assumed that he was on the other side of the duplex, guarding Eleanor. Lokan wasn't there either, but he might have left after doing his part.

When coffee and cocoa were served, Kian waited until everyone was done stirring and getting comfortable before he began.

"Some of what I'm going to tell you we've learned from Eleanor, and some of it we guessed. Regrettably, we discovered that she is not susceptible to compulsion either, and we had to coerce the information out of her."

"Did you torture her?" Ella asked.

Kian smirked. "Terribly. We tied her up and didn't let her go to the bathroom until she told us what we needed."

Ella arched a brow. "Seriously?"

He nodded. "Seriously. But her need to relieve herself was just part of the reason she told us where we could find Jin. It seems that you were right and that your aunt is a compeller. Eleanor is certain that Jin will refuse to come with us, claiming that Jin came voluntarily because she's a patriot who wants to help her country and because of the generous compensation she was offered."

"That sounds reasonable," Mey said.

"Yes. But when I said that we were willing to offer Jin a deal twice as good, Eleanor was still confident that Jin would refuse it. That, along with several other comments, convinced us that Eleanor compelled Jin to accept the offer."

"How did she find out about Jin?" Mey asked.

"From what Eleanor told us, she is an independent contractor rather than an employee of the organization, and her job is to lure in the talent. She is not the one who discovers them, though. They give her the names and addresses, and she travels to wherever they are and brings them in."

Ella shook her head. "Still, she is directly responsible for Jin being in the program even though she didn't discover her. If not for Eleanor, Jin wouldn't have agreed to join."

Kian nodded.

Ella slumped in her chair. "It's even worse than I imagined. She really is a rotten apple."

Julian wrapped his arm around her shoulder. "As you often say, people are not black and white. I'm sure your aunt has some redeeming qualities."

"So, what's the plan?" Mey asked. "How are we going to convince Jin to come with us if she is under Eleanor's compulsion? Are we going to force Eleanor to remove it?"

"Lokan is going to help us with that," Kian said. "He had to return to Washington, but he'll be back on Saturday to join us."

Kian flipped open his laptop and turned it around for everyone to see. It had a map of a mall displayed on the screen. "This is the Valley Mall, where Jin and the other new recruits are going to be dropped off on Saturday morning." He pointed at a spot across the street. "And this is where we are going to be waiting for the bus's arrival."

72

MEY

When Saturday morning arrived, Mey was running on pure adrenaline. She hadn't slept all night, and the nights before hadn't been very restful either. She'd kept tossing and turning and waking Yamanu up, not letting him get a good night's sleep either.

During the days, she'd been busy keeping Ella occupied so she wouldn't venture into the other side of the duplex and demand to see her aunt.

Now that Mey was leaving with the retrieval team, it would be Amanda's job to keep an eye on Ella.

The truth was that Mey had been tempted to go see the evil witch herself and give her a piece of her mind for forcing Jin to join the program. But that wasn't the only reason she wanted to go talk to Eleanor. None of them knew for sure what that program was all about, and Mey could think of several torture devices other than a full bladder to get that information out of her.

Except, according to Julian, he was keeping Eleanor drugged with opiates, which made her so loopy that she could barely utter a coherent sentence.

Still, perhaps she should go see the bitch before their team left to retrieve Jin and see what she could learn. It would be her last chance to do so.

The moment they got Jin, Kian was going to call Arwel. Julian was going to administer the drug that would make Eleanor forget the last few days, and he and Arwel would drive her back to the resort. After they dropped her off at the hotel room, they were going to drive to Washington to meet up with the rest of the team.

Naturally, some surveillance footage erasing would be done to remove every last trace of the operation.

It was amazing what her people could do.

Shimon would have flipped if she told him. But just as she couldn't tell Yamanu about her days in the Mossad, she couldn't tell Shimon about the clan of immortals she had joined.

"You're awake." Yamanu yawned, stretched his long arms over his head, and then turned to her with a big grin on his face. "Good morning, my lady Mey." He kissed her on the lips.

"What's the big smile about?"

His grin got even broader. "Every day that I wake up next to you in bed, I feel like I should open a bottle of champagne and celebrate my incredible fortune."

Wrapping her arms around his neck, she kissed him back. "And I thank God, the Fates, and my lucky stars for having you in my life. I love you so much."

"I love you too." He wiped a tear from the corner of her eye with his thumb. "Are you nervous about today?"

She nodded. "I couldn't sleep. I kept thinking about all the what-ifs and everything that could possibly go wrong."

"Like what?"

"For starters, like Jin not being on that bus. What will we do then? Attack the facility she is held in?"

"We can do that."

"No, we can't. We don't have enough people. And even if we had, it's way too risky."

"We can wait for next Saturday."

"What if there is no bus at all? What if Eleanor lied?"

Yamanu stroked her hair. "Don't do that. The what-ifs are infinite. What if an asteroid hit the earth in the next hour and eradicated all life? What if a massive solar flare destroyed all of our satellites and electrical grids? What if the Doomers are planning to attack our village as we speak? You can make an endless list of possible catastrophes, but what purpose would that serve other than adding to your stress? There is no upside to that."

Mey let out a long breath. "You are right. I need to think positively. Jin is going to be on that bus, Lokan is going to remove Eleanor's compulsion, and Jin is going to fall into my arms, overjoyed that I came for her."

Smiling, Yamanu leaned and kissed the tip of her nose. "That's the spirit, my love." He lifted his arm and glanced at his watch. "It's six-fifteen, which means plenty of time before we need to head out." He cast her a lascivious look. "I can think of a way to pass an hour or two and alleviate your stress at the same time."

She laughed. "Not this morning, my love. Your immense shrouding ability might be needed today."

He pouted, but then smiled mischievously. "I can still do something about your stress. My turn will just have to wait for later."

Mey's heart swelled with love. "You are so unbelievably selfless." She kissed his jaw. "But I'm afraid that I'm too nervous to enjoy myself. I prefer for both of us to wait for tonight." She smiled. "I can't think of a better way to celebrate Jin's liberation."

"Tonight, we are hopefully going to be in the air on our way home."

She arched a brow. "And your point is?"

He threw his head back and laughed. "Thank the dear merciful Fates for giving me the most perfect mate."

COMING UP NEXT
THE CHILDREN OF THE GODS BOOK 35
DARK SPY CONSCRIPTED

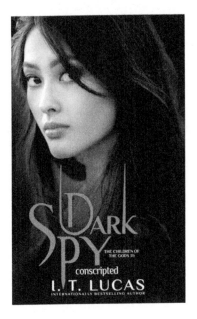

To read the first 3 chapters
JOIN THE VIP CLUB AT ITLUCAS.COM
and gain access to the VIP Portal

If you're already a subscriber and forgot the password to the VIP portal, you can find it at the bottom of each of my emails. If you are not getting them, your email provider is probably sending them to another folder, and you are missing out on updates and other goodies.

To fix that, add

isabell@itlucas.com

to your email contacts.

Dear reader,

Thank you for reading the ***Children of the Gods***.

As an independent author, I rely on your support to spread the word. So if you enjoyed the story, please share your experience with others, and if it isn't too much trouble, I would greatly appreciate a brief review on Amazon.

Click here to leave a review

Love & happy reading,

Isabell

THE CHILDREN OF THE GODS SERIES

THE CHILDREN OF THE GODS ORIGINS

1: GODDESS'S CHOICE

When gods and immortals still ruled the ancient world, one young goddess risked everything for love.

2: GODDESS'S HOPE

Hungry for power and infatuated with the beautiful Areana, Navuh plots his father's demise. After all, by getting rid of the insane god he would be doing the world a favor. Except, when gods and immortals conspire against each other, humanity pays the price.

But things are not what they seem, and prophecies should not to be trusted...

THE CHILDREN OF THE GODS

1: DARK STRANGER THE DREAM

Syssi's paranormal foresight lands her a job at Dr. Amanda Dokani's neuroscience lab, but it fails to predict the thrilling yet terrifying turn her life will take. Syssi has no clue that her boss is an immortal who'll drag her into a secret, millennia-old battle over humanity's future. Nor does she realize that the professor's imposing brother is the mysterious stranger who's been starring in her dreams.

Since the dawn of human civilization, two warring factions of immortals— the descendants of the gods of old—have been secretly shaping its destiny. Leading the clandestine battle from his luxurious Los Angeles high-rise, Kian is surrounded by his clan, yet alone. Descending from a single goddess, clan members are forbidden to each other. And as the only other immortals are their hated enemies, Kian and his kin have been long resigned to a lonely existence of fleeting trysts with human partners. That is, until his sister makes a game-changing discovery—a mortal seeress who she believes is a dormant carrier of their genes. Ever the realist, Kian is skeptical and refuses Amanda's plea to attempt Syssi's activation. But when his enemies learn of the Dormant's existence, he's forced to rush her to the safety of his keep. Inexorably drawn to Syssi, Kian wrestles with his conscience as he is tempted to explore her budding interest in the darker shades of sensuality.

2: Dark Stranger Revealed

While sheltered in the clan's stronghold, Syssi is unaware that Kian and Amanda are not human, and neither are the supposedly religious fanatics that are after her. She feels a powerful connection to Kian, and as he introduces her to a world of pleasure she never dared imagine, his dominant sexuality is a revelation. Considering that she's completely out of her element, Syssi feels comfortable and safe letting go with him. That is, until she begins to suspect that all is not as it seems. Piecing the puzzle together, she draws a scary, yet wrong conclusion...

3: Dark Stranger Immortal

When Kian confesses his true nature, Syssi is not as much shocked by the revelation as she is wounded by what she perceives as his callous plans for her.

If she doesn't turn, he'll be forced to erase her memories and let her go. His family's safety demands secrecy – no one in the mortal world is allowed to know that immortals exist.

Resigned to the cruel reality that even if she stays on to never again leave the keep, she'll get old while Kian won't, Syssi is determined to enjoy what little time she has with him, one day at a time.

Can Kian let go of the mortal woman he loves? Will Syssi turn? And if she does, will she survive the dangerous transition?

4: Dark Enemy Taken

Dalhu can't believe his luck when he stumbles upon the beautiful immortal professor. Presented with a once in a lifetime opportunity to grab an immortal female for himself, he kidnaps her and runs. If he ever gets caught, either by her people or his, his life is forfeit. But for a chance of a loving mate and a family of his own, Dalhu is prepared to do everything in his power to win Amanda's heart, and that includes leaving the Doom brotherhood and his old life behind.

Amanda soon discovers that there is more to the handsome Doomer than his dark past and a hulking, sexy body. But succumbing to her enemy's seduction, or worse, developing feelings for a ruthless killer is out of the question. No man is worth life on the run, not even the one and only immortal male she could claim as her own…

Her clan and her research must come first...

5: Dark Enemy Captive

When the rescue team returns with Amanda and the chained Dalhu to the keep, Amanda is not as thrilled to be back as she thought she'd be. Between Kian's contempt for her and Dalhu's imprisonment, Amanda's budding relationship with Dalhu seems doomed. Things start to look up when Annani offers her help, and together with Syssi they resolve to find a way for Amanda to be with Dalhu. But will she still want him when she realizes that he is responsible for her nephew's murder? Could she? Will she take the easy way out and choose Andrew instead?

6: Dark Enemy Redeemed

Amanda suspects that something fishy is going on onboard the Anna. But when her investigation of the peculiar all-female Russian crew fails to uncover anything other than more speculation, she decides it's time to stop playing detective and face her real problem—a man she shouldn't want but can't live without.

6.5: My Dark Amazon

When Michael and Kri fight off a gang of humans, Michael gets stabbed. The injury to his immortal body recovers fast, but the one to his ego takes longer, putting a strain on his relationship with Kri.

7: Dark Warrior Mine

When Andrew is forced to retire from active duty, he believes that all he has to look forward to is a boring desk job. His glory days in special ops are over. But as it turns out, his thrill ride has just begun. Andrew discovers not only that immortals exist and have been manipulating global affairs since antiquity, but that he and his sister are rare possessors of the immortal genes.

Problem is, Andrew might be too old to attempt the activation process. His sister, who is fourteen years his junior, barely made it through the transition, so the odds of him coming out of it alive, let alone immortal, are slim.

But fate may force his hand.

Helping a friend find his long-lost daughter, Andrew finds a woman who's worth taking the risk for. Nathalie might be a Dormant, but the only way to find out for sure requires fangs and venom.

8: Dark Warrior's Promise

Andrew and Nathalie's love flourishes, but the secrets they keep from each other taint their relationship with doubts and suspicions. In the meantime, Sebastian and his men are getting bolder, and the storm that's brewing will shift the balance of power in the millennia-old conflict between Annani's clan and its enemies.

9: Dark Warrior's Destiny

The new ghost in Nathalie's head remembers who he was in life, providing Andrew and her with indisputable proof that he is real and not a figment of her imagination.

Convinced that she is a Dormant, Andrew decides to go forward with his transition immediately after the rescue mission at the Doomers' HQ.

Fearing for his life, Nathalie pleads with him to reconsider. She'd rather spend the rest of her mortal days with Andrew than risk what they have for the fickle promise of immortality.

While the clan gets ready for battle, Carol gets help from an unlikely ally. Sebastian's second-in-command can no longer ignore the torment she suffers at the hands of his commander and offers to help her, but only if she agrees to his terms.

10: Dark Warrior's Legacy

Andrew's acclimation to his post-transition body isn't easy. His senses are sharper, he's bigger, stronger, and hungrier. Nathalie fears that the changes in the man she loves are more than physical. Measuring up to this new version of him is going to be a challenge.

Carol and Robert are disillusioned with each other. They are not destined mates, and love is not on the horizon. When Robert's three months are up, he might be left with nothing to show for his sacrifice.

Lana contacts Anandur with disturbing news; the yacht and its human cargo are in Mexico. Kian must find a way to apprehend Alex and rescue the women on board without causing an international incident.

11: Dark Guardian Found

What would you do if you stopped aging?

Eva runs. The ex-DEA agent doesn't know what caused her strange mutation, only that if discovered, she'll be dissected like a lab rat. What Eva doesn't know, though, is that she's a descendant of the gods, and that she is not alone. The man who rocked her world in one life-changing encounter over thirty years ago is an immortal as well.

To keep his people's existence secret, Bhathian was forced to turn his back on the only woman who ever captured his heart, but he's never forgotten and never stopped looking for her.

12: Dark Guardian Craved

Cautious after a lifetime of disappointments, Eva is mistrustful of Bhathian's professed feelings of love. She accepts him as a lover and a confidant but not as a life partner.

Jackson suspects that Tessa is his true love mate, but unless she overcomes her fears, he might never find out.

Carol gets an offer she can't refuse—a chance to prove that there is more to her than meets the eye. Robert believes she's about to commit a deadly mistake, but when he tries to dissuade her, she tells him to leave.

13: Dark Guardian's Mate

Prepare for the heart-warming culmination of Eva and Bhathian's story!

14: Dark Angel's Obsession

The cold and stoic warrior is an enigma even to those closest to him. His secrets are about to unravel...

15: Dark Angel's Seduction

Brundar is fighting a losing battle. Calypso is slowly chipping away his icy armor from the outside, while his need for her is melting it from the inside.

He can't allow it to happen. Calypso is a human with none of the Dormant indicators. There is no way he can keep her for more than a few weeks.

16: Dark Angel's Surrender

Get ready for the heart pounding conclusion to Brundar and Calypso's story.

Callie still couldn't wrap her head around it, nor could she summon even a smidgen of sorrow or regret. After all, she had some memories with him that weren't horrible. She should've felt something. But there was nothing, not even shock. Not even horror at what had transpired over the last couple of hours.

Maybe it was a typical response for survivors--feeling euphoric for the simple reason that they were alive. Especially when that survival was nothing short of miraculous.

Brundar's cold hand closed around hers, reminding her that they weren't out of the woods yet. Her injuries were superficial, and the most she had to worry about was some scarring. But, despite his and Anandur's reassurances, Brundar might never walk again.

If he ended up crippled because of her, she would never forgive herself for getting him involved in her crap.

"Are you okay, sweetling? Are you in pain?" Brundar asked.

Her injuries were nothing compared to his, and yet he was concerned about her. God, she loved this man. The thing was, if she told him that, he would run off, or crawl away as was the case.

Hey, maybe this was the perfect opportunity to spring it on him.

17: DARK OPERATIVE: A SHADOW OF DEATH

As a brilliant strategist and the only human entrusted with the secret of immortals' existence, Turner is both an asset and a liability to the clan. His request to attempt transition into immortality as an alternative to cancer treatments cannot be denied without risking the clan's exposure. On the other hand, approving it means risking his premature death. In both scenarios, the clan will lose a valuable ally.

When the decision is left to the clan's physician, Turner makes plans to manipulate her by taking advantage of her interest in him.

Will Bridget fall for the cold, calculated operative? Or will Turner fall into his own trap?

18: DARK OPERATIVE: A GLIMMER OF HOPE

As Turner and Bridget's relationship deepens, living together seems like the right move, but to make it work both need to make concessions.

Bridget is realistic and keeps her expectations low. Turner could never be the truelove mate she yearns for, but he is as good as she's going to get. Other than his emotional limitations, he's perfect in every way.

Turner's hard shell is starting to show cracks. He wants immortality, he wants to be part of the clan, and he wants Bridget, but he doesn't want to cause her pain.

His options are either abandon his quest for immortality and give Bridget his few remaining decades, or abandon Bridget by going for the transition and most likely dying. His rational mind dictates that he chooses the former, but his gut pulls him toward the latter. Which one is he going to trust?

19: Dark Operative: The Dawn of Love

Get ready for the exciting finale of Bridget and Turner's story!

20: Dark Survivor Awakened

This was a strange new world she had awakened to.

Her memory loss must have been catastrophic because almost nothing was familiar. The language was foreign to her, with only a few words bearing some similarity to the language she thought in. Still, a full moon cycle had passed since her awakening, and little by little she was gaining basic understanding of it--only a few words and phrases, but she was learning more each day.

A week or so ago, a little girl on the street had tugged on her mother's sleeve and pointed at her. "Look, Mama, Wonder Woman!"

The mother smiled apologetically, saying something in the language these people spoke, then scurried away with the child looking behind her shoulder and grinning.

When it happened again with another child on the same day, it was settled.

Wonder Woman must have been the name of someone important in this strange world she had awoken to, and since both times it had been said with a smile it must have been a good one.

Wonder had a nice ring to it.

She just wished she knew what it meant.

21: Dark Survivor Echoes of Love

Wonder's journey continues in *Dark Survivor Echoes of Love*.

22: Dark Survivor Reunited

The exciting finale of Wonder and Anandur's story.

23: Dark Widow's Secret

Vivian and her daughter share a powerful telepathic connection, so when Ella can't be reached by conventional or psychic means, her mother fears the worst.

Help arrives from an unexpected source when Vivian gets a call from the young doctor she met at a psychic convention. Turns out Julian belongs to a private organization specializing in retrieving missing girls.

As Julian's clan mobilizes its considerable resources to rescue the daughter, Magnus is charged with keeping the gorgeous young mother safe.

Worry for Ella and the secrets Vivian and Magnus keep from each other should be enough to prevent the sparks of attraction from kindling a blaze of desire. Except, these pesky sparks have a mind of their own.

24: DARK WIDOW'S CURSE

A simple rescue operation turns into mission impossible when the Russian mafia gets involved. Bad things are supposed to come in threes, but in Vivian's case, it seems like there is no limit to bad luck. Her family and everyone who gets close to her is affected by her curse.

Will Magnus and his people prove her wrong?

25: DARK WIDOW'S BLESSING

The thrilling finale of the Dark Widow trilogy!

26: DARK DREAM'S TEMPTATION

Julian has known Ella is the one for him from the moment he saw her picture, but when he finally frees her from captivity, she seems indifferent to him. Could he have been mistaken?

Ella's rescue should've ended that chapter in her life, but it seems like the road back to normalcy has just begun and it's full of obstacles. Between the pitying looks she gets and her mother's attempts to get her into therapy, Ella feels like she's typecast as a victim, when nothing could be further from the truth. She's a tough survivor, and she's going to prove it.

Strangely, the only one who seems to understand is Logan, who keeps popping up in her dreams. But then, he's a figment of her imagination—or is he?

27: DARK DREAM'S UNRAVELING

While trying to figure out a way around Logan's silencing compulsion, Ella concocts an ambitious plan. What if instead of trying to keep him out of her dreams, she could pretend to like him and lure him into a trap?

Catching Navuh's son would be a major boon for the clan, as well as for Ella. She will have her revenge, turning the tables on another scumbag out to get her.

28: DARK DREAM'S TRAP

The trap is set, but who is the hunter and who is the prey? Find out in this heart-pounding conclusion to the *Dark Dream* trilogy.

29: Dark Prince's Enigma

As the son of the most dangerous male on the planet, Lokan lives by three rules:

Don't trust a soul.

Don't show emotions.

And don't get attached.

Will one extraordinary woman make him break all three?

30: Dark Prince's Dilemma

Will Kian decide that the benefits of trusting Lokan outweigh the risks?

Will Lokan betray his father and brothers for the greater good of his people?

Are Carol and Lokan true-love mates, or is one of them playing the other?

So many questions, the path ahead is anything but clear.

31: Dark Prince's Agenda

While Turner and Kian work out the details of Areana's rescue plan, Carol and Lokan's tumultuous relationship hits another snag. Is it a sign of things to come?

32 : Dark Queen's Quest

A former beauty queen, a retired undercover agent, and a successful model, Mey is not the typical damsel in distress. But when her sister drops off the radar and then someone starts following her around, she panics.

Following a vague clue that Kalugal might be in New York, Kian sends a team headed by Yamanu to search for him.

As Mey and Yamanu's paths cross, he offers her his help and protection, but will that be all?

33: Dark Queen's Knight

As the only member of his clan with a godlike power over human minds, Yamanu has been shielding his people for centuries, but that power comes at a steep price. When Mey enters his life, he's faced with the most difficult choice.

The safety of his clan or a future with his fated mate.

34: Dark Queen's Army

As Mey anxiously waits for her transition to begin and for Yamanu to test

whether his godlike powers are gone, the clan sets out to solve two
mysteries:

Where is Jin, and is she there voluntarily?

Where is Kalugal, and what is he up to?

35: DARK SPY CONSCRIPTED

Jin possesses a unique paranormal ability. Just by touching someone, she
can insert a mental hook into their psyche and tie a string of her
consciousness to it, creating a tether. That doesn't make her a spy, though,
not unless her talent is discovered by those seeking to exploit it.

36: DARK SPY'S MISSION

Jin's first spying mission is supposed to be easy. Walk into the club, touch
Kalugal to tether her consciousness to him, and walk out.

Except, they should have known better.

37: DARK SPY'S RESOLUTION

The best-laid plans often go awry...

38: DARK OVERLORD NEW HORIZON

Jacki has two talents that set her apart from the rest of the human race.

She has unpredictable glimpses of other people's futures, and she is
immune to mind manipulation.

Unfortunately, both talents are pretty useless for finding a job other than
the one she had in the government's paranormal division.

It seemed like a sweet deal, until she found out that the director planned on
producing super babies by compelling the recruits into pairing up. When
an opportunity to escape the program presented itself, she took it, only to
find out that humans are not at the top of the food chain.

Immortals are real, and at the very top of the hierarchy is Kalugal, the most
powerful, arrogant, and sexiest male she has ever met.

With one look, he sets her blood on fire, but Jacki is not a fool. A man like
him will never think of her as anything more than a tasty snack, while she
will never settle for anything less than his heart.

39: DARK OVERLORD'S WIFE

Jacki is still clinging to her all-or-nothing policy, but Kalugal is chipping
away at her resistance. Perhaps it's time to ease up on her convictions. A

little less than all is still much better than nothing, and a couple of decades with a demigod is probably worth more than a lifetime with a mere mortal.

40: Dark Overlord's Clan

As Jacki and Kalugal prepare to celebrate their union, Kian takes every precaution to safeguard his people. Except, Kalugal and his men are not his only potential adversaries, and compulsion is not the only power he should fear.

41: Dark Choices The Quandary

When Rufsur and Edna meet, the attraction is as unexpected as it is undeniable. Except, she's the clan's judge and councilwoman, and he's Kalugal's second-in-command. Will loyalty and duty to their people keep them apart?

42: Dark Choices Paradigm Shift

Edna and Rufsur are miserable without each other, and their two-week separation seems like an eternity. Long-distance relationships are difficult, but for immortal couples they are impossible. Unless one of them is willing to leave everything behind for the other, things are just going to get worse.

Except, the cost of compromise is far greater than giving up their comfortable lives and hard-earned positions. The future of their people is on the line.

43: Dark Choices The Accord

The winds of change blowing over the village demand hard choices. For better or worse, Kian's decisions will alter the trajectory of the clan's future, and he is not ready to take the plunge. But as Edna and Rufsur's plight gains widespread support, his resistance slowly begins to erode.

44: Dark Secrets Resurgence

On a sabbatical from his Stanford teaching position, Professor David Levinson finally has time to write the sci-fi novel he's been thinking about for years.

The phenomena of past life memories and near-death experiences are too controversial to include in his formal psychiatric research, while fiction is the perfect outlet for his esoteric ideas.

Hoping that a change of pace will provide the inspiration he needs, David accepts a friend's invitation to an old Scottish castle.

45: Dark Secrets Unveiled

When Professor David Levinson accepts a friend's invitation to an old Scottish castle, what he finds there is more fantastical than his most outlandish theories. The castle is home to a clan of immortals, their leader is a stunning demigoddess, and even more shockingly, it might be precisely where he belongs.

Except, the clan founder is hiding a secret that might cast a dark shadow on David's relationship with her daughter.

Nevertheless, when offered a chance at immortality, he agrees to undergo the dangerous induction process.

Will David survive his transition into immortality? And if he does, will his relationship with Sari survive the unveiling of her mother's secret?

46: Dark Secrets Absolved

Absolution.

David had given and received it.

The few short hours since he'd emerged from the coma had felt incredible. He'd finally been free of the guilt and pain, and for the first time since Jonah's death, he had felt truly happy and optimistic about the future.

He'd survived the transition into immortality, had been accepted into the clan, and was about to marry the best woman on the face of the planet, his true love mate, his salvation, his everything.

What could have possibly gone wrong?

Just about everything.

47: Dark haven Illusion

Welcome to Safe Haven, where not everything is what it seems.

On a quest to process personal pain, Anastasia joins the Safe Haven Spiritual Retreat.

Through meditation, self-reflection, and hard work, she hopes to make peace with the voices in her head.

This is where she belongs.

Except, membership comes with a hefty price, doubts are sacrilege, and leaving is not as easy as walking out the front gate.

Is living in utopia worth the sacrifice?

Anastasia believes so until the arrival of a new acolyte changes everything.

Apparently, the gods of old were not a myth, their immortal descendants share the planet with humans, and she might be a carrier of their genes.

48: DARK HAVEN UNMASKED

As Anastasia leaves Safe Haven for a week-long romantic vacation with Leon, she hopes to explore her newly discovered passionate side, their budding relationship, and perhaps also solve the mystery of the voices in her head. What she discovers exceeds her wildest expectations.

In the meantime, Eleanor and Peter hope to solve another mystery. Who is Emmett Haderech, and what is he up to?

———————

FOR A **FREE** AUDIOBOOK, PREVIEW CHAPTERS, AND OTHER GOODIES OFFERED ONLY TO MY **VIPS**,

JOIN THE VIP CLUB AT ITLUCAS.COM

———————

TRY THE SERIES ON

AUDIBLE

2 FREE audiobooks with your new Audible subscription!

THE PERFECT MATCH SERIES

PERFECT MATCH 1: VAMPIRE'S CONSORT

When Gabriel's company is ready to start beta testing, he invites his old crush to inspect its medical safety protocol.

Curious about the revolutionary technology of the *Perfect Match Virtual Fantasy-Fulfillment studios*, Brenna agrees.

Neither expects to end up partnering for its first fully immersive test run.

PERFECT MATCH 2: KING'S CHOSEN

When Lisa's nutty friends get her a gift certificate to *Perfect Match Virtual Fantasy Studios*, she has no intentions of using it. But since the only way to get a refund is if no partner can be found for her, she makes sure to request a fantasy so girly and over the top that no sane guy will pick it up.

Except, someone does.

Warning: This fantasy contains a hot, domineering crown prince, sweet insta-love, steamy love scenes painted with light shades of gray, a wedding, and a HEA in both the virtual and real worlds.

Intended for mature audience.

Perfect Match 3: Captain's Conquest

Working as a Starbucks barista, Alicia fends off flirting all day long, but none of the guys are as charming and sexy as Gregg. His frequent visits are the highlight of her day, but since he's never asked her out, she assumes he's taken. Besides, between a day job and a budding music career, she has no time to start a new relationship.

That is until Gregg makes her an offer she can't refuse—a gift certificate to the virtual fantasy fulfillment service everyone is talking about. As a huge Star Trek fan, Alicia has a perfect match in mind—the captain of the Starship Enterprise.

Also by I. T. Lucas

THE CHILDREN OF THE GODS: BOOKS 1-6—INCLUDES
CHARACTER LISTS

THE CHILDREN OF THE GODS: BOOKS 6.5-10—INCLUDES
CHARACTER LISTS

TRY THE CHILDREN OF THE GODS SERIES ON
AUDIBLE

2 FREE audiobooks with your new Audible subscription!

FOR EXCLUSIVE PEEKS AT UPCOMING RELEASES & A FREE COMPANION BOOK

JOIN MY *VIP CLUB* AND GAIN ACCESS TO THE VIP PORTAL AT

ITLUCAS.COM

CLICK HERE TO JOIN

(OR GO TO: http://eepurl.com/blMTpD)

INCLUDED IN YOUR FREE MEMBERSHIP:

- FREE CHILDREN OF THE GODS COMPANION BOOK 1
- FREE NARRATION OF GODDESS'S CHOICE—BOOK 1 IN THE CHILDREN OF THE GODS ORIGINS SERIES.
- PREVIEW CHAPTERS OF UPCOMING RELEASES.
- AND OTHER EXCLUSIVE CONTENT OFFERED ONLY TO MY VIPS.

Printed in Great Britain
by Amazon

58560757R00180